Journey

to

Senia

Stan Niego

To Jo

STAN NIEGO

CONTENTS

STAN NIEGO

INTRODUCTION

It is said that everyone has at least one book in them. This is mine. You could say that I started on this story in the mid-1970s when one evening I walked along the beach at Crescent Beach, Florida, looked out over the ocean, and wondered whether there really could be life as we know it somewhere out there in the universe. Could the stories about flying saucers, which were prevalent at the time, actually be true? I wondered about how a saucer-shaped craft could actually fly through the atmosphere and be capable of disappearing from sight with a jolt. I thought it must have a way to control the effect of the Earth's gravitational field. It must have a centrifugal force mechanism that locks in to spin if off in a specific direction.

Many years later, when I started writing this story, I decided to build upon the concept of, you could say, reality-based science fiction. In the universe of our hero, Josh Rinaldi, there is no warp drive or suspended animation for traveling the long distances of space. They have to slog it out one day at a time at a mere ninety-five percent of the speed of light. They travel to the planet Senia, over sixteen light years from Earth, which orbits around the star known as Gliese 832 on Earth. There is no instant communication across the vast reaches of space. Communications travel at the speed of light and it takes many years for messages to be received. Nor is there a universal translator or food replicator. The Senians, who have observed Earth since Biblical times, want to make contact, but they cannot understand any of the myriad of Earth languages. The purpose of their mission is to obtain an Earth human to teach them an

Earth language so that they may make contact with Earth on their next space voyage many years later. Josh becomes that Earth human, voluntarily boarding their craft but having no idea of what lies ahead. With an unceasing effort over months and years, Josh and the beautiful Fela teach each other their languages and much more.

The Senians are a good people. They have learned how to live in harmony with their environment, which is not nearly as generous or abundant as that of Earth. They need some of Earth's uranium in order to maintain their defenses against the Corilian home world, which has fallen under a brutal totalitarian dictatorship of the Tskar, who has determined to destroy Senia's major cities with nuclear weapons if it does not submit to Corilian domination. The Tskar must conquer Senia as a stepping-stone to his conquest of Earth for its uranium and other resources.

Josh leaves Earth in 1977, returning forty years later in 2017. During that time, Earth enters the digital age and there is major upheaval in the geopolitics across the globe. The Berlin wall falls. The Soviet Union is dissolved. China becomes and economic powerhouse. Extremist Islamist elements become a major threat to a civilized world order. When the Senians return to earth in 2017, they have a major impact upon future events.

I describe historical Earth developments in some detail - hopefully not so much as to bore or distract you from the main story. I find it fascinating how much things have changed over the last 40 years, only to remain the same in many fearful respects.

I want to express my great appreciation and thanks to my wife Jo, who has always been there for encouragement and support over the more than forty years that we have been together, and to my dear friend, Kathryn Mennella, who assisted me in critiquing and editing this book, and also providing me with the confidence and encouragement to bring it in for a landing.

Stan Niego

CHAPTER 1 - UP, UP AND AWAY

This is a story about a journey; a journey through time and space that would ultimately alter the course of human history.

Josh Rinaldi just finished his first semester of law school at the University of Florida and is on the way in his Ford Econoline van for a few days of overnight camping at Crescent Beach. It was one of Josh's favorite destinations, a small beach town on the east coast of Florida, a little bit south of St. Augustine. After messing with a few broken down cassette players he purchased at garage sales, Josh finally broke down and bought a new player at Radio Shack for $120. A pre-recorded cassette of the favorite songs from his record collection is blaring Canned Heat's "On the Road Again" through the new speakers. Next comes "Fried Hockey Boogie." All is well with the world.

It is 9:30 a.m., June 15, 1977, and the morning sun is starting to shine brightly through the windows of his precious light blue van with windows all around. The ice box is loaded with ham, apple juice, raisins, nuts, Swiss cheese and an assortment of fruit. A beat up twin size mattress covers most of the floor with his trusty beat up nylon string guitar lying atop.

The previous day had seen the conclusion of Josh's first semester as a freshman law student at the University of Florida. It had been somewhat rough, as he actually had to go to class and try to keep up with the work during this latest bout with the educational system. Several years had elapsed since he finished his college studies in economics and political science, and the no-nonsense discipline of law school took some getting used to. Josh had been used to not getting serious about his courses until about two weeks before final exams. It soon became apparent to him that this approach would see him out the door sooner than would otherwise be desired and he was someone not prone to failure. So he buckled down and spent most evenings reading the casebooks to be ready for the next day's discussions. He liked participating in the discussions and generally enjoyed the intellectual law school atmosphere.

Grades would not be in for a few weeks, It was time to relax and unwind. Time to forget about the endless hours of study and listening to the professors pontificate. Time to become a "lay person" once again.

Maybe even lay another "lay person," he chuckled to himself as he rambled down State Road 84 on the way to Palatka.

With his left hand on the wheel, he scratched his head, bushing up his curly dark brown hair that had not been cut since he started the semester. It was starting to look a little outrageous, although not nearly as wild as it had looked during his college days. He would get it cut before going back for the next semester.

His beard was also starting to grow past the stubble point. There would be no shaving while on the beach, and probably not for the next two weeks of semester break. With his dark brown eyes, thin and lanky six-foot, two-inch profile, and near coke bottle glasses, he looked like he much more belonged on the streets on Brooklyn where he was born than in the rural hinterlands of northern Florida.

He had chosen law school at the University of Florida without a whole lot of thought, his main idea being to escape from the rigors of living in New York City. His Italian dad had struggled all of his life to build a moderately successful garment factory in Coney Island, making children's ware and ladies' dresses. Along with his uncle, they had started with just two sewing machines after the war in the late 1940s and built the business into a factory that employed about fifty people. One thing Josh knew was that he did not want to become trapped in New York for the rest of his life working in a formaldehyde-ridden garment factory. His dad grudgingly helped pay for his college education, but really wanted him to follow in his footsteps. His Jewish mom saw to it that he got the minimal support needed to make it through college. Florida, with its beautiful beaches and un-crowded cities and towns, was a wonder to him. He knew he would never return to New York City.

Josh's immediate plan was to get as far away from civilization as possible, unwind, and let the sun recharge his batteries. There was much to think about. Law school had completely stifled the creative side of his nature and he was hoping to revive these energies and perhaps write a few songs.

As he drove through Palatka, a paper mill town along the St. Johns River, whose glory days as a transit point for barge traffic along the river had long since passed, he spotted a moderately harmless looking fellow trying to thumb a ride. In days gone by, he would have felt guilty about passing someone up in his van. This was not the case today. Today, he was interested in escaping from other people as much as possible.

Better to let his mind drift and contemplate what little there was to plan about the trip ahead. He would drive south about seven miles down the beach to his favorite spot near the Matanzas Inlet. In the early seventies, when he first parked his van as far up in the sand as possible for an overnight stay, there were no houses for many miles from the inlet. Now there were a few, but the beach was for the most part empty.

Much of Josh's thoughts were spent contemplating world events. He was one of those people who became very absorbed with matters occurring in remote areas of the globe that most people hardly knew existed. The big issue of the day was what President Carter would do about the energy crisis. Jimmy had delivered a "fireside chat" in late April, in which he said the American response to the energy situation should be viewed as the "moral equivalent of war." Josh thought he had over-dramatized the situation a bit, but also thought that Carter's proposals did not go far enough.

As he passed by the Hastings potato fields, his thoughts again turned to the trip ahead. It was developing into a typical June Florida day. The sun had now fully burned its way up through the morning mist. A few small clouds began to form to the west, and it was likely the sky would be clouded over after a few hours. Hopefully, the sea breeze would keep the clouds pressed inland for most of the afternoon.

This was the first time he would spend more than one night at the beach. He had stayed overnight a few times without incident, but was always somewhat apprehensive about being out there alone without any protection other than a corroded fishing knife. Having grown up in various parts of New York City, Josh had developed a big city mentality about crime that he found hard to leave behind. Still, he was determined to not let the very low risk of trouble get in the way of having a good time. He could hold his own in a fight if necessary, so long as he kept his glasses on his head.

The beaches were nothing like he had ever experienced in New York. When the tide went out, the beach would be about 200 feet wide and very flat. There was plenty of room to run on the near level, well packed sand along the shore. Closer toward the dune, out of reach of the tide, the very fine sand was soft and lightly colored, unlike the coarse sand he was familiar with up north.

And you were allowed to drive a car on the beach, something unheard of in New York. To top it off, the beaches were generally empty, unlike the crowds at Coney Island and Jones Beach. The last few months seemed like an eternity as he contemplated laying in the soft sand and not getting up until dripping with sweat for a dip in the ocean.

Finally, he hit the home stretch along State Road 206 that would carry him to the rickety old bridge across the intra-coastal waterway and onto Highway A1A along the beach. The road was deserted and the surrounding area consisted of mostly pine plantations. He hit the gas pedal and brought the rickety van up to about seventy miles per hour. The engine coughed a few times as he picked up speed. The wobble in the front wheels evened out. Any faster and he could not be sure what would happen.

When he got to the beach he found it surprisingly empty, even for the middle of the week. He knew as he traveled down the beach there would be the inevitable temptation to casually pull up in the vicinity of a young lady or two, and after awhile, mosey over a strike up a conversation.

"Would you please watch my stuff while I go for a run?" was one of his favorite lines.

Then, upon return, thank the ladies for their help and offer them a beer from the cooler. This approach had, at least a few times, led to some success. This time, however, he was determined to go it alone, at least initially.

As he traveled the last seven miles to his spot, opportunities for diversion did arise, but he held his course and was pleased to find his spot absolutely empty. It was about 11:00 and the sun was starting to intensify. The sand dunes were as beautiful as ever, with the sun now casting sharp shadows though the sea oats along the dune line and the scraggly oaks that inhabited the wide sandy area between the dune line and the highway.

He grabbed a beer, spread out a few large beach towels, and collapsed into the sand.

The tide was almost completely out and there was ample room for the few cars that passed by on their way to the inlet. As he lay there, his thoughts once again turned to the stories he had read in *U.S. News and World Report* the night before. It wasn't that Josh particularly wanted to think about such things. But by process of elimination, there wasn't much else to contemplate, and Josh was intrigued by the complexity of world events. He had determined not to think at all about law, which had almost completely occupied his thoughts for the last four months.

Romance in his life at the time was virtually non-existent. He was getting too old to chase after the teeny boppers that frequented the streets of Gainesville. And so, the last few months, while gregarious in one respect, were very lonely in another. However, Josh generally didn't mind being alone. He was well aware of and comfortable with his thoughts and sense of being.

As he drifted off to sleep, his thoughts again turned to world events. Omar Torrihos was threatening that he could not guarantee the security of the Panama Canal Zone in the absence of a re-negotiation of the Panama Canal Treaty, while in the Middle East, the election of Menachim Begin of the Likud Party was widely viewed as a setback in the efforts toward a negotiated settlement. The civil war in Rhodesia was in full swing, with British and American diplomats seeking to convince Ian Smith to step down peacefully. As for the Soviets, they were becoming very dismayed with Carter's human rights initiative. They were pleased, however, with his talk of withdrawing American forces from Korea, which raised considerable consternation in the Far East and among American conservatives. On the domestic scene, the Richard Nixon interviews with David Frost were the topic of the day, along with Carter's inability to get a Democratic Congress to support his programs. Carter's veto of several pork barrel projects had pissed off a number of important people on the hill.

As Josh dozed there in the sand, Zfar, the ship's Captain and pilot, and Fedar, second in command, were drawing him into focus on the monitor from 100,000 feet overhead. The Earth human appeared to be a good candidate for what they hoped would be their next and successful attempt at getting one of the Earth humans to board their shuttle craft. The Senian starship was maintaining its position over the east coast of Florida, but they could not stay long. They had dodged about the planet on several prior unsuccessful attempts and were certain that they had been detected by Earth radar systems. There would be no attempt during the day, and they dashed off over the Atlantic Ocean out of the reach of coastal radar.

The Senians were correct in their conclusion that they had been detected on Earth. Both the Americans and the Soviets were alarmed about the presence of this possible UFO that would suddenly appear and then disappear on their radar screens. The Americans were ready to scramble to intercept the craft, but it never remained in one place long enough.

After about an hour Josh awakened to find the sun beating steadily overhead. Somewhat energized, he emerged from the sand ready for a dip in the ocean. Gingerly, he approached the breaking waves. The water felt very cold against his feet. Still, he needed to wash off all of the sweat that had accumulated and coat himself with salt water before applying the suntan lotion.

Better make a run for it, he thought.

With that, he briskly ran through the receding waves until the water was about three feet deep and then dove in.

The day passed uneventfully between laying on the blanket, going for short runs, and finally, a trip to the parking area at Crescent Beach to rinse off all of the salt and suntan lotion.

As the afternoon moved toward sunset, everyone except Josh left the beach. After finishing a ham sandwich, he went for another long walk while the sun was setting. As the sky slowly darkened and the nearly full moon came into view over the ocean, he reached for his guitar. Sitting on the back of his van with the doors open, he began to strum his guitar as he gazed out at the ocean and the evening sky. As usual, he began with his version of "Don't Think Twice, It's Alright," then swung into Dylan's "Tom Thumb Blues." From there, it was whatever in his usual repertoire came to mind.

It was an incredible evening; could not have been any better. This was the first true whiff of summer. There was a warm, soft breeze blowing across the ocean from the southeast as the waves gently rolled to shore. The sky was clear and it was easy to see the stars. The temperature was perfect. There were glimmers of faint light from the beach-front homes several miles down the beach.

As he sat there, he thought about the Earth and all of the challenges that it faced from the growth of humankind If there is anything meaningful in life, he thought, it involves doing something to help bring the Earth into balance so it could remain a habitable place for the human race. There was not much that he could do, but he would try to do what he could.

The Senian starship *Explorer* returned to its position over the East Coast of Florida. Zfar had a decision to make. Should they move within range to launch the shuttle craft? At their current 100,000 feet, he was unable to detect whether the Earth human was still on the beach. They needed to move to 10,000 feet for their infrared equipment to be effective. During the day, they had observed the rocket launching facilities at the Kennedy Space Center. They had also observed Elgin Air Force Base in the panhandle. Zfar thought it was likely that they would be detected and there would be precious little time to make the landing and return to the ship.

Zfar was a seasoned space veteran, sixty-one years of age. Still, he was also a bit of a gambler and decided to proceed. He programmed in the coordinates to place the ship 10,000 feet above the landing destination, about 100 miles from the Kennedy Space Center. The forward vertical thrusters changed the angle of inclination of the ship so that it slowly began to lose altitude. After about fifteen Earth minutes, the ship was in position. Fedar, second in command and also an experienced starship pilot, was in the shuttle craft, ready to proceed on command. Zfar could now see on the monitor that Josh's vehicle was still on the beach. He gave the command, and Fedar launched the shuttle craft.

Josh was still sitting on the back of his van, playing his guitar and looking out over the ocean as the shuttle craft slowly approached. He slowly became aware that he could hear a somewhat high pitched un-natural sound that seemed to be coming in from over the ocean. He set his guitar down and listened more attentively as the sound gradually became louder.

How could this be? he thought.

There were no lights that he could see, and it seemed to Josh that there should be some lights if there was a boat out there on the water, although it didn't sound like any boat engine Josh had heard before. It was a steady hum that was slowly growing louder.

Then suddenly, a light appeared directing a beam toward the beach. He could not see what was behind the light.

This is starting to get very strange, he thought.

He considered starting the van and making a quick exit. Instead, yielding to his curiosity, he decided to leave the van and hide in the nearby sand dune. He grabbed his guitar, perhaps to use as a club, then quickly grabbed his rusty fishing knife, and ran for the dune.

When he reached the dune he lay flat in the sand with his head barely peeking over the dune so he could see. The object, which now appeared to be some kind of vehicle, kept coming toward him over the water until it slowly settled down on the beach just past where the waves were meeting the shore. The guiding light was turned off and a very dim light appeared which illuminated the inside of the craft making it possible to discern its outer dimensions. It was now about 100 feet away, close to the van.

Josh could see that it was not a helicopter. He wondered how it could have descended so slowly, not stirring up the soft sand as it landed on the beach.

Then, the outline of a person who appeared to be male became discernable. Several thoughts ran through Josh's head.

Should he stay hidden and avoid the potential danger or approach whatever it was and satisfy his growing curiosity?

Fedar left the craft and began walking slowly toward the van, expecting to find the Earth human there. He was armed with a powerful laser pistol, purely for self defense, that he kept tucked into his belt in front of him beneath his loosely fitting long sleeve pullover shirt. Finding the van was empty, Fedar headed back to the shuttle craft.

Josh, watching Fedar's calm and measured movements, became more confident that this person was not belligerent. His curiosity was now overwhelming and he decided to move closer to check things out.

As Josh began walking, guitar in hand, toward the unknown, he muttered to himself, *curiosity killed the cat.*

To the extent that he could detect any vibes from the stranger, Josh didn't feel in danger.

The beach was a place where everyone had good vibes, right?

Josh was feeling in the best of vibes himself when this strange situation had developed, and he still had a reflection of the same peaceful mood, although tempered with a large measure of caution.

Slowly, he walked closer and closer, stopping about twenty feet away. He could see the person outside the vehicle had noticed him approaching. They stood there looking at each other. Josh could now see that the stranger was an older man, perhaps in his fifties, which was somewhat reassuring and alleviated some of his anxiety. An elderly person would not be someone who would normally present a threat. He appeared to be no more than about five feet, eight inches tall, and had a very thin frame, which also helped alleviate some of Josh's anxiety.

Fedar gestured with his hand in an inviting manner for Josh to continue to approach. Josh slowly moved closer and then, about ten feet away, suddenly stopped.

He could now see that the stranger did not appear to be human. His forehead was larger than that of a normal person; not much larger, but it gave his head a rather bulbous appearance that did not seem to be the result of an injury. His thin, blondish gray hair was very straight and combed back. His ears were those of a normal human and so was the rest of his face, with its finely shaped features and strong jaw. His body, although thin, appeared to be very strong as he stood tall and straight. There was a friendly smile on his face as he continued to gesture for Josh to approach.

Josh continued to slowly approach and was soon standing there several feet before the stranger, his guitar hanging by his side, ready to be used as a club, with his fishing knife in the pocket of his very well faded denim jeans. His curly brown hair was a bushy mess.

Fedar did not say anything, so Josh spoke first.

"Who are you?" he asked.

"My name is Fedar," Fedar replied in Senian.

Fedar could not understand Josh and knew that the Earth human could not understand him. Senian was a fluid tongue sounding like a mix of Spanish and Chinese.

Whatever the stranger said, he was pointing to himself and appeared to be saying his name. Josh did the same, pointing to himself.

"I am Josh."

Fedar smiled and pointed toward the shuttle craft, gesturing for Josh to follow him. He had some second thoughts about whether this wild haired Earth human would be suitable for their mission, but they had taken so much risk to get this far, he had no choice but to proceed.

"Please come with me," Fedar said.

They walked to the craft and Josh looked inside, hardly believing what he saw. Nothing appeared to be based on current technology, as far as Josh knew. There was no steering wheel or anything of that sort. He could see a bright screen, gently lit by a pale blue light, with red, yellow and orange touch buttons imbedded into the screen.

The craft did not indicate any visible evidence of a propulsion system. It was circular in shape, about ten feet in diameter. There were two seats in the front. The rear portion was a compartment that almost came up to the top of the seats. Josh guessed it might contain the propulsion system. A clear Plexiglas-like material encircled the upper portion of the craft, held together by curved supports that coalesced at the center of the top of the craft.

Fedar entered the vehicle, took a seat and gestured for Josh to take the other seat beside him. Josh was a smart guy and he began to add things up. The problem was that the conclusion he was coming to was totally implausible.

A vehicle had descended from the sky with no apparent propulsion system and landed on the beach. In the vehicle was a being that did not appear to be human. The vehicle itself did not appear to be anything that resembled any technology that Josh was aware of.

Was this person really from another world? he thought.

Could it be that there actually was something to the all of the stories about UFOs?

Josh definitely had an open mind to the possibility of there being life on other planets.

But why would someone from another world land at Crescent Beach, Florida, and be out there gesturing for Josh to step aboard his vehicle?

All of these thoughts ran through his head in an instant. He could not stand there forever. He had to decide. Would he step aboard or not? His curiosity was overwhelming. Almost instinctively, apparently without making a conscious decision, he found himself bending over and stepping into the vehicle, guitar in hand.

As he did so, he kept thinking to himself, *curiosity killed the cat.* Yet, he also had a sense of calm and wonderment as to what would happen next. The vibes he was getting from the strange being were not at all threatening.

Josh, of course, had no idea what was in store for him. He had barely given any thought to the possibility that his stepping aboard the craft could amount to what in essence would be a one way trip for the foreseeable future to a very distant world. He did not know how much time he would have to reflect upon that decision.

There was only about a one-foot step up onto the floor of the vehicle. Josh stepped in and sat down looking at the stranger to his left. There they were, now as close as could be. They looked at each other intently, each studying the other's facial expressions and perceiving the other's vibes. Josh could now see the fine lines of Fedar's face and his curious expression as he looked Josh over. There was a great intelligence in Fedar's eyes and no appearance of a sinister motive. He was clean shaven with a thin grey moustache.

Fedar looked at Josh and continued to wonder whether this Earth human was of sufficient intelligence to meet their needs. His unshaven growth of about three days, plus the bushy head of curly brown hair, tossed about by the wind, gave Josh a very primitive appearance to Fedar. Yet, Fedar could see in Josh's eyes that there was a degree of intelligence. And the Earth human had been willing to board the craft, another sign of intelligence prevailing over fear.

Josh could not remember what the alien had said to be his name. He was terrible anyway at remembering names after introductions, and in the excitement the alien's name had melted away into oblivion.

Josh pointed to himself again and said "Josh."

Fedar pointed to himself and said "Fedar."

Fedar knew it was time to move. There was no time to waste. Fedar quickly locked in his seat belts and motioned for Josh to do the same. There were two belts that crossed over each other from the waist to the shoulders. Josh complied. Fedar touched the screen and the door on Josh's side of the craft slid shut.

Fedar knew that they would need to reach the *Explorer* as quickly as possible if they were to safely rendezvous with the ship and exit Earth's atmosphere. He touched a series of control buttons and the propulsion system, which had been quiet, began to make its humming sound. The vehicle began to lift itself off the beach.

Josh could now see more clearly the yellow, orange and red touch buttons on the screen and a series of what appeared to be level meters, all identified with strange symbols that did not resemble any language he knew. There were no buttons to push or switches to flip, except for a movable lever control at the center of the console and a fader control on the right side of the console, similar to the volume control on Josh's stereo, but much larger.

He looked about to see what was propelling them upward but could not detect anything. There were no signs of conventional propulsion from expanding gases. The sand on the beach was not blowing about. The craft ascended straight up as Fedar pushed forward on the control. The whirring sound did not increase in pitch or intensity.

Fedar began to operate the air jets that encircled the craft and provided stability in Earth's atmosphere. Josh did not realize that the craft was designed specifically for Earth's atmosphere and that the Senian mission to Earth was for the sole purpose of bringing an Earth human back to Senia.

But how was it, Josh wondered, *that this craft could apparently defy gravity without any visible means of propulsion to overcome the force of the Earth's gravitational field?*

Had these aliens developed some type of anti-gravity field?

It appeared so.

Josh did not have time to wonder further about that as the unfolding events took over his full attention. They were now several hundred feet above the beach and ascending rapidly. He looked over at Fedar, who smiled back at Josh with a kind and friendly smile.

Am I being beguiled? he wondered. He did not know. He smiled back with a similar smile and they continued upward as the lights below started to fade. The guitar lay by his side on the floor; the fishing knife protruding slightly from his pocket. Fedar could see the knife, but decided to make nothing of it for now.

The lights on the outside of the shuttle craft were very dim, as the Senians did not want to be detected. The shuttle craft and the starship *Explorer* carried no armaments. Their only defense was evasive

15

action.

On their last trip to Earth, about 450 years ago, the Senians had observed many wars in progress using very primitive but destructive technologies and had determined that the Earth humans were not advanced enough in their social development to accommodate contact with beings from another part of the galaxy. It was too risky, as they would have no means of defense or escape if they landed and encountered hostilities.

This time, as they approached Earth, they were able to pick up radio and television transmissions showing the great extent of Earth's technological progress since the last mission. Still, it did not make very much sense to them. They did not understand any of the Earth's languages. It was a mystery to them why there were so many different Earth languages. On Senia, there was one written and spoken language.

The main purpose of the mission to Earth was to extract an Earth human who would be able to teach them an Earth language so that they would be able to communicate with Earth on the return mission. The Senians would then seek to gain Earth's support in their long standing struggle with the tyrannical forces that had taken control of their home planet, Corilia -- forces that would sometime in the future also endanger Earth.

Considering what conditions were like on their home planet after being overcome by tyrannical forces, the Senians regarded contact with Earth far too risky without first knowing how to communicate and understand something of Earth's political systems and the state of its world affairs. It would take a minimum of thirty-six additional Earth years to make further contact with Earth, but this delay was considered necessary in order to ensure the safety and success of the mission.

The Americans were not standing still while Josh and Fedar became acquainted and departed from Crescent Beach. The Senian ship had been tracked by radar from the moment it came within range of coastal facilities. Military satellites were also tracking the craft. Five fully armed F-16s had scrambled from Elgin Air Force Base and were rapidly approaching. The Kennedy Space Center was also on alert to intercept any transmissions.

Zfar communicated to Fedar about the approaching jets.

"We will need to take evasive action. Maintain your trajectory and we will return to the intersect coordinates."

"I will maintain position at 10,000 feet," Fedar replied.

Kennedy intercepted the transmissions and immediately forwarded them to NORAD Central Command at Peterson Air Force Base in Colorado. NORAD specialists, who spoke fluent Russian, advised their commanders that the transmissions were not Russian or any other language they knew. There was a sense of relief that it did not appear to be a Soviet intrusion into American air space. Instead, this provided additional confirmation that the craft could be a UFO.

The person immediately in charge of the situation at NORAD command was General Mark Boswell. The Pentagon had been notified of the prior intrusion several hours ago and word of the new development was buzzing through communications channels. General Boswell, however, as NORAD duty officer, had the authority to order the approaching F-16s to down the craft. He had a direct line to the pilots and on his command they would fire their Sidewinder missiles.

General Boswell was not of a mind to down the intruder. If indeed it was a UFO, their effort would be to direct the intruder to land at a secure military facility. The fighters were now within five miles of the starship, well within range to down it with a missile.

General Boswell spoke to Willie Johnson, the squad commander. "Do not fire unless fired upon. Photograph and immediately report your observations."

Willie replied: "Roger."

As the jets approached within a mile, Zfar decided it was time for evasive action. With a few touches on the screen, the starship suddenly jerked from its stationary position at the intersect coordinates in an easterly direction over the ocean and began to rapidly accelerate. The F-16s quickly swerved to the left to follow the ship. Then, with a sudden shift, the ship jerked to the south, far too quickly for the F-16s to adjust. They circled about, but by the time they were on course toward the intruder it was over ten miles away and rapidly accelerating faster than they could catch it.

Willy reported back to NORAD:

"It's gotten away from us. This is no ordinary airship. I think it's a UFO."

General Boswell replied: "Roger. Stay airborne and follow it."

"It's heading east, southeast. We'll stay with it as long as we can."

Fedar and Josh were looking up in awe at the aerial display as they approached the intercept coordinates. Fedar could maintain his position for about fifty Earth minutes, but then would have to land the shuttle if they were not able to board the starship. He waited anxiously for word from Zfar.

When they reached the intercept position, Fedar radioed to Zfar: "We are at the intercept position. What is your position?"

"We will be in position in about six quarseks," which was about eight Earth minutes.

Zfar then directed the starship to change direction to the intercept coordinates. The ship quickly began to reverse course. The fighter squad, losing hope that they would ever catch the ship, suddenly found themselves rapidly approaching the ship as it veered off to the right on their radar screens. Willy brought his jet around as quickly as he could, and the others in the squad followed suit. By this time, the UFO was again about five miles ahead of them and approaching the coast.

Zfar had no choice. He would be at the mercy of the Earth humans if he attempted a rendezvous with Fedar. He had to begin decelerating in order to be in a stationary position at the intercept coordinates. The Earth humans had not taken any hostile action thus far and, being the gambler that he was, he decided to chance it.

He entered the commands to bring the ship to a halt at the intercept coordinates. The *Explorer* began to rapidly decelerate as Fedar's shuttle came into view. Fedar breathed a deep sigh of relief as he saw the dimly lit starship approach. Josh was too amazed at what was happening to think rationally. He only hoped they would not be shot down.

Willy's squad rapidly caught up with the starship and streaked by with their cameras rolling as the shuttle approached the starship from below.

He radioed NORAD: "We just passed them. They're located at their original coordinates. What are my orders?"

General Boswell replied: "Same orders. Do not fire unless fired upon. Follow them as long as you can."

Zfar could not know how fortunate they were to have chosen the United States for their next attempt at extracting an Earth human. Had they invaded Soviet air space, it is likely they would have been shot down.

Fedar was now simultaneously working both of the manual controls as they approached the ship from beneath. Josh looked up and could see faint lights above him. They were stationary. The shuttle craft was slowing its ascent while the lateral thrusters moved them toward the lights.

As they moved closer, Josh could see the outline of the ship in the moonlight. It was circular and appeared to be about 150 feet in diameter. It was indeed saucer shaped and Josh could see that the lights were emanating from its underbelly.

There was a whirring sound that became louder as they got closer. When close to the ship, Josh could see that the outer edge of the ship was spinning at a rapid speed. They were moving up toward the center of the ship. When they neared the hull of the ship, the shuttle bay door at the bottom, about twenty feet in diameter, slid open. Fedar then used the stabilizer air jets to rotate the shuttle craft 180 degrees as it entered the ship.

Briefly, Josh could feel a release from the force of the Earth's gravity and blood rushing to his head as the seat belts held him in place as he clutched his guitar, which bobbled about in mid-air for a few seconds before he grabbed it. As they completed the rotation, this weightless sensation went away and the gravitational force was again coming from beneath them as he looked down at the Earth below. He laid the guitar back on the floor. They slowly entered the ship as Fedar gently pulled back on the joystick control. The craft rested on the floor of the shuttle bay and the shuttle bay door closed.

Willie and his squad circled back and forth by the starship. In the evening sky, they had not noticed the small shuttle craft as it approached the underbelly of the ship. Nor had it been detected by ground based radar systems.

The shuttle door slid open and Fedar gestured for Josh to exit. Leaving his guitar propped up against the shuttle seat, Josh stepped out. When his foot hit the floor of the ship, he was amazed to find that he felt much lighter. It was as though he had entered a different gravitational field. It felt to Josh as if there was just enough gravity to keep him on the floor.

He had in fact entered a different gravitational field. Over the course of several hundred years, the Senians had developed an understanding of dark matter and the sub-atomic particles that generate a gravitational field. This knowledge led to the development of electric powered equipment that could generate a gravitational field, and therefore, cancel out and even reverse an attractive gravitational force. They developed the ability to control and direct the output of the gravitational field generator with great precision.

These technological developments, along with many others, led to interstellar space travel thousands of years ago. The speed of travel was limited to about 97 percent of the speed of light. Above that, the increasing mass of the ship presented too much stress to the structure. In order to have some margin of safety, the maximum speed of the Explorer was about 95 percent of the speed of light, or about 271,700 miles per second.

Josh looked about. They were in an airlock. It was a circular room about twenty-five feet in diameter. The walls were a pleasant light brown color. There was nothing on the walls other than a control pad adjacent to a door that exited to the rest of the ship.

He could feel the air circulating very rapidly. It was being sucked out of a series of openings that were arranged vertically from the floor to the ceiling at four equidistant points along the circumference of the shuttle bay, while air was flowing into the airlock from a series of openings near the ceiling. What Josh didn't know was that the air was being rapidly run through a radioactive purifier and filter that would kill and remove any organisms in the air column. The Senians had learned to cope in varying degrees with numerous pathogens on their home planet and were highly sensitive to the danger associated with introducing pathogens from Earth into their environment. It would take about five minutes for all of the air to be treated.

Meanwhile, the F-16s continued to streak back and forth by the starship, taking no hostile action. Three Apache attack helicopters had been dispatched from Elgin and were on their way. They would arrive in about five minutes.

Willie attempted to communicate.

"Identify yourself," he repeated.

Zfar replied in Senian, "We are on a peaceful mission. We are not armed."

After a few such attempts, it became apparent to Willie that the intruders, although responding to his communication, were speaking a language he didn't understand. This provided additional confirmation that the intruder was indeed a UFO, which was now clearly visible to him as he sped past the ship.

Fedar placed his arm on Josh's shoulder and directed him toward the exit door and the control box. He pointed toward what appeared to be a counter. The symbols were changing.

Fedar said a sound that sounded to Josh like "fwa quarseks" and held up four fingers. Josh knew that Fedar was telling him in his language how much time would pass before they could enter the ship.

Josh smiled and said "yes."

Fedar nodded.

It seemed to Josh to take forever, but eventually the door opened and two Senian males wearing breathing apparatus entered the room. Each had a similar apparatus in his hand. One was given to Josh and one to Fedar. Fedar began to put his on and Josh understood that he needed to do the same. With some assistance from the Senians, he strapped a small tank made out of a light grey carbon composite material around his waist and placed the attached breathing apparatus over his nose and mouth. The Senian touched a control on the facial portion and air began to circulate.

Josh flashed a thumbs up to indicate that he was breathing well. The Senians looked at each other and smiled. The thumbs up was something new to them and they got a kick out of it. They mimicked his gesture with a thumbs up.

It was finally time to enter the ship. Once inside, the two Senians removed their breathing equipment. Fedar touched Josh on his shoulder and gestured that he was keeping his on and Josh should do the same. Josh began to understand that he was being isolated from the air in the ship in order to prevent the spread of possible pathogens. What he didn't know at that time was that both he and Fedar would have to spend twelve Senian days, which was more than ten Earth days, in isolation while their blood was carefully studied by Zofar, the Senian medical officer, to detect any possible pathogens.

The Senian knowledge of immunology had progressed to the point where they were capable of using the host's T cells to generate an antibody to a pathogen within about two weeks. These antibodies would then form the basis of a vaccine to protect other members of the crew, as well as treat the host.

This knowledge had allowed the Senians to survive their first visit to Earth, about 4,500 Earth years ago, or about 2,500 B.C., where they had spent about one Earth year on the planet and gained a great deal of familiarity with Earth's pathogens. The crew had been immunized for all known Earth pathogens, which were kept alive in facilities on Corilia and Senia in anticipation of further Earth voyages. However, there was always the possibility of a new pathogen, so it was necessary to follow strict quarantine procedures and take all possible steps to prevent the spread of a disease or illness that could jeopardize the mission.

For now, however, Josh's only interest was to see the starship. For the Senians, their only interest was to leave Earth's atmosphere as quickly as possible. The jets continued to streak back and forth by the ship without taking hostile action.

Zfar and Banar, the Information Officer, were on the bridge. They could hear the Earth human speaking from Kennedy on the monitor.

"You are in United States airspace. What is your mission? State your mission."

Zfar continued to reply in Senian: "We are on a peaceful mission. We are not armed."

Other than the tone of their voices, there was no way for either of them to understand what the other was saying. The tone of their voices, however, was calm and not threatening.

Kennedy Center continued: "You are directed to land at these coordinates." The coordinates were to land at Peterson Air Force Base in Colorado.

Zfar again replied: "We are on a peaceful mission. We are not armed."

The coordinates were meaningless to him as he did not understand the Earth's numerical system.

Fedar directed Josh to an elevator that was immediately across from the door that exited the shuttle bay. There was one touch screen button to summon the elevator. There were three touch buttons inside the elevator. Fedar touched the uppermost button that would carry them to the bridge - a circular flattened bubble about fifty feet in diameter that constituted the third level at the top of the ship. Josh had not seen the bridge, having approached the ship from its underbelly.

After they hurriedly entered the elevator, Fedar grabbed the handrails tightly and motioned for Josh to do the same. The elevator started to rotate. Josh again felt blood rushing to his head. This sensation began to diminish after about halfway through the rotation, and then once again felt normal as he completed the rotation. The elevator then carried them to the bridge.

When Josh stepped out of the elevator door he was absolutely amazed by what he saw. There was so much to take in - the ship and the starlit surroundings. But there in front of him stood what had to be the most beautiful woman he had ever seen, so she immediately became the focus of his attention. She was about five foot five with green eyes and beautiful brownish-blonde hair that lay gently on her shoulders. Her hips were something to behold. She appeared to be somewhat older than him, perhaps around thirty. He felt a rush inside and then suddenly became aware that his reaction to her was apparent to all the others. He gained his wits and looked about.

The compartment was something like the shuttle. It was transparent from about his shoulder height on up, so he could see the stars with great clarity. The support structure for the transparent dome consisted of six ribs that coalesced at the center of the top. It was a very tight space, unlike the extravagantly wasted space he was familiar with from watching Star Trek episodes. The space below the dome was packed with monitor screens and other equipment. There were five molded seats that circled around about one-half the circumference of the room.

There were three people standing there to greet him as he entered. Zfar, a somewhat elderly man, stood at the center with Banar, the ship's Information Officer, a younger man, at his right. The beautiful woman was at his left. Zfar looked very much like Fedar – thin, with strong facial features, but slightly shorter. His wavy hair, almost entirely gray, was a bit longer than Fedar's, but still very neat.

"Welcome" he said in Senian, making a welcoming gesture with his hand. Josh nodded with a slight bow of his head in the same type of gesture he would ordinarily make when approaching another person.

There was no time for introductions. Fedar quickly put his hand on Josh's shoulder and directed him to a seat, where he strapped himself in with Fedar's help. He was strapped in very securely. There was a waist belt and also two belts that crisscrossed across his shoulders. Fedar and the others quickly strap themselves in, as well.

Josh could see the F-16s whizzing by and understood the urgency of the moment. Then, in the night sky they all saw the fearsome looking Apache helicopters as they took up stationary positions directly facing the front of the bridge.

Josh could see the lights below all the way from Daytona on one side to Jacksonville on the other. He could not see beneath the ship, but then he noticed a large monitor that provided a view from the underbelly of the ship. There he could see faint lights along the beach and the brighter lights of St. Augustine. He could now see the spinning outer rim of the ship very clearly.

Willie established radio contact with the approaching Apaches.

"We are under orders not to fire unless fired upon."

"Roger"

"I've tried to make contact. They have responded to my communications, but are speaking some crazy language I never heard of."

"I'll maintain position and await your orders."

With the F-16s buzzing by and the Apaches now facing them, it was time for Zfar to make his exit. He touched his control screen several times and the pitch of the whirring outer rim increased along with the speed of rotation. Then, with one more touch on the control screen, the ship suddenly spun about like a ride Josh was familiar with at Coney Island. It was a slingshot effect as the ship hurled itself from a stationary position toward the Atlantic at a ninety degree angle from the facing Apaches.

Willie spoke to the Apache group commander: "How'd you like them apples!"

"I wouldn't believe it if I didn't see it myself," he replied.

"I'll give pursuit, but I think they're gone."

General Boswell and about twenty people at NORAD command were eagerly listening on the channel.

"This will probably be classified," he said. "Everyone is under direct orders not to discuss this incident with anyone."

About ten seconds later, the ship whipped around again as it increased its velocity and continued along the same course. The acceleration process continued about every ten seconds with ever increasing velocity. After the ship had traveled several hundred miles out over the Atlantic, Willie gave up the chase and the squad returned to base.

Having escaped pursuit, Fedar programmed the ship for a course toward Senia. They were beating it away from Earth as fast as they could, traveling along a horizontal line with the gravitational field generator pushing the starship ever further from Earth as they traversed its curved surface.

Josh was fixated between the view outside the ship and that on the monitor. Both views were absolutely breathtaking. He could now see the outline of the Earth against the darkness of the universe as they drew further and further away. Beneath the ship, he could see the clusters of lights becoming ever smaller. He did not have time to think about what was happening to him, he was so fascinated by what he was experiencing.

Josh would have enjoyed knowing that the beautiful woman, Fela, immediately felt attracted to him. Fela was actually about forty Senian years old, about thirty-eight Earth years. The Senian life span is longer than that on Earth, averaging about ninety-seven Earth years. On Senia, this was around 102 years, as the Senian year was about ninety-five percent of an Earth year. Senia was a smaller planet than Earth and orbited closer to its sun, the star known on Earth as Gliese 832.

When Fela and Josh first saw each other, she could sense his reaction to her. She was somewhat intimidated by his burly nature and his curly mess of dark brown hair that seemed primitive by Senian standards. Yet, he seemed to have a presence of mind she could relate to. She had not had sex with anyone since departing on the voyage to Earth over eighteen Senian years ago, so Josh's instinctual sexual response aroused her long suppressed sexual desires. Still, she knew that sex with the Earth human was not possible.

Before leaving on the voyage, Fela had been counseled by the Senian mission commander that it would be highly inadvisable for her to enter into a sexual relationship with a member of the crew. She desperately wanted to be a part of the mission and also understood the wisdom behind the advice she received. On a voyage that would take over eighteen years one way, if conflict developed among the crew over her affections, there would be no escaping the situation for many years. Contentious relationships among the male crew members could jeopardize the mission. Nor was the ship designed or sup-plied to sustain another person. All the crew members wanted her, despite the fact that some of them were many years older, and she knew that if she favored any one of them with her affections there was sure to be resentment from the others.

It was only after much debate among the senior mission com-manders that she was approved for the voyage. Due to the length of the voyage, there was a need to include a few younger crew members to offset the possibility that one of the older crew might die. Moreo-ver, having a skilled linguist to learn an Earth language and teach the Earth human the Senian language was the central focus of the mis-sion and required the very best talent. Fela was the best. She was well versed in the knowledge the Senians had acquired about some of the Earth's languages from their previous stay on Earth, and was also highly skilled in teaching the Senian language. This consideration trumped all objections and she was approved for the voyage.

Minar, the Assistant Engineer, was about her age, but Fela was not attracted to him. When she was around, he would strut about like a peacock, thinking that she surely must find him attractive over his older shipmates. His subtle smiles and occasional sexual innuendos only stiffened her resistance to him.

Fedar was the one crew member she found most attractive. She truly adored him and would have readily given herself to him if not for the circumstances of their voyage. Fedar sensed her unspoken affection for him and felt the same. They had settled into a sort of unspoken loving relationship that never entered the physical realm. When she would occasionally pleasure herself in bed at night, she would often think of Fedar and wonder if he was doing the same and thinking of her. He was, although not necessarily at the same time.

After about fifty Earth minutes, the *Explorer* escaped Earth's gravitational field. From that point forward, the acceleration would be minimal and hardly noticeable. It would continue for about six months until achieving maximum velocity. Then, without any signifi-cant resistance in the vacuum of space other than space dust, the ship would hurl its way toward Senia.

The ship was designed to accomplish the mission in as small a space as possible. The greatest danger in space during the voyage was space debris. Even a small bit of debris had the potential to breach the skin of the ship with catastrophic consequences. Hence, the saucer shape. With the sharp leading edge and an outer shell made of a carbon titanium composite material that was five times the hardness of a diamond, the ship's hull was capable of deflecting small bits of space debris. The ship also maintained a strong force field at its leading edge, utilizing the anti-gravitational system that was not needed for takeoff and landing during interstellar travel.

The most vulnerable area of the ship was the transparent portion of the bridge. This was made from a carbon silicate composite that was also extremely hard and resistant to breakage, also protected by a force field.

Larger space debris was a different story. Here, the ship's main defense was its low profile and the very low odds of a collision. Traveling at near light speed, it was virtually impossible to detect and navigate around an object such as a large meteorite.

The Senians had meticulously mapped all of the known asteroids and other identifiable space debris in this sector of the galaxy. Once the departure time from Earth and three dimensional space coordinates were fed into the onboard computer, the navigational system set the course for Senia, including any necessary corrections to account for the trajectory of space objects stored in the data bank. Fedar's role as navigator was simply to initiate the system.

A small nuclear reactor made of ceramic and carbon composite materials powered the ship. The reactor heated a circulating mixture of water and other fluids to drive a turbine electric generator. Senian nuclear technology included a mechanism whereby heat from the reactive process was dissipated through a series of heat exchangers that encircled the ship and the internal circulation system that heated the ship, as well as the horticultural systems located on the first level.

The generator powered a magnetic levitation system that suspended the ship's outer ring, causing it to spin. In order to move the ship, the electromagnetic field causing the outer rim to rotate in one direction could be quickly reversed so as to create a slingshot effect, propelling the ship forward. In the vacuum of space, each such movement accelerated the ship until it reached maximum velocity.

The ship was supplied with enough nuclear material to last about forty Earth years. The on-board gravitational field generators created the gravitational fields that kept things in place. Because the Senians were biologically adapted to a smaller planet, they required less gravitational force than Josh.

About fifty-five minutes had passed since Josh was given the breathing apparatus. Fedar replaced Josh's air tank and motioned for him to unstrap himself. Josh quickly sprang up and again felt the sensation of being very light on his feet. Fedar motioned for Josh to follow him as they began a tour of the ship.

They took the elevator to the second level and walked about twenty feet along a hallway to a five-foot wide corridor that encircled the ship close to its perimeter. The halls were the same pleasant tan color. What appeared to be grey and black storage lockers and compartment doors lined the side of the corridor closest to the outer rim. They made use of the space that was too low for any other purpose in view of the gently rising ceiling level as one moved toward the center of the ship. Josh immediately began to realize that no space on the ship was wasted.

Fedar walked past two doors facing the center of the ship and pressed a button similar to that of the elevator to open a door to a very small area. This was an airlock that was built into all crew quarters in case quarantine was necessary for any crew member. Fedar then opened another door to a room that was obviously crew quarters. As with elsewhere on the ship, there was no wasted space. On Josh's left as he entered was a very small bathroom. There was a shower with a sliding door, a toilet, and a vanity area with a sink, mirror, and some level surface area with cabinets above and drawers below. The walls throughout were the same pleasant tan color.

It did not appear to be lived in and Josh immediately concluded this would be his quarters. He was relieved to see that he would have private quarters and a private bathroom.

Josh's attention turned toward the room. On his left was a bed that butted up against the other side of the bathroom wall. The bed appeared to be just long enough for Josh's six-foot, two-inch frame. He sat down on the bed and stretched out to make sure. It would do. The mattress seemed very comfortable. It was a foam mattress and appeared to be about eight inches thick. Underneath the bed were sliding drawers for storage.

Josh noticed a large screen on the other side of the bathroom wall facing the bed. It appeared to be a television screen.

How could that be? he thought.

It was securely fastened to the wall and did not appear to be more than an inch thick. Josh checked the other side in the bathroom wall to make sure. Yes, it was only an inch thick.

Josh looked over at the opposite wall. There was a desk area with more cabinets above and drawers below, except where one could place his feet under the desk. Josh opened one of the dark grey cabinet doors. It was very thin and light, made of the same composite material Josh had seen in the corridor cabinets. There was a chair locked in place under the desk. Fedar unhinged it and slid it out for Josh to see. It was a comfortable looking reclining armchair that could be used to watch television.

To the right of the desk knee hole near the floor was what appeared to be a refrigerator. Josh opened it and confirmed it was a refrigerator, not yet turned on. Near the door opposite the bathroom was a closet with a sliding door. There was no door to the bathroom. Josh estimated the area was about ten feet wide and fifteen feet long and reminded him of a very well organized recreational vehicle one might expect to find on Earth. The space had a slight pie-shaped angle to it, reflecting the curvature of the ship.

It seemed that the room would do. Josh was very relieved that he had brought his guitar. With the examination of the living quarters, the reality that he wasn't going back to Earth anytime soon began to sink in. He was on a trip to who knows where. Surely, it would be somewhere very far from Earth, but he could not even hazard a guess as to where that might be. His guitar would bring him comfort and help pass the time.

Oh shit, my guitar!, he suddenly thought as he remembered he had left it in the shuttle. He motioned toward Fedar like he was strumming on a guitar. Fedar looked at him quizzically.

"My guitar," Josh said, somewhat exasperated. "In the shuttle."

Fedar still did not understand. He motioned for Josh to follow him.

They left Josh's quarters and continued down the corridor. Fedar skipped one door and opened another door that did not have an airlock to enter the exercise room. It was a much larger room, about twenty feet wide and twenty-five feet deep, with the same pie-shaped curvature to the walls. There were two bicycles, two pieces for running in place, and two rather complex looking pieces that most closely resembled Nautilus equipment to Josh.

From there Fedar opened the next door down the corridor and they entered the ship's medical facility. It was about twice the size of the exercise room, divided into two rooms. In one room there were two operating or examining tables, a dentist's chair with what looked like x-ray equipment, many cabinets, several had transparent doors, possibly refrigerators, and a variety of medical equipment, including three monitors adjacent to each other on one of the walls. The other room was the ship's medical lab, filled with a variety of Senia's most advanced medical equipment for detecting and combating pathogens.

Zofar, the ship's medical officer, who was also a dentist, was in the room wearing a white shirt that hung over his waist. Zofar was forty-eight Senian years of age. He also cut a strong presence, being about five foot-ten with a closely cropped thick head of straight black hair and a soft olive complexion. He was a very rare genetic type on Senia, having descended from one of the dark-complexioned original settlers, who had evolved from the equatorial area of Corilia where the Senian sun was the strongest. Due to the precautions the original settlers took against inbreeding, his genetic material had been largely diluted among the Senian population as it grew. It was very rare at this point in Senian genealogy for someone with Zofar's features to emerge.

Zofar greeted them with a welcoming gesture of his hand and a slight bow of his head. Josh returned the greeting in a similar fashion, pointing to himself and saying "Josh." Zofar pointed to himself saying his name. Josh looked around the room at the complex equipment, wondering what it all did.

I hope they are not planning to conduct experiments on me, he thought in a moment of sudden fear. He looked over at Fedar and Zofar with their pleasant smiles and was somewhat relieved.

As they were not capable of any further communication, Fedar said to Zofar that they would be back tomorrow and placed his hand on Josh's shoulder indicating it was time to leave.

They continued around the corridor. After skipping two doors, they entered a conference room, also without an airlock. It was a smaller room, just large enough for a conference table that would accommodate eight people, with eight chairs tightly fixed to the wall on both sides of the table. There were cabinets and shelves on the wall with the door. The opposite wall toward the center of the ship had a large video screen that almost covered the wall.

Leaving the meeting room, they entered another small room packed on all sides with monitors and electronic equipment. A console that ran the entire length of one wall, jutting out from the wall about two feet at a slight angle so that one could sit in front of the console and operate the controls that looked similar to those that Josh had seen in the shuttle craft. Banar, the Information Officer, greeted them with the same Senian greeting, bowing his head slightly, as they arrived. Josh returned the greeting staring about in wonder at all of the equipment.

Banar was typical Senian stock, about five foot-eight with a neatly cropped head of wavy light brown hair that was starting to show some peppering with grey at his 51 Senian years of age. He had a relaxed but intense manner about him as he looked closely at Josh, wondering if this very gruff human would be able to meet their needs after all of the risk and effort they had undergone.

"How is he doing?" he asked Fedar, smiling lightly at Josh.

"He seems to be doing well so far, not fearful like the other Earth humans; very curious."

"That is good. Perhaps our eighteen years in space will amount to something," he wryly replied.

"Yes, I hope so."

Fedar had now shown Josh all he needed to know about Level Two, except for what the crew called the "central area." The other rooms they had skipped were crew quarters, similar to Josh's, and supply closets. The crew quarters were two adjacent rooms, separated by the supply closets and other facilities designed so the crew would have more privacy and be spread throughout the second level of ship.

Fedar and Josh circled back to the elevator. Two corridors branched around the elevator compartment to a door on each side that opened into the central area. Josh was getting very tired, but his eyes opened wide when he entered the room. It was a large circular room, about sixty feet in diameter. Fedar had wanted to explain about the multiple activities encompassed by the central area, but could only let Josh take in what he could understand.

The multi-function nature of the room was apparent to Josh. There was an area with nine theatre-type chairs and a large screen against the wall, obviously a viewing area. The ninth chair was for Josh. A large rectangular table, obviously for dining, stood at the center, also with nine chairs fastened to the table. Some of the area was walled off for a very compact kitchen. A portion of the wall was a transparent glasslike material with an opening and table area for passing food, similar to any sleazy restaurant on Earth. There were two adjacent couches against the wall, some small tables and chairs, and other amenities denoting an area for the crew to relax and be social.

In all of the other areas Josh had seen, the walls were consumed with storage compartments. Here, some of the walls were devoted to Senian art and pictures of Senia. Josh walked over and looked. Most of the pictures were natural landscapes, depicting an unspoiled planet with an ocean, rivers, forests, and wide open grasslands, similar to many areas on Earth.

It was now about two hours after midnight, Earth time, and Josh was very tired. He yawned and Fedar noticed. Josh had reached his limit and wanted to lie down so he could digest the day's events like any other day and go to sleep.

Fedar decided Josh could see the ship's first level tomorrow. He motioned for Josh to leave and Josh followed him back to the quarters Fedar first showed him. Fedar opened the bathroom wall cabinet and showed Josh where his drinking and other utensils were located. Then, he nudged Josh's breathing apparatus to indicate that it could come off. Josh understood and placed it on the desk.

Josh pulled the fishing knife from his pocket, along with his wallet, keys, and some loose change, and laid them on the desk. Fedar looked at the fishing knife and then at Josh. It would not be wise, he thought, for Josh to keep the knife, although he had a sense that the Earth human would not harm anyone. He walked over to the bathroom, grabbed a small towel, and used it to pick up the knife, reinforcing Josh's understanding of the quarantine he was still under. Josh showed no objection to Fedar taking the knife.

Fedar patted Josh on the shoulder and gestured with his hand that he should lay down in bed. Josh nodded his understanding and sat on the bed. Fedar then pointed to the door and moved his arms back and forth over each other with a frowning expression, trying to convey to Josh that he should not go outside. Josh now fully understood that he was being quarantined. He nodded his head up and down and gave Fedar a thumps up. Fedar smiled, gave Josh a thumbs up, and left.

As he lay in bed staring up at the ceiling, there was so much to think about, but his eyes began to draw shut. Josh glanced at his watch. It was 2:20 p.m. It was a self-winding watch and Josh thought this might be the only record he would have as to the passage of time on Earth.

He thought back to his last view of Earth receding in the distance, and understood that he was going somewhere deep in the universe. His thoughts then turned to the beautiful woman he had seen. She seemed to be the only female on the ship. Would she become his fantasy woman? He thought not. He did not want that, because fantasy women had a way of never becoming reality. Josh wanted to leave open the possibility that this beautiful woman might actually become his bedmate. In the meantime, his fantasies would have to rely upon the usual standbys, women he almost seduced during his college days, some of the hotter looking women at law school, and whomever else his memory or imagination might be able to conjure up.

He started to wonder about what his parents and others would think had happened to him. He did not have any strong attachments after his first semester at law school. There was a brief liaison with another law student, and they were still friends. People would probably think that he was murdered and his body dumped somewhere. What a pleasant thought. No one would ever think that he had been carted off into outer space, voluntarily no less.

He wondered how it could be that the aliens were so similar to Earth humans. Were they from a common genome or had they evolved separately from Earth? If they were from a common genome, that raised many questions. Had the aliens influenced evolution on Earth? Josh knew a little bit about human evolution and the development of human civilization. There was a period of time between about 25,000 years ago and the beginning of recorded history about 3,000 years before the birth of Christ when humankind went from a primitive hunting and gathering existence and the use of crude stone and wooden tools to the development of agriculture, metalworking, and many other technological advances. It was a very large technological leap that to Josh's understanding was largely unexplained.

And there were the mysteries of Stonehenge, Easter Island, and the pyramids, and how and why they were constructed thousands of years ago. Was there a connection between those events in human history and alien intervention as some had speculated? Josh could only wonder. He realized that he might gain knowledge that could provide an answer to many of these questions.

Somehow, in those closed quarters, with everything so orderly, he felt safe. He had made the decision to put his life on the line, and now he was going along for the ride. He would see about getting his guitar tomorrow. His eyes shut for the last time and he drifted off into a deep sleep.

CHAPTER 2 - DAY TWO

It was early the following day, 8:05 a.m., Eastern Standard Time on Earth. The *Explorer* was now more than 300,000 miles from Earth. The moon loomed large, showing its many craters in great detail, with the blue Earth shining in the background. Mars, Venus, Saturn and Jupiter could also be seen in the distance across the great panorama of the solar system. Josh was still soundly asleep. Fedar, Zfar, Fela, and Banar manned the bridge. The rest of the crew were in their quarters.

There wasn't much to do on the bridge. At this point, the *Explorer* was on its trajectory toward Senia. If all systems worked properly, there would not be any need for navigation for about seventeen Earth years. In the coming days, however, there would be more to direct the crew's attention.

First on the list was receiving and digesting all of the information that would now be coming toward the ship from Senia. Traveling away from Senia at 95 percent of the speed of light meant that, as time passed on Senia, most of the transmissions about events there would not reach the ship until the return voyage. Some transmissions did reach the ship, but they were about one twentieth as fast as the passage of time on Senia. That meant that when the ship reached Earth, the Senians were only aware of events that had last occurred a little more than sixteen Earth years ago on Senia.

The opposite would be true on the return voyage, when Senian transmissions would reach the starship at almost twice the speed of the passage of time on Senia. The daily Senian transmissions would now be received twice daily, Senian time, instead of once every twenty Senian days. There was much to be apprehensive about.

Several years before launching the Earth mission during Earth year 1960, the Senians had successfully intercepted and destroyed an interstellar nuclear ballistic missile that had been launched from the Corilian home planet and was intended to cause incalculable damage on Senia. The missile was similar in design to the Senian starship, except that it was much smaller, as it did not require any environmental or other systems necessary to sustain a crew. Vondar, the new Corilian Tskar, had decided to up the ante in the Corilian effort to reassert dominion over Senia.

Senia was initially settled by Corilian explorers a little more than 4,700 Earth years ago. This resettlement was the first leg of Senian interstellar space exploration, the next leg being the initial voyage to planet Earth. The Corilians had developed the technology that enabled them to determine with a fair degree of certainty those star systems that contained planets that, like Earth, would be habitable to human life.

Senia was smaller than Corilia with conditions that were not as habitable, but still adequate for establishing a colony. Water was much scarcer, covering only about twenty-eight percent of the planet's surface. Rainfall was much less frequent. The sky was mostly devoid of clouds and the Senian sun could be intense. The planet was volcanically active and there were several large mountain ranges that trapped moisture from the prevailing winds, creating rainfall that found its way through rivers and streams to the great Senian Sea. The majority of the planet most closely resembled the savannahs on Earth's African continent.

It was a beautiful planet, largely unspoiled. The ocean was filled with abundant aquatic life that served as the protein staple of the Senian diet. The afternoon sky filled with shades of orange and red during the sunset while light clouds drifting slowly across. The Senians largely settled along the coast and near the rivers and streams leading to the coast.

There was no form of human life on the planet before they arrived. The many terrestrial creatures that traversed the great savannahs, not unlike antelope and other animals on Earth were the highest forms of life. The Senian environment was largely devoid of trees except near rivers and streams. The terrestrial rain forests that gave birth to the primates that became the predecessors to humans on Earth did not exist on Senia.

The first voyage to Senia consisted of two starships very similar to the starship the Senians were now using to travel to Earth. One ship contained supplies and returned to Corilia, along with a minimal crew. The other ship remained on Senia as a means of exit for the settlers should conditions become threatening or unbearable. Fifteen Corilian settlers remained to establish the colony.

The settlers were not lacking in the technical knowledge necessary to develop a complex technological society on Senia. Still, it would be several hundred years before they discovered and fully developed the minerals needed for their technology. For many years, life was mainly a struggle for survival against the elements and a continuing effort to build the settlement.

After about two hundred Earth years, the Senians had developed sufficient nuclear technology and felt secure enough in their existence on Senia to commission the first Earth exploration mission. The ship they had retained from the original Corilian voyage was used for the mission, its fuel supply replenished from the scarce uranium resources they were able to locate on Senia.

The mission was considered a great success, as they were able to establish peaceful contact with various populations across the planet. Still, there was no means of communicating with the Earthlings, who spoke in a variety of seemingly crude languages and were only beginning to develop the rudiments of written language. The Senian explorers concluded that many hundreds or thousands of years would be needed before the Earth populations had developed to the point that communication with Earth was possible in any meaningful way.

The Senian population grew slowly at first and then accelerated until the planet reached its carrying capacity of about five hundred million people.. Senians were then encouraged to maintain replacement fertility of no more than two children per woman. Due to the strong sense of community that had developed on Senia as a result of the ongoing struggle to settle and develop the planet, it was not necessary to implement any coercive policies to maintain replacement fertility.

As the population of Senia slowly grew, there was some settlement of the large land mass, known on Senia as the "Expanse." Vast water projects were developed to move fresh water inland as agricultural production increased and minerals were extracted from the Expanse.

As time passed, the Senians developed their own democratic means of governance and only paid lip service to governance from Corilia. The vast distance across space, about sixteen Earth light years, made it impractical to transport any minerals from Senia to Corilia, with the exception of highly refined uranium, which was of limited supply and was in constantly increasing demand on both Senia and Corilia. The Corilians did not seek to impose any taxes on Senia, and were content to have Senian cooperation in exploitation of the uranium resource.

For the first thousands of years of human life on Senia, the two planets maintained a relationship of friendly cooperation. This benign relationship fell apart about four hundred Earth years ago when Corilia fell under totalitarian rule. Soon after that, the Tskar, as the new Corilian tyrant came to be known, sent a mission to Senia seeking to install a new leader there who would faithfully implement his commands. By that time, Senia had achieved its full population and there was simply no way the Senians were going to accept a hand-picked tyrant from the home planet.

There was really nothing the home planet could do about it. The vastness of space made it impossible for the Corilians to send a military mission that could take physical control of Senia. All the home planet could do is threaten Senia with destruction. The Senian leadership graciously refused to accept their new leader, sending him back to Corilia after a brief stay.

It would be at least thirty-six Senian years before there could be another visit from Corilia, assuming the Corilian ship returned to Corilia before another mission was launched. The Senians used this time to develop their defensive technology and became very adept at intercepting and destroying missiles in space. A network of satellites encircled the planet and provided the early detection system. The Senians maintained a constant awareness of the trajectory a missile launched from Corilia would take as the planets shifted their positions in the galaxy. They continually stood ready with starships capable of intercepting and destroying such a missile.

More than seventy-five Senian years would pass before there was another attempt by Corilia to assert control over Senia. A single Corilian ship entered the Senian protection zone. Contact was established and the captain asserted that their mission was peaceful. After much debate, the Senians agreed to meet the ship in space where they would inspect it to determine whether it constituted a threat.

Following the inspection, Corilians were allowed to land on Senia. Discussions ensued. The Senians were presented with assurances that they would be allowed to retain their democratic form of government if they pledged allegiance to the Tskar and allowed the Corilians to establish a military outpost on Senia from which they could continue to explore the galaxy. If the Corilian proposal was refused, the envoy said, the Tskar would declare a state of war against Senia and use all means at his disposal to destroy the colony on Senia.

After much debate, the Senians decided to reject the Tskar's proposal. They knew that there could not be any assurance that the Tskar would not attempt to gain control over Senia once the Corilian military was allowed to establish an outpost. The Corilian commander was told that Senia would only re-establish ties with Corilia if it returned to democratic government, and that, from that point forward, Senia would consider itself to be in a state of war against Corilia. Any incoming vessels would be destroyed.

The steely Senian response gave the Corilians pause, and there were no further attempts to establish contact with Senia or take hostile action for several hundred Senian years. The Corilian rulers were having considerable difficulty maintaining totalitarian control over Corilia. Word had leaked of the Senian refusal to submit to Corilian rule, and this gave encouragement to those on Corilia who sought a return to democratic institutions. Corilia was in a constant state of rebellion, with ever more stringent and egregious measures taken against those in the population who sought to challenge the ruling elite.

The Corilian leadership had degenerated into a corrupt regime that greatly favored those in control of the political and economic apparatus, while the general populace was ever more suppressed and disadvantaged in its economic development. An underground movement developed that included people in positions of power and at academic institutions, who did their best to keep the spirit of democracy alive. Corilia had all of the trappings of a totalitarian society, with secret police, torture, betrayals, and executions. Yet, the underground movement persisted to the present day.

After word of the Senian refusal leaked out on Corilia, the Corilian underground sought to establish contact with Senia through high energy radio transmissions from facilities used to study the galaxy at the observatory on Mount Vilara. It would take about sixteen Earth years for the transmissions to reach Senia. The Senians intercepted the transmissions, but hesitated to respond because a response might be detected by the Tskar and expose the Corilian underground. These communications continued until the present day undetected by the Corilian authorities. Over time the Senians began to trust the reliability of the information received.

This situation persisted until Vondar, the latest Corilian Tskar, decided that it was absolutely imperative that Corilia re-assert its dominion over Senia in order to establish a base from which it could extend its control over that sector of the galaxy, including Earth. The degeneration of Corilian society had led to reckless exploitation of the planet's natural resources, and the Tskar had designs on establishing control over Earth by subjugating or eliminating its population, making this lush planet into a new Corilian colony and mining its uranium for use on Corilia.

In order to do so, it was necessary to go back to the original plan for development of the Senia colony as a point of embarkation for the journey to Earth. The Corilians had no idea to what extent Earth had developed technologically since their second and last mission almost 500 Earth years ago. After the rebellion on Senia, it was no longer possible for Corilia to send further Earth missions.

The Tskar thought it wouldn't be difficult with the threat of nuclear destruction to overcome the planet if the Earth's technology was anywhere near as lacking as it had been during their last visit. They did not land on the planet during that mission, but did obtain extensive aerial photography showing the state of Earth's technological development.

It was through the most recent Senian underground transmission, received after Zfar and the others had departed for Earth in Earth year 1960, that the Senians learned of the Corilian plan to send a fleet of thirty starships to attack Senia. The Corilians thought that, in sufficient numbers, they would be able to overwhelm the Senian planetary defenses. If only a few ships got through, they would be capable of destroying all of the major cities on the planet.

Constructing thirty starships capable of carrying weapons of war would be a massive undertaking. These warships would be considerably larger than a non-military starship, as they would carry weapons and the crew to maintain and operate these weapons. The ships would be more vulnerable to space debris and it was possible that some would be lost in the journey to Senia.

The information was transmitted to Senia from the Corilian underground while the military effort was still in the planning stage. The Senians conservatively estimated that it would take about eleven Senian years for the Corilians to construct these ships, mine and refine the uranium necessary to power the ships, and train the necessary crew. The transmission took about seventeen Senian years to reach Senia. Therefore, when the transmission was received, the Corilian fleet was already about six Senian years into the voyage and would reach Senia in about twelve Senian years, or eleven and one-

43

half Earth years.

Word of the impending Corilian attack was immediately transmitted to the Earth mission. This information would not reach the starship until it was about eleven Earth years into the return voyage. It was possible that, if all went well and their estimates were correct, the Earth mission would return to Senia several months to a year before the Corilian attack.

As was their usual procedure, Banar checked for incoming transmissions. There were none. Banar ran some calculations and informed the others that it would be about two milseks, or one Earth hour, before the next transmission. It would be a continuation of the previous transmissions, and reflect events on Senia about seventeen Earth years ago. Now that the frequency of transmissions would increase by a factor of forty, *Explorer* crew members were eager to catch up with the progress of events on Corilia.

Before they left Senia, a transmission from the Corilian underground described the increasing militancy of the Corilian rulers, along with their increasing belligerency toward the Corilian population. It was even possible, as they hoped against hope, that the increasing oppression would precipitate a revolution on Corilia that returned the planet to democratic government.

Fedar briefed the others regarding his impressions of Josh.

"I think we may have succeeded. He appears to be very intelligent and understands that he is leaving his home planet."

Zfar: "Does he understand that he is under quarantine?"

Fedar: "Yes, I think so. He should be able to deduce that from the fact that he was not required to wear breathing equipment in his quarters. I locked the outside door to his quarters, but I don't think he will test the door."

Zfar turned to Fela: "When should we start the language sessions?"

"I would like to start today, if possible." As she spoke, Fela could feel her excitement over meeting Josh welling up.

Fedar replied: "I will show him the first level and then we can start the language sessions and see how he responds."

They all were greatly relieved that things appeared to be working out well with the Earth human. One of the precepts of the mission was that the Earth human not be abducted against his or her will. They knew the likelihood of their gaining cooperation in learning their language and teaching them an Earth language, as well as the geopolitical circumstances on Earth, would be greatly diminished if the Earth human was abducted.

The Senians had made several failed attempts at other locations to obtain an Earth human. In the most isolated and sparsely settled areas, the Earth people had cringed in fear and refused to approach the shuttle. They then decided to try a location closer to a populated area, finally leading to success at this phase of the mission.

Banar, Zfar, Fela and Fedar spent some time chatting about how happy they were to be finally heading in the direction of Senia.

Banar: "At last we're headed home. Only eighteen years to go."

Fedar: "I can't start thinking of Senia yet. It will only make it seem longer. I'll start when we're about one year away."

Fela, in her usual cute and somewhat coy manner, wondered: "What will I do without all you gentlemen to keep me entertained?"

Fedar replied: "I don't think you will have any trouble finding someone to amuse you," thinking that he would like to be that person.

Banar: "I know the first thing I'm going to do when I get back to Senia."

They looked at him inquisitively.

"Take a leak on the grass. I guess I'll have to wait until after all of the reporters leave."

Fela: "You can count me out on that."

They all laughed.

All of them had dedicated a great part of their lives to this mission. When they returned, friends and family would be much older and some would have passed away. None of them were married. As on Earth, it was the custom on Senia to mate for life. Whatever attachments they had were broken off before departing, some with the understanding that they would seek each other out when and if they successfully returned to Senia.

It was indeed a very lonely voyage for all of the crew. They relied upon each other for companionship and had formed strong bonds of friendship. There was a very subtle competition for Fela's amusement, if not affection, but it never went further. With the exception of Minar, they knew and accepted that Fela most adored Fedar.

At last, they received the next Senian transmission. It was completely non-eventful, just a continuation of the last dreary transmission. There was no news about the Corilians, which was the only thing that really got their attention. News on Senia was mostly about the next government project, usually to do with water, and the business, sports, and weather news. During the political season, the candidates appeared to discuss and debate issues. There was virtually no crime on Senia. The economy hummed along at full employment and the Senians had a great deal of time for recreational pursuits. They had invented a variety of sports, many similar to those on Earth.

There was nothing more to do on the bridge, so all except Zfar left for their quarters and the central area. The ship continued to accelerate with the slight jolts they were all very accustomed to.

Fela could hardly wait for the day's events to begin. She sat in the central area by herself, sipping on freshly brewed tea, thinking about Josh. Fedar thought him to be very intelligent. She had sensed that too in the way he quickly adjusted to his circumstances. She had only a brief glance at him. He was so tall and burly looking.

Were all of the Earth humans like him? she wondered.

There was so much she wanted to ask him about Earth, but knew that would take many months, or years, before they would be able to converse freely.

Josh suddenly awakened from a deep sleep. He glanced at his watch. It was 9:15. There were no windows and he did not know how to work the television.

First things first, he got up and went to the bathroom. Oh, how he wanted a good shower. There was no mechanical shower control, just two buttons and a small glasslike screen above the top button. He pressed the top button and water started to pour out in a high pressure, very light flow, similar to the water conserving shower heads that were starting to show up at hardware stores. A meter above the top button lit up. He pressed the button again and the flow stopped. He found the soap in a drawer by the sink and finally started to shower. The water was cold. He tried the second button and the meter moved to the right. The water quickly warmed and Josh concluded that the meter showed the water temperature. He had just finished washing all of the soap from his body when the shower stopped. Josh then surmised that the showers were for a set time, about five minutes.

The sink was a religious experience. He was thirsty and needed something to drink. He found a glass tightly bound inside a drawer in a molded grey bedding and went to the bathroom sink, only to be confounded by no handles to turn on the water.

There they are again, those darn buttons, he thought, again with a small glasslike screen above the top button.

What is wrong with a simple mechanical faucet?

He pressed the button and water came out of the faucet in a slow, steady stream. It was cold. Josh filled his glass and started to drink. The screen above the button was lit, again showing a temperature meter with strange symbols. Josh pressed the button again. The flow stopped and the screen became dark.

He had just finished brushing his teeth when he heard the outer compartment door opening.

There was a knock and he said "enter."

Fedar took Josh's utterance to be permission to enter. He was wearing his breathing apparatus and carrying an air refill for Josh's breathing apparatus and a small plate with two greenish brown wafers about one-half inch thick. He held the plate toward Josh and gestured for him to eat. Josh was hungry and curious.

Is this what I'm going to have to eat for the rest of this journey? he wondered.

His mind immediately went to *Soylent Green*, a pretty lousy movie he had seen years ago. He chuckled and picked up one of the wafers. To his surprise, it did not taste that bad. It was crunchy and mildly sweet. Josh quickly consumed the two bars while Fedar watched with a smile.

Josh put on his breathing apparatus and they took the elevator to the bridge. Josh was astonished as he stepped out into the room and could see the stars of the universe with greater clarity and abundance than he had ever seen from Earth. The Earth, its moon, Mars, Venus, Saturn and Jupiter seemed larger than life, illuminated by the Sun against the backdrop of the stars.

Zfar, Banar and Fela were on the bridge. They all noticed Josh's eyes open in amazement. Although the space view was a very routine site for them, they took pleasure in seeing Josh's reaction to the wondrous expanse of the universe.

Fedar and the others discussed the plan for the day. Josh would first have blood drawn at the medical facility for testing. Then he would be shown the first level. After that, they would meet Fela at the conference room for the opening language session. Then, they would all gather for the midday meal at the central area.

Fedar motioned for Josh to follow him and they took the elevator to the second level. Zofar was waiting when they arrived. He greeted Josh with a smile and gestured for him to take a seat on one of the operating tables. Josh's apprehension factor skyrocketed. Zofar observed Josh's trepidation and he patted Josh on the shoulder, trying to reassure him that nothing drastic was about to happen. Zofar obtained a syringe and extended his arm, gesturing for Josh to do the same. Josh was greatly relieved. This was just an ordinary blood draw. He was a little squeamish about blood draws, but survived them without fainting.

He thought with a smile: *Where was the tri-coder device from Star Trek that flashed a few lights and told you everything you needed to know about the condition of the human body?*

After the blood was drawn, Zofar approached a circular scanning device that stood vertically at one corner of the room. Josh noticed the device was large enough to accommodate a human body. He gestured for Josh to enter. It sort of looked to Josh like Woody Allen's "orgasmatron" from *Sleepers*. Not so.

After Josh entered, the compartment door slid shut and the scanner descended from the top to the floor and then back up. The scan would provide Zofar with a wealth of information about Josh's circulatory and nervous system and the state of his organs in order to ascertain whether Josh was in sufficiently good health to survive the voyage. Zofar then obtained a urine sample and took Josh's blood pressure. With that, the medical exam was complete.

It would take Zofar several days to analyze the blood and urine samples for viruses and other pathogens. If all went well, Josh would remain in quarantine for about ten more Earth days.

It was now time for Josh to see the first level, which contained the guts of the ship. They stepped into the elevator. Fedar grabbed the handrails on the side of the circular compartment. Josh did the same. The elevator began its descent to the first level. As they descended, Josh could feel his blood mysteriously rushing to his head as his body became lighter and lighter and began to float over the floor of the elevator. It was the same strange sensation he had felt when he first ascended to the bridge after entering the ship. The elevator came to a halt at the first level and started to rotate. As they rotated, the sensation of blood rushing to his head diminished until all felt normal when the 180 degree rotation was complete.

Josh did not realize that "down" was a relative term aboard the ship. The ship's center of gravity was between the first and second levels. The direction of the gravitational force was the same on the second level and the bridge. The reversal of the gravitation field for the first level was necessary so there would be a flat floor on the first level and no wasted space beneath the floor on the saucer shaped ship. In order to accommodate the change in gravity fields, it was necessary for the elevator to rotate 180 degrees when traveling between the first and second levels. There were no stairs between these levels, as it would have been impossible to ascend a set of stairs with the reversing gravity field.

The elevator compartment contained a gravitational field generator at its base. This operated to neutralize and reverse the gravitational field emanating from the field generators between the first and second levels in order for the elevator to rise to the third level and descend to the first level. The elevator compartment rotated 180 degrees after descending to position on the first level. There were no cables or motors to move the elevator between levels. It would work forever, so long as the gravitational field generator was maintained.

They left the elevator and entered a vestibule area with three doors. Fedar pressed a button, the door opposite the elevator slid open, and they entered the shuttlecraft bay. Josh's guitar was there where he left it.

"My guitar," he said, pointing to it.

"Guitar," Fedar slowly replied, please to have learned an Earth word.

"Yes." *I'll leave it here for now,* he thought.

Josh studied the craft, still wondering how it could fly. He could see no propulsion mechanism other than the small air exhausts that encircled the craft.

They exited the shuttle bay and then entered the horticultural portion of the ship. It extended from the ship's perimeter to the outside edge of the shuttle bay, there being no perimeter corridor on this level. The ceiling was about five feet high at the perimeter and fifteen feet high toward the center of the ship. Along the perimeter, which was similar to the second level, Josh could see an array of instruments, cabinets, and doors. It was an open space and appeared to take up about one fourth of the lower level.

Bandar, the Horticultural Systems Officer, was there to greet them. He was a small person, about five-foot five, with curly brown hair, closely cropped. He appeared to Josh to be about thirty-five years old. Actually, he was forty-one Earth years of age, which amounted to forty-three Senian years.

From habit, Josh put out his hand to shake Bandar's hand, but then realized that there could not be any physical contact between them. Instead, he bowed his head slightly and Bandar did the same.

They walked about the area. It was a maze of plants, shelving, clear plastic tubing, and other equipment. There was a large tank against the inner wall filled with very small shrimp-like creatures. At the highest point, three levels of plantings extending from the floor to the ceiling. Josh saw a great variety of fruits and vegetables of many different colors. Some resembled vegetables that he was familiar with, such as green beans and lettuce. Others were completely strange to him.

Josh wandered through the area, gazing up and down while Fedar told Bandar about Josh. As there was nothing they could say to Josh to explain how things worked, Fedar motioned for them to leave. Josh bowed toward Bandar, who did the same, and they departed through the door from which they'd entered.

They returned to the lobby-like area by the elevator and opened the door to the ship's engineering area. It was a very large space that encompassed the remainder of the first level. Elar, the Chief Engineer, and Minar, Assistant Engineer, were busy monitoring the ship's systems as they entered the control area at the center of a vast array of monitors and control panels that ran along the inside diameter of the space opposite the shuttlecraft bay. As with other areas of the ship, there was no wasted space.

Opposite the wall containing the control panels, Josh could see a maze of equipment, pipes and control panels with narrow access isles throughout. This area contained the ship's nuclear propulsion system and the engineering systems that digested and recycled human wastewater to the horticultural area, while water from the sinks and showers was purified and recycled to the sinks and showers to be used again.

The nuclear reactor generated the heat necessary to power a steam turbine, which generated electricity to power all of the ship's systems, except heating the ship, which was done with waste heat from the reactor. The remainder of the waste heat was disbursed into space through heat exchangers along the perimeter.

Josh gazed about for several minutes while Fedar conversed with Elar and Minar. As he stood there looking at the maze of equipment, the enormity of his situation began to sink in. Up to now, he had been consumed by his amazement at what was happening. He had passed out last night before having much chance to reflect on things. Now, as he stood there, he thought about how that equipment somehow enabled the ship to defy gravity on Earth and fly through the universe.

What technology enabled these people, who are not that much different from humans on Earth, to accomplish this? he thought.

He determined that he would do whatever he could to learn the aliens' technologies. There was going to be the challenge of first learning their language.

If this technology could be learned on Earth, it could be of great benefit. Or perhaps they possessed technologies so destructive, like the atom bomb, they would best be left unknown. They apparently had the ability to neutralize the effect of gravity without a propulsion system, unlike Earth rockets. Earth rockets required so much energy that the weight of all of the needed fuel greatly added to the gravitational force that needed to be overcome.

Fedar waved to Josh that it was time to leave. Josh had now seen the entire ship, and it was time to meet Fela in the conference room. He spoke into the communicator on his wrist.

"Fela, I'm on my way to the conference room."

When he said "Fela" the communicator knew to connect him with Fela.

She replied, "I'll see you there."

Individual communications did not go through the central broadcast communications system. One could communicate throughout the ship by first saying "broadcast." Otherwise, communications could be initiated between individuals or groups.

Before they left, Elar replenished their air supplies. They entered the elevator and gripped the sidebars as the elevator rotated. Josh still did not understand what was happening but was getting the routine.

When they arrived at the conference room, Fela was there to greet them. She smiled at Josh and he smiled back. Her green eyes sparkled, and so did his, as they gazed into each other's eyes, unable to communicate in any other way. The interplay lasted perhaps a moment too long, when Fader motioned for Josh to take a seat.

They sat down around the table. Fela opened a small tablet computer to a page that contained thirty symbols. There were twenty symbols and beneath them in a separate paragraph were ten additional symbols. Josh understood that he was being shown the Senian alphabet. He correctly figured that the first twenty symbols were the equivalent of letters, while the next ten symbols were numbers.

There appeared to be a great logic to the Senian alphabet. Some symbols were based upon a circle with lines across the circle on the horizontal, vertical and diagonal in both directions. It was not at all like the English alphabet with its flowing letters that led into the next letter.

Josh was eager to show them the English alphabet. He motioned that he wanted to write. Fela got up and came over to him. Leaning over his shoulder, she placed her tablet computer in front of him. She opened it up and moved a pen-like implement across the screen. As she did, a line appeared on the screen. As usual, Josh was fascinated with the new device. He thought about how this resembled the Etch-A-Sketch he used to play with as a child. However, you didn't have to shake it up to make it work.

The device had a keyboard with the same symbols Fela had shown him in the book, along with a number of additional keys. This confirmed to him that this was a writing device, and he was looking at the Senian alphabet.

Josh wrote out the English alphabet followed by the numbers from one to twenty in order to show the additive nature of the numerical system. Fela and Fedar looked at each other, surprised at how perceptive Josh was.

Fela said: "This may not be so difficult after all."

Fedar nodded his agreement.

Fela then wrote out the Senian numbers one through 20 and showed it to Josh. He looked at it and saw the symbols repeating themselves in the same manner as the numbers he had written out. His face lit up and he looked over at Fela and Fedar, giving them his thumbs up, which they all found so amusing.

They all laughed. They now knew that they shared a common numerical system based upon a root of ten.

Since they would soon run out of air again, Fedar stood up and motioned to Josh that it was time to go. Fela stood up and handed Josh the tablet computer that lay on the table. Josh smiled with a slight bow of his head and she did the same. They then left as Fela stood there watching them go.

Fela was even more impressed with Josh than before. The other Earth humans they had attempted to make contact with had been so afraid, giving the Senians the impression that the Earth humans were still somewhat primitive, although their civilization had greatly expanded and advanced in so many ways. Josh, however, appeared to be at their level, or close to it, with only a language barrier separating them. This boded well for the success of the mission in establishing contact with Earth and learning much more about its development and geopolitics.

It was just about time for the mid-day meal. This was a time when the crew gathered in the central area for food, conversation, and amusement. The ship did not have a cook, as there was little to cook and what little kitchen work there was did not support the need for another crew member. Bandar, the horticulturalist, was as close as they came to a chef. He would gather up the fresh fruits and vegetables for the day and set them out on the counter by the dining table. The crew would then help themselves and cut them up into a salad or whatever else they wished. Sometimes, Bandar would cut up the vegetables and steam them in the microwave oven. There were no fossil fuels on the ship to supply a gas stove and a very limited supply of vegetable oils and spices that needed to be rationed over the entire voyage, although some spices and vegetable oils were grown on the ship.

Protein was most precious. The small shrimp-like creatures in the large tank in the horticultural area were the primary source of protein. They were processed, along with dried fruits and vegetables, into the brownish green wafers that Fedar had given to Josh. There was a dish full of these wafers on the table.

Neither Fedar nor Josh would be able to eat with the crew, as they were under quarantine and had the breathing apparatus to contend with.

Fedar led Josh around the corridor to the central area. All the crew was there except Zfar and Fela. Now that Josh had met everyone, they did not attempt any further formalities. The crew went about their business chatting and preparing their meals, hardly taking notice of Josh.

Zofar asked Banar: "Any news from Senia?"

Banar wryly replied: "Yes, it looks like the drought broke – seventeen years ago."

Zofar: "Game of Bayaki later?"

As the ship's medical officer for a crew that was almost always in great health, Zofar had a lot of time on his hands. He had become a Bayaki addict and was constantly trying to improve his game. Banar was the best player on the ship. Bayaki, a complex board game on a par with chess, was a favorite with most of the crew, who spent countless hours improving their game.

Banar: "Don't you ever get tired of losing?"

Zofar: "Makes winning feel that much better."

Elar: "Our new passenger seems to be very inquisitive."

Zofar: "He didn't offer any resistance when I drew blood."

Elar: "How long will it be before we know if we have a problem?"

Zofar: "If all goes well, we will be able to release him from quarantine in eleven days."

Elar: "What about Fedar?"
Zofar: "Same."

Fedar's risk of infection was very small, as he had minimal unprotected contact with Josh. Still, there was some risk. They had decided, however, that it was worth this risk to leave Fedar unprotected when he first landed the shuttle on Earth in order to increase their chances that the Earth human would not be frightened away by his protective suiting. This also gave them a Senian baseline that would help identify any Earth pathogens, as Fedar's blood would be analyzed for pathogens and compared with the analysis of his blood before landing on Earth.

Fedar motioned for Josh to follow him to the counter with the food. He filled a plate with fruits, vegetables, and two protein wafers and gave it to Josh. Then, he drew a glass of cold water, gave it to Josh, and motioned for them to leave.

They returned to Josh's quarters. Josh placed his food and water on the desk area opposite his bed, took off his breathing apparatus, and sat in the chair. He was hungry and anxious to know what the Senian food tasted like. He tried the yellowish-orange fruit about the size of a plum, finding it was very sweet and delicious. Then, he tried the vegetable that resembled a green bean, recalling how, as a child, he used to eat green beans raw. It too was very palatable. He looked up at Fedar and gave him the thumbs up. Fedar smiled and gave Josh the thumbs up.

Fedar then opened a drawer that held the control for the monitor on the wall. He showed Josh the "on" button and turned it on. To Josh's surprise, it instantly turned on to show an incomprehensible menu system. Fedar demonstrated how to use the control to navigate through the menu system. Then, he tuned in to the forward space monitor, which displayed in stunning clarity a three dimensional view of space from the bridge. He then selected some of the other menu items, including now ancient news broadcasts, dramas, and sports events.

Josh was astounded that a device no more than an inch thick

could have such incredible picture quality, and in 3-D no less. He compared it with the eleven inch black and white television at his apartment, with its manual control for changing the channels.

This technology alone would make me a zillionaire on Earth, he thought.

Fedar showed Josh how to turn the monitor off and gestured that he was about to leave. He felt frustrated by his inability to tell Josh anything about his quarantine. He again gestured for Josh not to leave his quarters. Josh shook his head up and down to indicate that he understood. Fedar then returned to the central area, got his food, and went to his quarters to eat, where he too would have to stay, except for a forty-five minute break that he would take with Josh later that day.

Josh turned the monitor back on, set his plate on the desk, and started to work his way through the menu while crunching down the vegetables and savoring the fruit. He knew there was much he would want to look at later, but for now, what he wanted to see was the view of outer space.

It wasn't so "outer" now, he thought. He was in it. The Earth was not visible on the forward view and who knows how many thousands or millions of miles away by now.

He thought of the time he had driven out west after finishing college, and how the Rocky Mountains first appeared in the distance as a slight elevation and then grew larger as he drew closer, ever so slowly, after driving hundreds of miles. It was as though the ship was not moving in the vastness of space. Yet, he could feel the ever present jolts as the ship continued to accelerate.

He was still sitting in the chair transfixed on the monitor of the universe about an hour later when he heard the door signal that someone was seeking permission to enter.

"Come in," he said.

The door opened and there to his great pleasure and surprise stood Fela wearing a breathing apparatus.

Fela, who like Fedar was anxious to let Josh know how long he would be quarantined, had had a brainstorm. She sat down on the bed and opened the writing device Josh had used to write out the English alphabet and numerical system. She then drew a circle around the number eleven and pointed toward the breathing apparatus.

Josh looked at her quizzically.

She then pointed to her breathing apparatus.

Josh understood. He was very relieved to know that he would only have to wear a breathing apparatus for eleven more days, which was actually a little over ten Earth days.

"Thank you," he said with a smile.

Fela, pleased that her plan had succeeded, smiled, got up, and turned to leave. As she left, Josh finally got a good chance to take in her rear view. It was absolutely stunning, as close to perfection as anyone could expect from a woman on Earth, and apparently in the galaxy as well. Josh thought to himself how hard it would be to resist having Fela become the woman of his fantasies. He started to imagine how nice it would be to have her lying in the bed beside him while he gently slid his hand over her beautiful bottom and slowly removed her slacks. He could feel his excitement rising. He stopped himself because he wanted to keep the dream alive that he might actually make love to her someday.

Josh spent the next several hours going through a tremendous amount of viewing material on the monitor, as one leafs through a magazine before choosing something to read. He began to get a picture of Senian life that was not very different from life on Earth – at least the better aspects. There was a channel that showed only natural scenes of the planet. He gazed with wonder at the three dimensional views of the Senian sunrises and sunsets over the beautiful unspoiled landscapes of the savannahs, rivers, forests and ocean. Many of the scenes reminded him of some of the remaining unspoiled areas on Earth.

There were views of the cities too. The buildings appeared to be a sort of desert style of architecture that featured a large amount of glass, but not so much as some of Earth's large office buildings. To his surprise, Senian structures were not very tall by Earth standards, the largest appearing to be about ten stories high. He did not see any decrepit or decaying buildings or slums like one would find on Earth.

"Perhaps that was because these programs are just showing the best part of the planet," he thought.

After several hours, Fedar arrived with some cooked vegetables and two protein wafers. He gave Josh a new air tank and they embarked for the central area.

Most of the crew was there. Zofar and Banar were intently playing Bayaki. Fela, Elar, Bandar, and Minar were watching the large viewing screen. Josh and Fedar sat down and watched for a few minutes. Josh thought it might be a detective story. It was some sort of drama, but the actors did not appear to be very emotional, sort of like watching a British drama. There were scenes of Senian life inside homes and offices and out on the streets of the city. The cars, which traveled on the ground, were very futuristic looking to Josh. He wondered why they did not travel above ground, as they apparently were able to overcome the force of gravity. There were a few vehicles that looked like military or police that traveled slowly above the ground, propelled by two large fanlike devices across the back.

After awhile, Fedar took Josh up to the bridge. Zfar was keeping an eye on the ship's systems. They had received another transmission about ten Earth hours after the first transmission. Although it could be dismissed as old news, to the crew it was still very much news. They eagerly awaited each transmission, which was immediately forwarded to the monitors in the central area and the crew quarters.

Zfar turned toward Fedar: "How did he do today?"

Fedar, speaking through his breathing apparatus and sounding something like a high pitched wren, replied: "Very well. He showed Fela the Earth alphabet and numerical system. Their numerical system is also based on the root of 10."

Zfar replied: "Good. Fela will have much to do."

"Yes, she seems to like him."

"Let's hope she doesn't like him too much."

Fedar hated the thought of Fela being attracted to Josh: "No, not Fela," he replied, not knowing whether his assurance was just wishful thinking.

They stayed on the bridge silently viewing the panorama of the universe until their air was running low. Fedar took Josh back to his quarters and bid him goodbye.

Josh hastily removed his breathing apparatus, which was starting to become an annoyance. As Fedar was walking out the door, Josh suddenly remembered about his guitar left in the shuttle bay.

"My guitar," he quickly exclaimed to Fedar.

Fedar turned and stopped.

"Guitar," he said in English. "I will get it for you," he said in Senian, giving Josh the thumbs up.

Josh smiled and said, "Thank you."

Minutes later, Fedar returned with Josh's guitar.

"Play it for me," Fedar said, as he handed it to Josh.

Josh assumed that Fedar wanted to hear him play. He sat up on the bed, quietly beginning his usual routine of Dylan's "Don't Think Twice, It's Alright," and then, Josh's version of Dylan's "Tom Thumb Blues."

Thank you, Lord, he thought, *for having me bring my guitar.*

Hearing Josh sing and play, Fedar thought about how different the Earth music was from the music they listened to, which can best be described as resembling "new age" music on Earth. Yet, he found the music pleasing. Simple, but pleasing. Josh would make a good addition to the gatherings they held about once weekly to play their instruments. After a few songs, he stood up and bid Josh farewell with his thumb up as he went though the door.

Josh strummed on for about an hour, until sleep began to call him. He laid his guitar on the floor in the closet and settled back in bed. So much had happened during the day to digest, not the least of which being the beautiful Fela.

He now felt assured that the aliens were not going to hurt him and pondered what it would be like after he could communicate with them. They appeared to have a lot of time on their hands. Apparently, there was no Star Trek warp drive allowing them to travel through the universe in a flash, or suspended animation in order to sleep through the voyage. He would have to slog it out one day at a time.

It dawned on Josh that, wherever they were going, it was going to be a long, slow journey, like the trek across the Great Plains looking at the ever distant Rocky Mountains. He had made the fateful decision to step aboard that craft on the beach, and now his fate was in the hands of the unknown. What lay ahead? Would he ever see Earth again? He rolled over and fell into a deep sleep.

STAN NIEGO

CHAPTER 3 - GETTING TO KNOW YOU

Three months had passed since Josh boarded the *Explorer*. The quarantine had been lifted after eleven Senian days, and Josh was now free to roam the ship. Each day, he rushed to the conference room for his morning session with Fela. She was there when he arrived, happy to see him. They had grown closer and closer, although there had been no physical contact between them other than the occasional pat on the back or touch on the arm.

Josh, speaking Senian, asked: "What shall we do today."

Fela, speaking English, replied: "Let's continue to expand our vocabulary."

It had been an arduous three months of intense effort on both their parts in order to reach the point where they could have simple conversations. Their effort began with phonetics, with Josh pronouncing the English alphabet and Fela doing the same with the Senian alphabet. From there, they began to identify words based upon objects that they both could see. Slowly, this led to an understanding between them of many words, from which they began to form sentences.

Josh found himself in the dual role of an English teacher and language student. He was good at English and had a reasonably comprehensive English vocabulary. Learning a foreign language was another matter. He hated memorization. Many times, he recalled how he happily tossed away his college German text after completing the college language requirement, thinking he would never have to learn a foreign language again.

Still, learning the Senian language was the order of the day and he set himself to the task. Fela did the same with the English language and proved to be much more adept than Josh. He had not yet tried to explain to Fela English grammatical intricacies, and the same applied to Josh. Their effort thus far had focused on memorization of key phrases and sentences that Josh needed to function on the ship.

Josh spent many hours writing out an English dictionary and an English – Senian dictionary on the tablet that Fela had given him, while Fela worked on a Senian – English dictionary. The keypad was of no use to him in writing out the English dictionary, so he started by writing it out by hand on the tablet. With much effort, Banar was able to program alternate keys to the English alphabet and numerical system and develop the related characters in the tablet's software. It was a struggle to learn the Senian word processing software, but Josh had made some rudimentary progress that allowed him to function at a minimal level.

The tablet contained a Senian dictionary, so he worked like a detective, trying to build his vocabulary of Senian words while also thinking of English words for which he would then write out a definition in Senian.

Josh was eager to show Fela the new English words he had defined in English: "I've defined some new words and will transmit them to your tablet," he said in English.

Fela replied in English: "Good."

Josh sent Fela an updated version of his English dictionary with the new words that he had defined highlighted.

Fela looked at the new words. She noticed that Josh had gone from defining common objects to describing human emotions.

He wrote: "happy - the state of happiness; to feel good; to feel joy."

Fela slowly replied: "Hap-py?," not pronouncing it quite right.

Josh replied: "Hap-py."

Fela looked at him quizzically. She understood "good," but the word "feel" was throwing her off. "State" was also an unknown word.

Josh was in a good mood. He stood up with a smile on his face, threw is hands in the air, and started to jump about.

"Happy, I am happy," he said as he jumped about, waving his hands and kicking his feet.

Fela laughed. Now she understood, at least she thought. This was the Earth way of conveying a pleasant state of mind. The Senians were not as prone to displaying their emotions. However, she found it amusing to see Josh jumping about. Somehow, this stirred her repressed feelings toward him.

Josh tended to define things in opposites. He thought it would help with understanding.

The next new word was: "sad - not happy; feeling bad."

Fela said "sad," again not pronouncing it quite right.

Josh said "sad," making a sad face and feigning starting to cry. "I am sad."

Fela understood.

Then Josh put on his happy face and they laughed.

This was how they slowly progressed through their separate vocabularies. They went on for several hours, working through most of the new words Josh had defined, with Fela providing Josh with her understanding of the Senian equivalent. Josh would then add the Senian word to his English definition. In the process, they spoke short sentences and slowly became familiar with English and Senian sentence structure, including the use of verbs, nouns, and pronouns in their respective languages.

After a productive morning, lunchtime approached. Josh said to Fela in his broken Senian, "Eat food?"

Fela said, "Yes" in Senian.

When they arrived at the central area, Zofar and Banar were locked in board game combat, as was usual for them at this time of day. Josh now understood the Senian game of Bayaki and was slowly improving at it, although he still had yet to win a game. He had also made up a backgammon board with some of the *Explorer*'s precious paper supply, carving out the chips from the protein wafers.

"I play winner," he said in Senian.

Zofar looked up. "That will be me."

Banar scoffed. "Not so fast."

They were speaking Senian, but Josh got the drift of their banter.

Messages were now coming in at the rate of two each day. The crew gathered in the central area, except Fedar, who had the bridge. They would watch the messages on the large screen before eating. The messages had the unique characteristic of being both news and history at the same time. Nevertheless, the Senians always watched with a great amount of trepidation. They did not know if today would be the day, however so many years ago, that a starship or missile would come hurling in from Corilia, laden with death and destruction. Each day that didn't happen was a day for which to be grateful.

Fortunately, the news from Senia was still largely uneventful, but provided them something to talk about over lunch, as events on the ship did not generate much of anything new to discuss. Josh had been the big news, but now that he was learning the Senian language, they needed to take care not to talk about him in his presence.

After lunch, Fela and Josh headed back to the conference room to continue their work. Josh had been mischievous, and defined the word, "<u>kiss</u> - an expression of affection between two people."

Fela looked at him with her beautiful green eyes wide open.

"Kiss? I do not understand."

The definitional terms "expression" and "affection" were unknown to her.

Josh stood up and said, "I will show you."

He could hardly believe what he was about to do. Maybe it was that he could not keep his feelings for Fela bottled up any longer. Maybe it was because he was wearing very large horns after three months working closely with Fela and having no more physical contact than an occasional pat on her back. Whatever the case, he found himself approaching her.

He placed his hands around her shoulders and pulled slightly for her to stand up. She did. And then, with the beautiful Fela standing before him, he gently moved forward and placed his lips on hers for a soft and gentle kiss.

Fela felt an incredible rush of excitement move through her. She did not know what to say or do and stood there looking into Josh's eyes, which conveyed his longing for her. She wanted to move forward and kiss him again, this time with much more passion and commitment.

"I have to go," she hurriedly said in Senian, realizing that she needed time to catch her breath and think about what she should or could do.

Josh went back to his quarters, wondering whether he had made a terrible blunder, or instead, whether Fela had the same feelings for him as he had for her.

Damn! I should not have done that, he muttered as he nervously walked down the corridor.

Fela hurried back to her quarters, not wanting to have any contact with another crew member. She could not be sure what her eyes or emotions would convey. A voice inside her was telling her in very strong terms, *you cannot do this!* It was the voice of her mentors and commanders, who tried to convey to her in every subtle or overt way that to enter into a sexual relationship while on the voyage could only lead to trouble. It was an unspoken condition for her acceptance on the mission. Nevertheless, it did not go so far as being a direct order.

She thought, *What would Fedar think!*

She had denied him her affections for so many years, now to give them to this primitive-looking stranger from Earth. Everything she could rationally think told her that she should deny Josh's advance.

And so, the rational part of her brain prevailed for at least that afternoon. She worked in her quarters on adding the new definitions Josh had given her to the Senian - English dictionary.

That evening, when the crew gathered for food and refreshments in the central area, she gently smiled at Josh but did not go over to speak to him. Josh also did not seek to approach her. Relieved by her smile, he smiled back.

Instead, he amused himself playing backgammon with Zofar. When he first showed the Senians backgammon, he would win repeatedly, but that was short lived. Now, he was still able to put up a very good game and win often enough so that the Senians did not think him a complete idiot.

Fela did not stay long after the evening's food was consumed. Josh hung around, playing backgammon and Bayaki, and watching a Senian game of zorecki, a ball game that resembled soccer, which they frequently replayed, as it was a championship match up between Vilarian Province and Monorian Province.

He was among the last to leave the central area when he went back to his quarters.

Fela did not seem terribly angry, he thought. *Maybe it would not be too bad.*

He was thinking about how he would approach Fela tomorrow when the entry chime to his quarters sounded.

"Come in," he said, expecting Fedar with instructions about something or other.

Instead, there before him stood Fela, not saying a word – just looking at him with an eager longing for his embrace. He could see what she was feeling in her eyes. He stood up and they embraced without a moment's hesitation. Fela could not deny her feelings any longer. This time, their kiss was passionate and long, as they savored every moment. Excitement ran through their bodies, as Josh gently lowered his hands along her waist, the side of her buttocks, and down her thighs.

That was all Josh needed. He was becoming erect very fast. He did not want to overwhelm Fela with his excitement and moved to the side as they slowly descended onto his bed. Fela was wearing what she usually wore, loosely fitting slacks with a loosely fitting knit, long sleeve top.

Now was the moment for the fantasy he had steadfastly resisted to come true. Their lips barely parted as they descended to the bed. The kiss continued as Josh stroked the side of her body, coming ever closer to and then over her beautiful bottom. He would go slow and easy.

Fela sat up, pulled off her top to reveal her beautiful breasts. Josh quickly pulled off his shirt and they embraced again. From that point, there was no question of stopping. The bottom half of their garments were quickly shed and they were making love. This was certainly the best sexual experience of Josh's twenty-six years of existence, and he wanted it to be the very best experience for Fela too. He would be a firm but gentle lover.

Fela was lost in a sea of ecstasy. It has been more than seventeen Earth years since she had made love to anyone. She'd had only one lover before signing up for the voyage. It had been a wonderful relationship and she thought of it often, but it was nothing like what she was feeling now. She could hardly believe the sensations running through her. She wondered how much of her excitement was due to her feelings for Josh, or rather the fact that she had been so long without sex. There was something primitive about her desires, which at first she tried to deny but no longer could.

As Josh moved rapidly toward his orgasm, Fela was in perfect sync with him. He did not want to leave Fela unsatisfied. And so, with somewhat muffled screams of excitement, because they did not want to make noise that would carry to Elar's adjacent quarters, they experienced the most intense orgasm either of them had ever had.

Afterwards, they lay there looking deeply into each other's eyes almost in a state of shock over to what had just transpired between them.

Josh said to Fela in English, "I love you."

Fela repeated the same to Josh in English and then in Senian.

Josh then said, "I love you" to Fela in Senian.

They kissed and kissed again and again, until Fela realized that she needed to get back to her quarters undetected. It was quiet on the ship, and the monitors in the corridors were turned off. Normally, they were only used in case of emergency. This was considered an element of privacy that the crew did not have to sacrifice in favor of security. They simply did not like being watched as they moved about the ship.

Fela kissed Josh one last time and said in English, "I must go now."

Josh returned the kiss and said, "I will see you tomorrow."

Then she was off through the door, leaving Josh to contemplate what had just happened. He could hardly stop thinking about it, he felt so good. Soon, however, he drifted off into a pleasant sleep.

Fela, on the other hand, could not sleep. She lay there for hours thinking about the potential consequences of what she had done.

What should she do about telling the rest of the crew?

Should they try to keep it a secret, or should she come out with it?

Could she become pregnant?

Were Senian and Earth humans genetically similar to the extent that their DNA would match enough to produce another human being?

There were Senian accounts of the first Senian Earth explorers having sexual relations with Earth humans. They had not stayed on Earth long enough to know if these liaisons had produced any off-spring. Perhaps she would provide the answer. She fervently hoped not.

She decided that she needed more time to think, and would not say anything to anyone tomorrow. Perhaps she would decide to call it off, although that was not what she was feeling. Still, she needed more time to think it over. Slowly, the worry faded away and she was left with the memory of what it had been like to make love to Josh and the resulting contentment that still ran through her. Eventually, she too fell into a deep sleep.

Back on Earth, three months had elapsed since Josh's disappearance. General Boswell's command to maintain secrecy about the alien encounter proved to be correct. The President, National Security Council, and Joint Chiefs of Staff had decided that the contact with the alien starship should be classified top secret. The aliens had come and gone, and there was no action required for the foreseeable future. It did not seem that anything could be gained by making knowledge of the encounter public. The consequences of public knowledge were too unpredictable to risk starting a panic, or in any case, a huge media headache. They decided, as was the case with many governmental decisions, to take a "wait and see" approach until the next encounter.

Following the encounter, examination of the aerial photography appeared to reveal the shuttle craft approaching the starship, but the photos were not entirely conclusive. The FBI was called in to investigate whether there had been any reports of missing persons in the area. They soon learned the van of a law student named Josh Rinaldi had been found empty on the beach. After a day, it was towed and impounded by the St. Johns County Sheriff and never claimed.

The Sheriff had classified Josh's disappearance as a potential homicide. Josh's family in New York was notified of his disappearance by the Sheriff's office. Josh's parents and family suffered much grief and consternation, not knowing what had actually happened and whether Josh was dead or alive. Over the last three months, the family's grief eventually gave way to acceptance that Josh had somehow perished, probably as a result of drowning or murder. Josh was a good swimmer, so unfortunately murder was the most likely conclusion.

A brief story about Josh's disappearance appeared in the *St. Augustine Record*. This prompted one of the residents along Crescent Beach to report to the *Record* that she had noticed unusual activity and what appeared to be lights in the sky on the beach about three miles south of her residence. Sally Post, an ambitious young reporter, attempted to follow up on this lead by checking with other residents along the beach, but it led nowhere and the matter was eventually dropped.

CHAPTER 4 - IT CAN'T BE, BUT IT IS

Fela was pregnant. It happened the first night, although she did not realize until about six Earth weeks later. She had kept putting off the decision as to whether or not to tell the rest of the crew about her relationship with Josh. Now, the decision was made. She would have to tell.

She and Josh had continued to secretly make love every few days as the passion between them continued to grow. They met as frequently as they could. There were many kisses when they were alone in the conference room, but they knew better than to go any further there. Instead, Fela quietly came to Josh's quarters after all of the crew had gone to their quarters for the evening.

Now that she was pregnant, she would have to seek medical attention from Zofar. She would tell Fedar before consulting Zofar. Knowing how Fedar felt about her, she wanted to try to explain to him what had happened in a way that would not hurt his feelings. As this was a matter of concern to the mission, however, she realized Zfar should be notified before Fedar. This she dreaded doing.

First, she had to tell Josh. Their ability to communicate was steadily improving. That morning, when they met in the conference room to begin their language session, she drew Josh close giving him a warm kiss. This was not unusual, but Josh could see in her eyes there was something else.

"What is it?" Josh said to her in English.

"I am pregnant," she said in Senian, not knowing the English word for pregnant.

Josh looked at her quizzically, repeating the Senian word in a questioning manner.

"Baby," she said in Senian, again not knowing the English word.

Again, Josh did not understand.

Then, she placed her hands over her belly and patted her belly.

This time, Josh understood.

"Pregnant?" he said in English

"Yes, pregnant," she repeated in English.

For an instant, Josh was shocked and surprised. Then, he realized that he was very happy about it. He truly loved Fela. If she was happy about it, he would do everything he could to keep her that way.

He smiled and said, speaking English: "This is good. Very good. I love you. Are you happy?"

"Yes, I am happy," she replied. "I must tell Zfar."

Josh became apprehensive. "Yes, how will he respond?"

"Respond?" She did not know that word.

"Will he be angry?"

"I do not know."

"When will you tell him?"

"Today."

"Should I be with you?"

"No."

They looked at each other then glanced at the tablet computers lying on the table. They both realized they would be unable to concentrate on their language duties with something like this on their minds.

"I must go now," she said, with apprehension in her voice.

"Yes, I will be here when you return."

Fela made her way to the bridge. Zfar and Fedar were there seated across from each other with a small portable table between them on which they were playing backgammon. They found the new Earth game very amusing, if not that challenging.

Fela said to herself, *Oh well, I may as well tell them both together.*

"I have something very important to tell you," she said, the apprehension in her voice being very apparent.

They both turned toward her, wondering what it might be.

"I have been having a sexual relationship with Josh and I am pregnant."

There, it was out, she thought, looking intently at them, awaiting their response.

Fedar looked down and away not wanting anyone to see the shock and disappointment that he was feeling. Then Zfar and Fedar looked at each other. Neither of them knew what to say. As Zfar was the captain, he felt it was up to him to respond.

"Are you sure?" he said in a very measured tone.

"As sure as one can be after six weeks. I'm sure."

"This is enormous. I need to think about this."

Voice trembling, Fela said: "You don't have to say anything now. I love Josh. I'm very sorry for this complication."

Zfar replied in a kind and reassuring tone: "You shouldn't be sorry about being in love with someone. We will figure this out."

"Thank you for being so understanding." Fela felt a great sense of relief that he hadn't responded with anger.

Overwhelmed by his personal thoughts and emotions, Fedar remained silent. Fela meant so much to him. He wanted her so much, but had never overtly expressed his feelings toward her. Now, this rather primitive Earth human had won her affections and her passion in just a few short months. He would have to get his emotions under control.

Fela turned and left.

Zfar turned to Fedar: "What will we do? The ship isn't designed for another person."

Fedar, despite his mixed emotions and hurt feelings, wanted to help Fela. "All we can do is the best we can. The child will have to stay with her. We should be able to sustain another person."

"The child will be seventeen years old when we reach Senia."

"Yes, this is going to be very interesting. It will have great scientific value."

"Now we know for certain that Senians and Earth humans can propagate."

"Yes, it's hard to contemplate that Senians and Earth humans could have evolved separately into such similar life forms."

"Indeed it is, but this is what it appears to be. There is no other answer."

Fedar wondered aloud: "Could the people of both Senia and Earth have been the descendants of human life that evolved somewhere else in the galaxy?"

"No, I don't think so," Zfar replied. "There is too much evidence of the evolution of human life on Corilia, and I would expect that it would be the same for Earth."

"Just think about this," said Fedar. "The human form must be the culmination of the evolutionary process for it to have evolved in such a similar manner in two isolated parts of the galaxy."

Zfar pointed out: "We appear to be a little bit more evolved than they are."

"Yes," Fedar replied. "Our cranial capacity is nine percent greater."

Zfar wondered, "It doesn't appear that we are much more intelligent than the Earth humans."

"Well, we only have one Earth human. His intelligence might be above the human average. We will know more when we learn their language and can talk to him."

"Yes," Zfar replied. "Josh and Fela are making good progress. The crew is also starting to learn the Earth language."

"One thing we have is time," Fedar said, with a wisp of longing in his voice. "I'm sure by the time we reach Senia, we will all be speaking the Earth language, and Josh will be fluent in our language."

He then suggested, "We will have to report this development right away to Senia."

Zfar laughed, "Yes, the message will arrive there about a year before us."

Fedar countered: "But what if we never arrive?"

Zfar agreed: "You have a point."

In the conference room Josh and Fela were still unable to think about working on language.

"How was Zfar?" said Josh in English.

"He was good. Fedar was quiet."

Josh tried to reassure her. "Fedar will be good too."

"I hope so," she said, not very reassured. "What are we to do today?"

Josh quickly replied, "Today, we celebrate."

"Celebrate?" not understanding the meaning of the word.

"Be happy."

"Yes, let's be happy. I love you."

"I love you."

They embraced and shared a tender kiss. The announcement had not gone as badly as one might have expected.

Suddenly, the thought hit him. "Should we not get married?" Josh said in English.

"Married?" Fela did not understand the word.

Josh grabbed her hand tightly and held it up.

"Married," he repeated, looking intently into her eyes. "Man and wife."

Fela thought she understood. "Yes," she said in English.

They embraced again.

"Will you speak to Zfar?" Josh inquired.

"Yes," she said, "but first I must talk to Fedar."

"Why Fedar?" Josh wondered. He had sensed a closeness between Fela and Fedar, but assumed it was just a sort of fatherly affection.

"Fedar loves me, and I care for him," Fela replied.

Josh wondered if they had ever been intimate, but dared not ask. He just nodded and smiled and hugged her again.

Later that day, after the evening meal was over, and the crew settled into their usual routine of board games and visual entertainment, Fela decided that she would talk to Fedar. Alone, up on the bridge, he was still trying to sort out his feelings about Fela's intimate attachment to the Earth human. He didn't want or expect to see Fela. As he gazed out at the view of space, the elevator door opened.

There she was, as beautiful as ever with a sad and concerned expression. She approached and took the seat next to him. She had thought a great deal about what she would say. When it came down to it, however, she found herself passing the buck to Fedar.

"You didn't say anything today. I want to know how you feel about what has happened between Josh and me?"

"I'm happy for you, but you must know how I feel about you."

"Yes," she replied. "And I've had the same feelings for you. I always resisted those feelings because of the mission."

"Then what happened with the Earthling?" he said, raising his voice in exasperation.

"It just happened. I was unable to resist, and I can't explain it, even to myself. I hope you will try to understand." Tears started to well up in her eyes.

Fedar took a deep breath, pulling himself together. Above all, he didn't want to hurt Fela.

"I've never said it before, but I will say it now. I love you and I want you to be happy. I'll always love you and you can always count on me to be there for you if you need me."

Losing her composure completely, Fela's tears flowed. Fedar moved to her, enfolding her in a comforting embrace.

An understanding passed between them during those few moments. Words were unnecessary. Fedar felt his anger melting away. He could now accept the sudden turn of events despite his feelings, knowing that he had at last told Fela how he felt about her and she returned his affection. It was probably all that they would ever have together, but it was more than they had before and would have to be enough.

Wiping the tears from her eyes, Fela asked Fedar:

"Josh and I have decided to marry. Would you give me away at our wedding? There is no one that I would rather it be than you."

Fedar replied: "Yes, I am giving you away. I wish that was me you were marrying."

Her smile of gratitude said she was not only grateful for his willingness to participate in the ceremony but also for his continued friendship.

She hugged Fedar again saying, "I will talk to Zfar tomorrow."

With that, she turned for the elevator, waving goodbye to Fedar as the elevator doors slid shut.

Fela wanted to tell Josh she had spoken with Fedar and had gotten his blessing, but preferred not to go back to the central area yet, as she was still flush with emotion. Instead, she headed to her quarters. Since Josh never came to her quarters during the evening, she would see him later in his quarters after everyone had retired for the day.

Still preoccupied with how he would tell the crew about Fela's relationship with Josh and their soon-to-be new entrant, Zfar headed up to the bridge to relieve Fedar and check on things. He found Fedar staring into space with a lost look on his face.

"What's with you?" he said.

Fedar replied: "I just spoke to Fela. They want to get married."

Zfar knew how Fedar felt about Fela and now understood why he looked so forlorn.

"First things first," he said. "I'm trying to decide how to break this to the crew."

"Just tell them," Fedar replied. "There are many positive aspects. Emphasize the positive."

"Right," replied Zfar. "I'll break the news tomorrow after lunch."

"What about the marriage ceremony?" Fedar asked.

Zfar thought for a moment and then replied: "We will have to try to make that something special. I will discuss it with Fela."

Zfar hit his communicator. "Fela, can you meet me in the conference room now?"

Fela, sitting restlessly in her quarters, replied: "I'll be right there."

Fela, with an apprehensive look on her face, was in the conference room waiting when Zfar arrived. She still wasn't sure how Zfar would react to the situation after giving it some thought.

Zfar, not taking a seat, spoke first. "I'm planning on making an announcement to the crew after lunch tomorrow. Have you told anyone?"

"Just Fedar," she said, also standing.

"Good. I understand you and Josh want to get married."

"Yes. Would that be possible?"

"Yes. I want this to be a happy occasion. Something to be celebrated."

"Oh, thank you so much," she said, wanting to give him a hug, but hesitating because she didn't know how he would react. Instead, she just leaned forward and projected her warm feelings toward him.

"I was so worried that you would not look favorably upon this."

"I would rather it hadn't happened. It will present some problems, but nothing we can't deal with. But Fela, please know there must not be any more children until we reach Senia."

"Yes, I understand. That will not happen."

"Have you thought about the wedding ceremony?"

"I want it to be simple. I will talk to Josh."

"Very well. We will discuss that later."

Zfar could think of nothing else to say. Fela stood before him with a very nervous and unsure expression. He held out his arms for her to come to him. In all of the long years about the ship, they had barely touched. Fela came to him, laying her head on his chest as he gently patted her back. Fela could feel tears of relief welling up inside. She hadn't wanted to become emotional with Zfar and drew back with a relieved smile on her face.

"Thank you so much for being so understanding," she said with a smile.

"This will make life interesting aboard this ship," Zfar replied. "We will have the first Senian-Earth human aboard this ship, born in space. That should make for a few headlines when we return to Senia."

"Yes, and even more when we return to Earth," she said with a laugh.

The hours passed slowly for Fela and Josh as they anxiously awaited Zfar's announcement to the crew after lunch. Finally the time came. Fedar was on the bridge, but everyone else was in the central area finishing up their lunch and about to disperse. Unsure as to whether he would be able to hide his feelings, Fedar preferred not to be there for the announcement and was happy to man the bridge.

Zfar knocked his clinched knuckles against the table for attention.

Speaking in Senian, he said: "I have an important announcement to make. We are going to have a wedding aboard ship. Fela and Josh have fallen in love and want to be married. They are going to have a child."

Fela smiled and looked shyly about at her crewmates. Josh could not fully understand what Zfar had said, but comprehended the gist of it. He anxiously gazed around the room for the crew's reaction.

The crew's initially stunned expressions slowly gave way to smiles. Elar went over to Fela, putting out his hands to her, which she quickly grasped.

"Congratulations," he said. "This is quite an event, a child to be born between Senia and Earth. I hope you and Josh will be very happy?"

Other crew members followed suit, offering their congratulations. Even Minar, who had long coveted Fela as his would-be bedmate, grudgingly managed to give the appearance of acceptance and support.

There followed much conversation in Senian between the crew that Josh could not fully understand, but their reaction appeared to be very positive. After congratulating Fela, they came over to Josh. He extended his hand to shake hands, a gesture they were not familiar with, but went along with in Josh's enthusiasm.

Zfar knocked the table again. "We will have our challenges with a baby and raising a child. The *Explorer* is not designed for that. We will have to share our provisions with another person, who will be seventeen years old by the time we reach Senia."

Banar inquired: "Do you know the gender yet?"

Zofar replied: "No, not yet. This is new to me."

Zfar continued: "We are going to have a wedding soon. It will be an occasion for great celebration."

With that, Zfar was finished. The crew continued to buzz about Fela and Josh while he left the room.

Zofar went over to Fela and said: "Can you see me this afternoon."

"Yes," she replied. "I'll be there as soon as I leave here."

Fela and Josh went to see Zofar as soon as the conversation died down and they could leave. He ran a scan of Fela in the "orgasmatron," as Josh called it, which confirmed she was indeed pregnant. It would be a few more weeks before he would be able to confirm the child's gender.

Greatly relieved at the progress of the day's events, Josh and Fela returned to her quarters. There would no longer be any need for them to be surreptitious about their love affair. In broken English they agreed to have a simple wedding in the Senian tradition as soon as it could be arranged.

Two days passed while Fela, Josh, and Bandar made arrangements for the wedding ceremony. Zfar, as ship captain, would marry them. Fedar would give Fela away. Josh decided not to bring up the Earth tradition of having a best man at the wedding. He was most friendly with Banar, the board game addict, but didn't want to favor one crew member above the others.

The wedding went off without a hitch. Fela looked absolutely stunning. There was not much they could do about clothing to make it special, as all of the crew had similar dress of loose fitting tops and slacks, and Josh had a choice between the jeans and tee he was wearing on the beach and somewhat tight fitting clothes that he had been given by Zofar, who was the closest to his size. He chose the Senian garb. Bandar managed to conjure up some flowers for Fela to wear, decorate the room and provide the broadest possible array of fruit.

The Senian ceremony was very similar to a ceremony on Earth. They took vows of fidelity and loyalty to each other. Fela worked painstakingly with Josh beforehand to translate the ceremony into English so Josh would understand the Senian vows that he would be taking. Elar helped out with the rings, crafting two rings from the limited store of platinum and copper wire that he had for repairs.

After the ceremony, they broke out their precious stash of Senian brandy for a toast. This was the first time Josh had ever seen the Senians toast to something, and he was amazed at the similarity in customs that had developed in such distant parts of the galaxy.

Zfar raised his glass first and the others followed.

"Let us wish Fela and Josh the very best for their lives together, and for the life of their child to be, that we all arrive at Senia safely so that we can share the joy of the first Senian-Earth human with the people of Senia."

Fela responded in Senian: "I am so thankful for the kindness and understanding that Zfar and all of you have shown to Josh and me." Tears started to well up in her eyes and she put down her glass.

Josh could not understand all of what was said, but he was very happy to see that their union had been cheerfully accepted by the crew, with the possible exception of Minar, who had a more brooding facial expression at times, but went along with the festivities as well.

Throughout the ceremony and the festivities afterwards, Fedar was most gracious and adoring to Fela and courteous to Josh. He had put his feelings behind him, at least for the moment.

After it was over, they settled in Josh's quarters. Even though they were now married, they decided it would be best not to spend the entire night together. They were sensitive to how the crew would react to them having an all night love fest.

That did not mean they would not make love. They practically ran back to Josh's quarters and embraced after the door closed. Their clothing quickly ended up on the floor. Soon the passionate lovemaking would be over as Fela became more pregnant, but not tonight. Josh was at his best. All of the tension that had built up in him over the last few days poured out into Fela in a sudden burst of excitement and relief.

As they lay there afterwards, Josh looked into Fela's beautiful green eyes, wondering what would become of them.

Would they ever reach Senia?

Would they ever return to Earth?

How would they be received on Senia?

What would their child look like?

Would he or she be deformed, some aberration of the attempt to mix the two humanoid life forms?

What would become of their child?

All he knew was that at that moment, he could not have been any happier. The future would hopefully take care of itself.

"We have much to be thankful for," he said in English, not wanting to express his many fears to Fela.

"Yes," she said in English. "I am very happy."

CHAPTER 5 - A NEW ARRIVAL

Seven and one-half months later, it was time for Fela to give birth to a girl. As one would expect, the crew was at first unsettled about the prospect of having to raise a child aboard ship. Over time, those feelings gave way to excitement and anticipation over the birth. A child would certainly brighten things up on the dreary and seemingly endless voyage through the depths of space. Zofar had kept close tabs on the child's development and everything pointed toward the birth of a normal human being. Her cranial features would be Senian. Over time, the great element of uncertainty as to whether Senian and Earth humans could successfully bear children had been all but removed.

After much deliberation, they had decided to name her "Rosilea." It was a fusion of the Earth name, Rosalind, for Josh's mother, and the Senian name, Ledar, for Fela's father.

Fedar's feelings for Fela were not diminished, but he did not want to bring any discomfort or unhappiness into her life. He and the crew had come to feel that the child would be theirs too, as they would all have a hand in some way in raising her.

Josh and Fela had made tremendous progress in their mutual understanding of Senian and English. For someone who had hated language, Josh was utterly consumed by his desire to understand Senian and have them understand English.

Josh had actually moved ahead of Fela, having the benefit of the Senian dictionary on his computer. After about six months, he had reached a critical mass where he understood enough Senian words that he was able to use the Senian dictionary to learn new Senian words. He would then add the new Senian words to his English - Senian dictionary and Fela would add the words to the Senian - English dictionary. His work was made available through the ship's network to the entire crew, who all spent at least an hour or two every day working on learning English.

The crew was impressed with Josh's intelligence and he had come to be thought of as another member of the crew. Josh would spend many hours with Bandar in the horticultural area and with Elar in the engineering section. He wanted to understand as much as he was capable of understanding about how the ship functioned and the technology behind it. He was still limited by his ability to understand Senian, but he pressed on and helped out wherever he could.

They were busy working in the conference room when Fela started to go into labor. Fela grasped her greatly protruding belly as she felt the pain start in her groin and run through her body.

"I think it is time," she said with a gasp.

Josh went over to her and helped her get up.

"Let's go to medical."

He helped her slowly down the corridor.

Zofar had the room prepared. Bandar would assist with the birth. Zofar helped Fela onto the operating table. Everything appeared to be fine. The baby was in the correct position.

Bandar communicated his excitement to the rest of the crew.

"Fela is in medical ready to give birth. Please stay at your stations. We will let you know as soon as anything happens."

The significance of her birth was not lost on them or any other member of the crew. Everyone was hoping with every fiber of their being that things would go well.

Josh sat and then paced about anxiously as Fela continued with her labor pains. After over seven long and arduous hours, Rosilea finally poked her little head from inside Fela's body. It was now late in the evening. Without Bandar, there was nothing to eat except protein wafers and some left over fruit, but no one was hungry anyway. The crew was now gathered in the central area awaiting word from Bandar, while Zfar manned the bridge.

In a few more minutes, Fela pushed her last push and Rosilea emerged. Zofar gave her a slap on the back and she started to cry.

Bandar spoke into his communicator.

"All is well. Rosilea has arrived. She looks fine."

They could hear the faint sound of a loud cheer coming from the central area.

After Zofar had cut the umbilical cord and gently washed Rosilea with a hand towel, he placed her in Fela's arms. She beamed with joy, excitement, and relief. Rosilea was beautiful. Everything was in correct proportion. One could see right away that she would one day be a beautiful lady. She had a small clump of brownish hair, darker than Fela's. Josh's genes had dominated there. Fela's genes dominated the shape of her skull, which was very much Senian, and her eyes, which were a beautiful dark green. She was a large baby, over seven pounds, probably due to Josh's influence.

One by one, the crew came by to see the newborn and wish Fela well. After all of the commotion had died down, it was finally time for Fela and Rosilea to leave medical. They were doing well, and there was no apparent need from them to stay in medical under Zofar's supervision. He would not be far away if a situation developed.

Josh wheeled Fela down the corridor to her quarters with Rosilea cradled in her arms. A portion of the desk and cabinetry had been removed and converted into a crib for Rosilea. Fela was not ready to place her in her crib. She settled into her bed with Rosilea in her arms. Josh settled back in the desk chair.

Fatherhood was not something that Josh had anticipated or aspired to, but now that it was here, he was overwhelmed by the emotions he was feeling. He looked at them both with great happiness and affection.

"She's beautiful, just like you."

"Will you stay with me tonight?"

"Wild horses could not pry me away tonight."

"Wild horses?"

"It's an English expression. It means that nothing could keep me from staying with you tonight."

She still did not quite understand, but presumed it meant that Josh would stay.

"She will be seventeen years old when we reach Senia," Fela said, as she gently patted the top of Rosilea's head.

Josh now understood the Senian timekeeping system. He quickly converted that to about sixteen years in Earth time.

"Yes, we will teach her Senian and English," he said.

"There is so much to do," Fela replied.

"And we have all the time we need to do it. So much time," Josh said wistfully.

"She will keep us occupied."

"I know. I could not be happier."

Josh snuggled in beside her and they lay there listening to Senian music on the monitor. He thought about getting his guitar to serenade them with the minimal assortment of folk and rock songs he knew, and some songs that he had written, but was too comfortable snuggled in with Fela and Rosilea to go back to his quarters. His guitar had proven to be a real blessing, both for his comfort and for helping him become thought of as a member of the crew. They loved to hear him play, even though he played the same songs over and over again. The music was so different than what they were used to and they loved rock and roll. After a few months, he was able to work his way into participating in their weekly music sessions, picking out lead lines that blended with the Senian music

It did not take long for Fela to fall asleep with Rosilea in her arms. Josh took Rosilea and placed her in her crib. Then he settled in beside Fela, thinking over how much his life had changed after he stepped onto Fedar's shuttle craft.

He now knew the basic character of the Senian mission to Earth and his role in it. He would someday return to Earth, which gave him great comfort. By his rough calculation, assuming he spent about a year on Senia, he would be in his mid-sixties when he returned.

How would life have changed on Earth since he left? he wondered.

Would there have been a nuclear war?

How much would the Earth have advanced technologically?

To say the least, Josh was utterly astounded by his tablet computer and all of the other computational devices on the ship. The last he knew of computers was the large monsters that filled a room with tubes, and the transistorized computers used for Neil Armstrong's trip to the moon. Some microchip computers that did basic calculations were also starting to come on the market. He was in constant amazement at what the computers on the ship were able to do and where the technology could lead Earth.

Much time had been spent learning to use his tablet, which opened up the Senian world to him to a great degree. There was also the monitor in his room. He came to find it contained a wealth of information about Senia, its art, history, science, government, and culture. There was virtually no time where he felt bored. Certainly, not with Fela there to fill up his time.

There was so much to learn about Senian life. He had come to learn that his watch was useless, except for keeping track of the passage of time on Earth. The Senian day was shorter than an Earth day. There was no a.m. and p.m. in the Senian time system. There were 10 Senian hours, or milseks, in one Senian day. One Senian milsek equaled about 2.1 Earth hours. Each Senian milsek was divided into 100 Senian minutes, or quarseks. One quarsek equaled 1.26 Earth minutes. He had deduced that one could learn much about Senia by first considering units of or multiples of 10. It was somewhat difficult, but Josh finally became accustomed to the length of the Senian day, which consumed twenty-one hours in Earth time.

He found what he had learned about the Senian week most fascinating. There were eight days (farseks) in a Senian week (biran). The Senian week was modified as Senia reached its carrying capacity and zero population growth. Previously, like Earth, the Senian year was divided into seven-day weeks. Like Earth, most Senians worked five days and took two days for personal leisure and recreation. The economy was focused on maintaining the growth necessary to build Senian civilization and sustain the growing population.

As Senia reached zero population growth, the demand for goods and services began to stabilize. The highly efficient productive technology had eliminated the need for much of the labor force and there was a large problem with structural unemployment, as there were not enough jobs in the high technology areas of the Senian economy to employ all of those who had been displaced by automated production facilities. This created some social friction regarding how to provide for the unemployed. Some argued that they were simply seeking to get a free ride at the expense of those who were employed. Others recognized the need to provide financial assistance to families without gainful employment.

After much debate, it was decided to revise the Senian calendar to increase the length of a week from seven to eight days, ultimately leading to full employment. The amount of time the average Senian had for recreational pursuits increased, offsetting the diminished need for labor to produce non-recreational goods and services, while greatly increasing the need for recreational goods and services. Those who had previously worked a five-day week generally continued to work five days, with one extra day for recreation. Recreational businesses and occupations flourished, creating many new jobs that were not high tech.

Senian factories, hospitals, utilities, transportation facilities, or other entities that needed to operate continually found the change to be very beneficial. Instead of having to schedule personnel for a four or five-day work week that overlapped with the work week of other personnel, all personnel could be scheduled to work four days each week. This created a tremendous amount of new positions, with many gaining the benefit of working four days and having four days of leisure time.

In this way, available work continued to be allocated among the population as the Senian economy shifted from growth to stability. It was a great adjustment for Senian economists and government and business leaders to change their thinking from being fixated upon a growth oriented economy to an economy that was in equilibrium based upon a population that was also in equilibrium.

Josh had now lost about fifteen pounds. He had become accustomed to the rigidity of the limited food aboard ship and felt much healthier and energetic. Still, he would often think about how much he would like to be able to stop at Nathan's in Coney Island, as he used to do on his way to work at his dad's factory, and have a hot dog and the world's best French fries. That would be the first thing he would do when he got back to Earth – or perhaps a trip to Katz's deli in Manhattan for a pastrami sandwich.

Speaking of Earth, over ten and one-half months had now elapsed since Josh first boarded the *Explorer*. Events on Earth plodded along with no major upheavals. President Carter vigorously pursued the first year of his presidency, focusing on energy policy and making progress toward peace in the Middle East. He shocked the Pentagon by declaring that he wanted to cancel production of the B-1 bomber program in favor of more reliance on cruise missiles. There was also discussion as to whether the U.S. should develop a "neutron bomb," which would kill people with radiation without destroying property. Opponents believed it would lower the threshold for use of nuclear weapons, making a nuclear confrontation more likely. Proponents felt that it would be a very useful addition to the country's arsenal, as it would counter the vast superiority the Soviets had in conventional weapons in Europe, while avoiding the most destructive aspect of nuclear weaponry, including long-term radioactivity.

Relations with the Soviets under Brezhnev had greatly deteriorated, but negotiations continued on a new treaty to limit strategic nuclear arms, known as SALT II. Many experts questioned whether the U.S. still had a sufficient nuclear deterrent to prevent a Soviet first strike attack. Communist parties across Europe were rebelling against Soviet dictates, which was thought to be partly attributable to Carter's human rights initiative.

In China, a pragmatist, Deng Xaioping, who had been purged during the Cultural Revolution of the 1960s, and believed that China should stress economic and scientific development over ideology, assumed the top leadership role. The U.S. sought to improve relations with China, but was stymied by the need to finesse its defense treaty with Taiwan with China's insistence that Taiwan was a part of China.

The debate over the effect of greenhouse gases was just beginning. Scientific thinking was shifting from thinking that the climate was entering a new ice age to the effect of greenhouse gases on global warming. A leading researcher at Columbia University was quoted as saying that the effects of burning coal, oil and natural gas could become the single-most important issue of the next 30 years.

Congress approved a new Cabinet agency, the Department of Energy, to focus on implementing Carter's energy plan. The Secretary of Transportation wanted to impose a 30-cent per gallon tax on gasoline to bring the price up to around $1.00 per gallon in order to discourage consumption. The energy plan had passed the House virtually intact, but was all but decimated in the Senate due to opposition from oil and gas interests and lack of public support.

President Carter doggedly pursued his effort to bring the Israelis and the Arab States to the negotiating table, with a key stumbling block being whether the Palestine Liberation Organization should participate in the discussions and whether it would recognize Israel's right to exist. Then, in November 1977, Egypt's President, Anwar Sadat, addressed the Israeli parliament, which completely changed the chemistry of peace negotiations. Despite strong opposition from Syria and others, Sadat expressed a willingness to make a separate peace with Israel.

By April of 1978, nothing much had changed. Negotiations between Israel and Egypt proceeded slowly, with talk that they were bogged down. Inflation roared in the U.S. economy. Tense SALT II negotiations continued, while the Senate, after much debate, finally approved the treaty President Carter had entered into to turn sovereignty over the Panama Canal to Panama in 1999. In April 1978, President Carter deferred production of the neutron bomb after the Dutch Second Chamber voted against its deployment and 50,000 people in Amsterdam demonstrated against the weapon.

CHAPTER 6 - BAD NEWS FROM SENIA

It was 3:47 Senian time, December 15, 1989 on Earth. Eleven Earth years have passed since Rosilea was born.

Zfar, Fedar, Banar and Josh were on the bridge awaiting the next transmission from Senia. By now, these transmissions had become a routine. The time of arrival, twice daily, was known with great precision. The message would arrive in a few minutes. It would include the daily news broadcast by the Senian public news service, along with various coded messages. Messages from friends, loved ones, and family were coded to specific crew members. Messages of the highest priority relating to the mission were coded to Zfar, Fedar and Banar.

There was no expectation that today would be any different from the previous eleven years. In came the usual news broadcast along with a mission-coded message. Before opening the message, Banar made eye contact with Zfar and then looked over at Josh. Zfar nodded approval for Banar to open the message. Josh was now fluent in Senian, but Zfar could not see any reason why Josh should not be privy to the message.

It was a video transmission from Dinar, the Senia – Earth mission commander. His expression was very grim and they knew immediately that it would be very bad news.

"We have received a transmission from the Corilian underground today that the Tskar has determined to attack Senia with nuclear weapons. We are advised that the Corilians are planning to build a fleet of thirty attack starships. We have estimated that it will have taken the Corilians eleven years to build and launch these ships. If you are on your scheduled course, the Corilians should be six years away from Senia when you receive this message. We estimate that you will return at least several months before the Corilian attack.

Acknowledge receipt of this message, but do not comment regarding its contents, as it may be intercepted by the Corilian attack fleet. I will follow with additional transmissions as more becomes known. Return safely."

They all looked at each other, their eyes filled with shock, anger, astonishment, anxiety and disappointment.

Zfar spoke first. "I will call a meeting to relay this to the crew."

Fedar: "Yes, we cannot keep this from them, although all it will do is cause them great anxiety until we return to Senia."

Zfar: "We will not be able to hide our anxiety."

Banar: "I agree. We are all together on this mission. We should not elevate ourselves above them in terms of this knowledge."

Zfar: "Josh, what do you think?"

Josh: "I agree. I don't know how I could keep this from Fela. She will sense that something is wrong and want to know. But we must not let Rosilea know."

Zfar: "Then it is decided."

Zfar then broadcast a message for all crew members to immediately assemble in the conference room.

Josh hurried over to Fela's quarters. She was there sitting in the desk chair watching a Senian drama on the monitor with Rosilea stretched out on the bed. Rosilea was now a beautiful, exotic looking eleven year old blend of Josh's and Fela's genes, with beautiful wavy dark brown hair and green eyes. Fela had a pleasant, happy expression on her face that quickly turned to concern when she caught a glimpse of Josh as the door slid open.

Josh didn't want to alarm Rosilea. He reverted to a cool expression and said: "There's a meeting being called soon about planning for the return to Senia," and motioned for Fela to join him.

Fela got up, leaving Rosilea happily engaged with the program she was watching.

"What is it?," Fela said with some apprehension as soon as they exited their quarters.

"You will find out at the meeting," Josh quickly replied.

With that, they dashed down the hall, Fela being very anxious to know whatever it was that so troubled Josh.

The crew, except for Zfar, had quickly gathered in the conference room. Fedar and Banar were not saying anything, waiting for Zfar to break the news.

Bandar broke the tension: "It must be news from Senia. The last transmission should have been received at 4:02."

Fedar replied: "Yes, its news from Senia, and not good. Zfar will be here soon." He called Zfar on his communicator: "They are all assembled."

Zfar was sitting alone on the bridge staring into space, trying to come up with the words to break the news to the crew. He was at a loss. There was no way to put this news in any sort of perspective that would make it less ominous or foreboding. He sprung up from his chair after receiving Fedar's message and headed for the conference room.

When he arrived, they all stood up from their chairs as he entered the room. As the door slid shut, standing up, he came out with the news.

"We just received a transmission indicating that the Corilians have launched an attack with thirty starships carrying nuclear weapons. We should arrive at Senia several months before the attack ships. There are to be no transmissions to Senia mentioning that we know of the attack. Let's sit down."

Everyone took their seats.

Zofar spoke first: "I suppose it was inevitable that this would happen. It looks like nothing has changed on Corilia since we left."

Banar: "Once the attack is launched, after about seven months they will not be able to call it back even if there is a change on Corilia."

Zfar: "I suppose if there is any good news in all of this, it is that we have had advance warning of the attack. Imagine if they had suddenly appeared with no advance warning."

Banar: "If my rough calculations are correct, they would have received the message from Corilia about six years ago. That will have given them twelve years to prepare for the attack."

Elar: "That should be just enough time to add more ships to the defense fleet. I would say that we could build about twenty ships in that time if they made an all out effort."

Zfar: "Yes, we should be able to match their numbers, but if only one of their ships gets through, it will cause incalculable destruction."

Fela: "Somehow, we will defeat them. We must!"

Zfar: "Nothing changes for us. I will send them a message confirming receipt of their communication, our position and arrival date."

Zfar stood up to leave, and said:

"Let's try to go about our business as we normally would. This is going to take some time to assimilate, but there is nothing we can do other than bring this ship safely back to Senia. We are well on our way to accomplishing our mission. We now all know an Earth language and are prepared to return to Earth and make contact. The Corilians have chosen to make war against Senia. This war will not end with this attack, even if we are successful in downing every ship before it reaches Senia. This situation has existed for hundreds of years and cannot continue any longer. Corilia must be returned to democracy."

Minar: "Perhaps a military defeat will lessen the military's grip on Corilia."

Fedar: "We can only hope."

With that, Zfar opened the door and left, with the others proceeding out behind him.

Fela was stunned. She and Josh hurried back to Rosilea.

What kind of world would Rosilea be returning to? she thought.

Suddenly, the tranquility of their mission had dissolved. It would still be over six Senian years before they would reach Senia. There was nothing they could do to help Senia prepare for the attack. They had hoped to stay on Senia for at least one year before returning to Earth. Now, perhaps, they might never be able to return to Earth. It was just too much to think about.

They entered Fela's quarters. Rosilea looked up.

"What was the meeting about, mom," she said, now bored with sitting in their quarters.

Fela didn't want to lie to her, but had to think of something.

"Just another meeting about supplies and that sort of stuff."

Josh and Fela still needed to talk.

"Would you like to go up to the bridge for awhile?" Josh asked.

"Yes," she replied.

Josh took Rosilea by the hand and they went up to the bridge, where she sat in an empty chair next to Zfar. Fedar and Banar were there and they were engaged in intense conversation.

"Can she stay here for a little while?"

Zfar replied, "Yes, but don't be gone too long."

They turned their attention to amusing Rosilea, while Josh hurried back to Fela.

Speaking Senian, Fela immediately queried Josh as he entered the room.

"What will we do? Will we stay on Senia or will they send us back to Earth before the attack?"

Josh thought for a moment and responded: "It would not make much sense to send us back to Earth not knowing whether they would survive the attack and have a civilization to represent to Earth."

She replied: "I did not mention that at the meeting."

Trying to calm Fela, Josh said: "We're getting ahead of ourselves. There is an Earth expression: What will be will be. It's useful when things are happening that you do not have any control over."

"What will be will be," she said in a questioning tone. "Well, of course, what will be will be. So what! I don't understand."

"Well, you'll have to hang around on Earth for awhile. Then you will understand."

Still not relieved, she said: "Let's discuss this with Zfar and Fedar when we have a chance."

They hugged a very long hug and Josh dashed off to get Rosilea.

The crew's assessment of what would happen on Senia was right on the mark. A meeting of the Supreme Council was convened soon after the transmission about the Tskar's attack plan was received. The Supreme Council consisted of two representatives from each of Senia's nine provinces, along with the Chancellor, Vice-Chancellor, head of the Central Defense Command, Chief of Intelligence, and the heads of the five central ministries for energy, social welfare, transportation, education, and commerce.

Immediately, an intense debate began as to whether the Senian population should be informed of the invasion threat. At the time the message was received, they estimated that it would be twelve Senian years before the ships reached Senia. An intense effort would be needed to prepare their defenses. They considered whether they would be able to engage in the necessary preparation without the population knowing of the invasion threat. There had never been any significant opposition to maintaining a defense force to protect the planet from the Corilians. Still, it had now been many years since the Corilian missile attack, and it was likely that a vast increase in defense expenditures at this time would encounter substantial public opposition if the populace was not aware of the imminent threat. This had to be weighed against the unpredictable harm that might occur if the population was informed. They could only guess at how this knowledge would affect productivity and social conditions. Certainly, there would be an increase in general anxiety for many years. Perhaps the population could be spared this anxiety, at least for awhile.

There was also the consideration that, if their knowledge of the attack was made public, there could be a Corilian spy on Senia, who would transmit word to the incoming fleet that Senia knew of the attack. The Senians, as well as the Corilians, were counting on the element of surprise. The Corilians had lost that element and it was now incumbent upon Senia to maintain its element of surprise over the Corilian fleet, which hopefully would still think it was engaged in a surprise attack against a much smaller Senian defensive force.

They decided to proceed one step at a time. For the present, the population would not be informed. The option always remained to inform the population should it later prove necessary.

Senia's existing planetary defense system included ten ships that were capable of escaping the planet's gravitational field and shooting down an incoming ship or missile with four missiles and two powerful lasers. They were of the same basic design as the interplanetary starships, except that most of the ship was devoted to armaments. The on-board propulsion system was capable of great maneuverability with a much larger store of propellant.

There could be no assurance as to how much advance notice the Senians would have. If their technology was the same as the Senians, the Corilians would have to decelerate from near light speed. Starlight reflected from the ships would then move faster than the ships toward Senia and might be able to be detected. The ships would surely be designed for stealth and it was entirely possible that they would not be able to detect reflected starlight.

It was also possible that the orbital radiation detectors would provide an advance warning of their approach. The ships' nuclear reactors would be well shielded, but certain radioactive particles, such as neutrinos, would escape and leave a trail.

In addition to the outer defenses, the Senians possessed about seventy heavily armed fighter jets, which were capable of destroying a Corilian attack ship that penetrated the outer defenses. The Senians did not know if there would be sufficient time for this force to be useful, as it would only be a matter of a few minutes after entering the Senian atmosphere that the nuclear weapons would be deployed. Nevertheless, the force would be increased, if possible, to 150.

There was no time for redesign. Existing plans would be used to construct twenty additional starships, making for a total fleet of thirty. Equal numbers, along with the element of surprise, was felt to give the Senians some advantage. In any case, it was not possible to assemble and train the crews for any more ships.

The planetary detection systems would also be increased, although they were already quite adequate. It was decided that additional redundancy could become very important when the planet came under attack.

While the Senians were scrambling to make initial preparations for their defense, the Corilian attack fleet was hurling through space at near light speed. Zenar, the Corilian commander, had no stomach for the mission he was ordered to carry out. But he was a dedicated military officer, and had risen through the ranks by strict adherence to military protocol and chain of command.

He tried to not think about the death and destruction that his and the other starships would be bringing to their brethren on Senia. Thousands of years had passed since the original Corilians had settled Senia, and any kinship ties that existed between these original settlers and those now on Corilia had long since faded into oblivion. Still, he could not help himself from thinking that the people who would be suffering so greatly at the expense of the Corilian dictatorship were of the same blood as him.

He understood the essential need for Corilia to establish a base on Senia in order to have a way station for travel to Earth. Corilia's uranium resource was virtually depleted. The Corilians knew from their initial exploration of Earth that it contained an abundant supply of uranium. It would have to be refined on Earth before being transported back to Corilia. To accomplish this, in the mind of the Tskar, it was necessary to establish dominion over Earth.

Zenar wondered why this could not be accomplished peacefully. He wondered the same thing with regard to Senia. Why was it necessary for Corilia to reestablish domination over Senia? Could they not recognize the Senian's right to exist independent of Corilian control and seek cooperative ties?

This was simply not the way the Tskar or the other members of the Corilian dictatorship conceived of things. He and any others who were of the same mind were fearful of expressing their point of view or even confiding in each other. It was a culture of fear and isolation where no one could be trusted and everyone had to blindly follow orders from the chain of command on penalty of death or imprisonment. Usually it was death, as the Corilians were not inclined to keep prisoners unless it served the purpose of obtaining information.

He also knew that, after hundreds of years of mistrust, it would be difficult for Corilia to ever gain the right of peaceful entry to Senia, and that the Senians would never cooperate with a mission to forcefully exert dominion over Earth.

Despite his deep reservations, he would carry out his mission. Failure was not tolerated on Corilia. He and his family would suffer greatly if he were to fail. He was a professional military officer and would execute the plan of attack with great precision.

They were counting on the element of surprise, but not in the sense of the Senians lacking any advance notice of their attack. They would have to begin the deceleration process about six months before reaching Senia. The Senians would most likely know they were coming several weeks before they reached the planet. Still, they would make every effort to conceal their attack. The ships would travel in a tight formation through space so that any signal would appear to be that of a single ship.

The main element of surprise would be the Senian's inability to prepare for such a large attack force. They did not have any intelligence as to the extent of Senian defenses, but presumed the Senians would not have designed their defenses to repel an attack by thirty starships.

The plan of attack was simple and dictated by the limitations of space travel. The ships would fan out and enter into a stationary orbit over their targets about 150 Earth miles above the planet. The gravitational field would be just strong enough at this point to maintain orbit. Then, the gravitational field generators would be used in reverse to attract the ships toward the planet, compounding the effect of Senia's gravity. They would descend as quickly as the atmosphere allowed, and then, the gravitational field generators would be slammed into reverse at maximum capacity, stabilizing the descent at about 20,000 feet. From there, it would only be a matter of a few minutes for the ships to reach their targets and release their bombs.

Even if the Senians knew they were coming, it would be exceedingly difficult for them to successfully defend against this scale of attack. They would be out of the range of Senian jets until about 50,000 feet above the planet. Above 50,000 feet, only a starship could operate, and then it would have to be capable of reaching and precisely targeting their starships while rapidly descending through the atmosphere for a period of a little over seven Earth minutes. Below 50,000 feet, the attack ships were equipped with a powerful laser that could disable or destroy an incoming jet in an instant.

Once they reached Senia, five ships would be initially diverted from the attack to destroy the planetary communications satellites and orbital detection systems. Then, these ships would follow the initial attack to key targets to provide a layer of redundancy in case the initial attack failed to hit all of the targets.

Those ships that survived the attack would return to Corilia. During the attack, the Corilians would transmit an ultimatum to Senia to accept Corilian domination or prepare to suffer the consequences of another similar attack. It was anticipated that the substantially weakened and destroyed Senia would conclude that it had no choice but to submit.

The Corilians had virtually no intelligence about the areas they would need to target on Senia. The last time a Corilian had set foot on Senia was when the Senians rejected their offer of separate governance hundreds of years ago. The Corilians used their entry to gain as much photographic and other intelligence as they could. Population centers could have shifted, and they had no intelligence as to the location of Senian military installations and the capability of Senian defenses. All of their targeting intelligence would therefore have to be developed as they approached the planet.

The Senian military and intelligence services spent hundreds of hours discussing precisely how the Corilians would attack their planet and what they would do if they were planning the attack. They designed an attack plan that was startlingly similar to the Corilian attack plan. They knew the Corilians would have to decelerate from near light speed, which would provide them with some advance notice of the attack, although the precise amount of notice could not be determined. Once at orbital velocity, they would have to break orbit as quickly as possible and attack.

The Senian defenses were built around the hypothetical Corilian attack plan. There would be three layers of defense. The Senian starship fleet would lay in wait on the opposite side of the planet from which the Corilians would approach. At the last possible moment, the fleet would leave their positions to intercept and disable or destroy the attackers just before they altered their course from Corilia to disburse and enter into orbit around Senia. The ships would split up, with ten ships circling the planet from one direction and ten ships circling the planet from the other direction, so that they would outflank the incoming starships from both sides, hopefully with the element of surprise.

The ships that got through the initial line of defense would be met by the remaining ten ships of the Corilian starship fleet as they attempted to enter orbit. Whatever was left of the initial twenty starships would protect the Senian communications and defense satellites.

The third line of defense would be a fleet of approximately 150 attack fighters dispersed over the planet. On the assumption that the orbital communications systems would be destroyed during the attack, the Senians would also intensify their ground based radar and other systems. They knew that there would be little time to intercept and destroy an incoming starship that made it through the first two lines of defense. Ground based missile systems would also be substantially increased.

Even with all of these defenses, they knew that they would indeed be extremely fortunate if they were able to intercept and destroy all of the incoming starships before they were able to release their weapons of mass destruction.

The preparations for the Corilian attack were kept secret from the general populace for over three years. At first, the increase in defense spending was not that noticeable, but as time went on the geometric increases could not be justified based merely upon a desire for increased military preparedness.

When the various defensive systems started to be assembled and deployed, it was no longer possible to keep the situation secret. The Supreme Council decided that it would be better to inform the people of the situation, rather than have it leak out and be subject to speculation, fear, and uncertainty. At least they would then know of the extensive effort that was being made to defend the planet, which would help mobilize the population and relieve some of their fear and anxiety. After three more years, the Corilian attack fleet was well on its way toward Senia, so the die was cast.

The Senians were very mindful about how the announcement would be made. There was no danger at that point in time that a message would reach Corilia in time to make any difference. However, if the communication was intercepted by the incoming starships, their chances of success would be drastically altered by losing the element of surprise. Satellite communication systems could not be used. This presented a great problem, as Senian communications were almost entirely dependent upon satellites. There was no alternative but to use nearly defunct printed media and the mail system.

The first to be advised were the various forms of news media. They were assembled at Avilia, the Capitol city. Chancellor Baldar made the presentation. The main purpose of the meeting was to advise the media of the need to maintain secrecy of the fact that Senia was aware of the impending attack. The media was instructed that they could not use any broadcast media, the global communications system, commonly known as "GCS," or any other form of communication that was dependent upon satellite technology, including telephonic communications, to discuss the attack. Basically, they were told that they were out of the picture in terms of communicating this grave news. Those media that still maintained print outlets could transmit the news in that manner. The journalists now understood why the government had sought to maintain secrecy as long as possible.

On the same day the Chancellor met with the media, members of the Supreme Council called special closed sessions of their legislatures. They too were cautioned of the need to maintain secrecy regarding Senia's knowledge of the impending attack. Lastly, a message from the Chancellor was mailed to every known address on the planet, stressing the importance of not discussing the situation by phone or through GCS with any friends or family members.

The Supreme Council could only hope that the populace would abide by the communications restrictions. On the positive side, no further questions were raised about defense spending and the preparation effort. Those who were directly involved in production and assembly of the starships, fighters, and other equipment redoubled their efforts. There was a noticeable increase in productivity. Everyone was willing to work very long hours to get the job done.

Remarkably, there was little fear or panic. The commonality of the threat gave everyone some measure of assurance. They were all in this together and would suffer the same fate if they fell apart in confusion, dissention, and panic.

On balance, the Supreme Council was pleased with the outcome. They could now devote their full efforts toward preparing for the Corilian invasion without any further probing by the news media and with the population's full support.

While the Corilian attack fleet careened toward Senia and the Senians calmly and methodically prepared their defenses, the starship *Explorer* continued its lonely course toward Senia. Over the course of many years, after Josh was able to converse freely with Fela and the others, Josh conveyed to them the nature of the situation on Earth with regard to the forces of good and evil as he saw it. The Senians had an endless curiosity about the intricacies of American and world politics and they would go on and on with their questions, with Josh responding to the best of his knowledge. He loved it as he was a political buff and there was no one around to dispute his point of view. Still, he tried to be objective and present the issues of the day from all sides.

His knowledge of history did not go back to World War I in any great detail, but he was well familiar for a person of his age with the causes and consequences of World War II. He told the Senians about the rise of the Nazis in Germany after World War I. They all listened intently, thinking about how similar it was to the fall of Corilia to totalitarian rule. He explained that it was the United States, the Americans, where they had landed, that had freed Europe and Asia from the grip of dictatorship, defeating the Nazis and the Japanese aggressors in Asia and restoring democratic government and institutions.

He discussed the bipolar world that developed after World War II, where the Soviet Union continued to pursue a doctrine of militaristic expansion, and that a "cold war" had developed after the Soviets tightened their grip over many of the nations of Eastern Europe, preventing them from developing democratic government, ruling through proxy governments, and threatening the other nations of Europe through a buildup of military forces.

He discussed the Cuban missile crisis of 1962, and how the Americans were the first to develop a nuclear bomb that brought about an abrupt end to World War II. He explained that the Americans did not use their nuclear power to prevent other nations from developing a nuclear weapon, and as a consequence, soon after the American development of nuclear weapons, the Soviets developed a nuclear weapon. Then, three other nations developed nuclear weapons. Two of those nations, England and France, were democratic governments in Europe that were saved from totalitarianism by the Americans. The other government, China, was hostile to the Americans, but also not very friendly with the Soviets.

The Senians came to understand Earth's geopolitics and realized how fortunate they were to have chosen American airspace for their last incursion. From the description of their previous incursions, Josh believed they had made attempts in Asia and Africa. In both of those instances, they had not been confronted by military jets.

The Senians related the history of their separation from Corilia and the danger that had persisted for hundreds of years that Corilia would seek to reassert control over Senia. They discussed the Corilian underground, which Josh easily related to the French underground during World War II.

Josh and the others also spent much time exchanging information about their political systems. He came to learn that Senian democracy was organized very differently from American democracy. The planet was divided into nine provinces. Each province had a single legislative body comprised of elected representatives from throughout the province. Legislative districts were sized to be approximately equal in population. Because the Senian population was basically stable in size and location, it was very infrequent that a legislative district would need to be adjusted.

Within each province, the voters directly chose their provincial representative, provincial leader, two representatives to the Supreme Council, and the Chancellor, who acted as the head of the Supreme Council and was responsible for administering the planetary government in accordance with the instructions of the Supreme Council. The provincial leader had complete authority to administer the executive and administrative branches of provincial government, subject to the laws enacted by the provincial legislature. There was no legislative body at the planetary level.

The Chancellor's powers were much more limited than the American President. All major planetary decisions were taken by a majority vote of the Supreme Council, with the Chancellor having one vote. It had never occurred that a vote was so close that the Chancellor's vote amounted to the tie-breaking vote.

The majority of governance occurred at the provincial level. As there were no nation states on Senia, the provincial governments became somewhat equivalent to nation states on Earth.

There was no dispute about the authority of the Supreme Council to implement the planetary defenses, coordinate economic activity and commerce between the provinces, and administer the judicial system to resolve disputes between the provinces. With regard to matters such as education and social welfare, the Supreme Council oversaw administrative agencies that were primarily focused on maintaining coordination and cooperation between the provinces. Infrequent disputes between the provinces that could not be settled by the Supreme Council's administrative agencies or through the judicial system were submitted to the Supreme Council for binding resolution.

One day, with a very captive audience of Fedar, Fela, Zofar and Banar, Josh explained the American system of government.

"In America, the country is divided into fifty states, which are similar to your provinces. There is also what we call the federal government, which is similar to your Supreme Council. There are two legislative bodies at the federal level of government, the House of Representatives and the Senate. Each state elects two Senators, regardless of the population of the state. Members of the House of Representatives are chosen based upon the size of the population within each state."

Fedar inquired: "Why are there two legislative bodies? How can you pass legislation with two legislative bodies?"

Josh replied: "It is very difficult to pass legislation. Very often, legislation will be passed by one legislative body, only to fail in the other. Sometimes they are able to come together and compromise and pass legislation that way. And even if legislation passes both legislative bodies, it can be vetoed by the President. The veto can only be overruled by a two-thirds vote of the House and Senate."

Fedar: "Senia could never function under such a system."

Josh: "Somehow our government manages to function, but not very well. When the Constitution was drafted, there was a great fear about government abusing its power. The country had just broken away from being ruled by the King of England, another nation state. So the power to enact legislation was not concentrated in a single body."

Josh explained about the political parties.

"In America there are basically two political parties, the Republicans and the Democrats. The country is basically divided politically between people of higher and lower income. The Republicans represent higher income people and business interests. The Democrats represent lower income people and organized labor."

Zofar commented: "It's somewhat like that on Senia, but there are no political parties. People of similar points of view just get together to discuss their ideas."

Josh asked: "How does one pay the costs of getting elected without a political party?"

Zofar replied: "Elections are not that costly. Most of the elections are for seats in the provincial legislatures. Candidates use GCS to put forth their qualifications and ideas and seek contributions. Contributions are made through GCS. It's the same for representatives to the Supreme Council and the Chancellor."

Josh responded: "Is there a limit to the amount of a contribution? Wouldn't it distort the election if one person or a corporation or labor union could give a very large amount of money to a candidate?"

Zofar explained: "Only individuals are allowed to contribute to a candidate. That question has come up, but contributions are disclosed on GCS. When people see that a candidate is receiving large amounts of money from a few people, they usually will not vote for that candidate."

While over twelve years had elapsed in space with virtually nothing changing except the birth of Rosilea, events on Earth saw a major transformation, the most significant of which were the Camp David accord, the rise of militant Islam, the beginning of the digital age, the rise of China as an economic powerhouse, and the dissolution of the Soviet Union.

No one could have foretold that the first ripple of the Iranian revolution, when a group of Iranian students occupied the Iranian Embassy at Wassenaar, Netherlands in August of 1978, would usher in a wave of Islamic militancy that would end up consuming much of the Earth's attention in the Twenty-first Century. The Ayatollah Khomeini was exiled by Mohammad Reza Pahlavi, the Shah of Iran, for his persistent resistance to the Shah's steps toward greater integration with western nations. Living in Iraq, he spearheaded the efforts of the Iranian Revolution with leaflets and cassette tapes. The Shah, who employed the ruthless SAVAK secret police to maintain control, was widely unpopular among a populace that hungered for democratic government. This hunger would not be realized, as the Shah's tyrannical rule was quickly replaced by Khomeini's religious autocracy, enforced by the Iranian Revolutionary Guard.

The Iranian Revolution proceeded rapidly. In September 1978, the Iranian army fired on Khomeini followers in Tehran, killing hundreds. In November 1978, Iranian troops fired on anti-Shah protesters by Tehran University. The Shah then placed Iran under military rule, which only lasted until the end of 1978, when he named as premier Shapour Bakhtiar, a democratic nationalist who had opposed the Shah's rule, and asked him to form a civilian government. In early 1979, the Shah fled Iran for Egypt as Bakhtiar formed a civilian government that sought to transition to democracy. Bakhtiar freed all political prisoners, lifted newspaper censorship, relaxed martial law, dissolved SAVAK, and sought to hold elections in three months to elect a constituent assembly that would determine the fate of the monarchy and Iran's future form of government.

This was not enough for Khomeini and his followers. Four days after the Shah left Iran, over 1,000,000 Khomeini supporters marched in Tehran. At this critical juncture, President Carter failed to provide Iran's fledgling attempt at democracy any material support. In February 1979, Khomeini returned to Iran after fifteen years of exile. Mr. Bakhtiar resigned shortly thereafter and Ayatollah Khomeini seized power.

In spring of 1979, Iran proclaimed an Islamic Republic and press censors started massive book burnings. Mass executions ensued, which were finally ended on Khomeini's orders in October 1979. Later that year, 500 Iranian "students" took ninety Americans hostage at the U.S. Embassy in Tehran. Although Khomeini did not plan the takeover, he sanctioned the hostage taking and declared the United States "The Great Satan" several days later. At the end of 1979, Iran adopted a new Constitution, declaring an Islamic Republic with

Ayatollah Khomeini as its Supreme Leader, having the power to overrule actions of the legislative body.

President Carter's astonishing success at Camp David, where, after weeks of negotiations an accord was reached between Egypt and Israel in September 1978 (resulting in a March, 1979 peace treaty), was overshadowed by the Iranian hostage crisis that ensued shortly thereafter and continued for 444 days until the hostages were finally freed after severe mistreatment. While the hostages remained in Iran, as if to add insult to injury, Soviet troops invaded Afghanistan in December, 1979. All of this projected an image of weakness abroad that led to the presidential election of Ronald Reagan, a conservative Republican who was viewed as a "hawk" in foreign affairs. On January 20, 1981, as President Reagan completed his inaugural address, the 52 remaining American hostages were released.

Things changed dramatically in Washington D.C. with the new President. An influx of conservative thinkers sought to keep President Reagan's campaign promise to cut taxes and balance the federal budget, while dramatically increasing military spending to counter the growing Soviet threat. It soon became apparent that the Americans could not "have their cake and eat it too" as the budget deficit continued to dramatically increase, despite some cuts in social spending. Something had to give, and it would not be the increase in military spending, so the budget deficit continued to grow. President Reagan's Budget Director, David Stockman, ultimately resigned in 1985. By the time President Reagan left office in 1989, the national debt had increased from $997 billion to $2.85 trillion.

President Reagan had decided that the United States, having a substantially larger economy than the Soviets, could better afford an arms race, which would ultimately break the Soviets economically if they tried to keep pace. He espoused what became known as the "Reagan Doctrine," which abandoned the idea of simply containing Soviet expansionism in favor of actively supporting fighters that resisted Soviet efforts to control foreign governments in the name of spreading communism. The U.S. actively supported anti-Soviet movements in Angola, Cambodia, and Nicaragua, but the most significant application of this doctrine was in supporting the Mujahideen in Afghanistan, a coalition of various alliances and tribal groups that steadfastly resisted the Soviet occupation. The Soviets ultimately withdrew from Afghanistan after the loss of over 14,000 troops and security forces and the death of over 850,000 Afghan civilians.

President Reagan's resistance of the Soviets went beyond countering foreign expansionism. Under his policy of "peace through strength," the B-1 bomber program was reinstated and the first B-1 bomber went into active service in 1986. There was a major across-the-board increase in overall defense spending, which the Soviets failed to match due to their faltering economy. The MX multi-warhead ballistic missile was produced and, under his "Strategic Defense Initiative," he called for development of a missile defense system capable to intercepting incoming Soviet missiles, which came to be known as "Star Wars."

He employed vociferous rhetoric against the Soviets. In a 1982 address to the British Parliament, he said that the "forward march of freedom and democracy will leave Marxist-Leninism on the ash heap of history." In a 1983 speech he referred to the Soviet Union as an "evil empire." In a 1987 speech at the Berlin Wall separating East and West Germany, he called on the Soviet leadership to "tear down this wall."

The Soviet Union underwent a fundamental change during the Reagan era. After two successive aging Communist bureaucrats died while holding the leadership position, the Politburo elected Mikhail Gorbachev General Secretary in 1985. Gorbachev favored political and economic liberalization and improved relations and trade with the western democracies. He implemented the policies of "Glasnost" (openness) and "Perestroika" (free markets). The loosening of the Communist Party's tight grip over the satellite nations of Eastern Europe, combined with an unwillingness to use brute force to maintain control, as had been done in the past, led to the development of independence movements throughout the Soviet empire. Beginning with the Solidarity movement in Poland, the populations of Eastern Europe revolted against their Communist puppet governments, culminating in the fall of the Berlin Wall in 1989. Open public debate gradually increased within Russia during this period, and by the spring of 1989 there were multi-candidate elections.

Russia's willingness to loosen its grip over the satellite nations of Eastern Europe led to a dramatic improvement in relations with the U.S. and the democracies of Western Europe. There were four summit meetings between President Reagan and Secretary Gorbachev. In 1987, they agreed to eliminate an entire class of intermediate range nuclear weapons. At the fourth summit in Moscow, when President Reagan was asked if he still considered the Soviet Union an "evil empire," he said "No, I was talking about another time, another era." The Cold War with the Soviets was officially declared over at the Malta Summit in December 1989.

Dramatic change was also occurring during this period on the other side of the Earth in mainland China. During the 1980s, China, a nation of over one billion people, began its transformation from a largely rural economy held back by Communist ideology to a modern industrial giant. The story of China's economic transformation was the story of the leadership of one man – Deng Xiaoping, who, although never holding a formal position of government or Communist Party leadership, was known as China's "paramount leader" from when he first consolidated his control over China's government in 1978 to when he officially retired from public life in 1992. Relations between the U.S. and China thawed considerably after President Richard Nixon visited China in 1972, resulting in the Shanghai Communiqué, whereby it was agreed that the thorny issue of Taiwan's legal status would be resolved peacefully. Starting in 1979, President Carter established full diplomatic relations with mainland China, breaking off diplomatic relations with the "Republic of China" on Taiwan.

Deng had been an active member of the Chinese Communist Party since the 1920s. He fought against the Chinese Nationalists, led by Chiang Kai-shek, who ultimately lost to the Communists after World War II and had to flee to Taiwan. He participated in the

"Long March" of 1934 when the Nationalists caused a Communist force of about 10,000 men to flee to the northern province of Shaan-xi. His Communist Party credentials were strong enough to prevent him from being removed from a leadership position during the purge against Communist Party members who did not go along with Mao Zedong's economic philosophy during the "Great Leap Forward" of the 1950s. Deng was a "pragmatist" who had worked since the 1950s to improve China's economic situation by developing policies that emphasized economic development over ideological dogma.

After being purged during the Cultural Revolution and forced to work in a tractor factory for four years in the 1960s, he re-emerged to a leadership position after Mao's death in 1976, and skillfully maneuvered against his opponents to obtain de facto leadership of China in 1978. From this position of power, he began to open the floodgates for China's economic development, espousing the "four modernizations" in economy, agriculture, scientific and technological development, and national defense. He set aside Mao's policy of economic self-reliance in favor of developing an export oriented economy that depended heavily upon foreign investment, including the creation of "Special Economic Zones." Western economies, including the U.S., which was in the throes of a wage-price spiral in the late 1970s, began to make much greater use of China's low cost labor supply by moving production to China, making considerable investment in Chinese employment while also transferring a great amount of technical know-how.

Deng's "four modernizations" did not include any liberalizing of the political system, which ultimately led to a massive protest movement developing in Beijing's Tiananmen Square in 1989. The movement started rather haphazardly, with people gathering to protest against the short shrift given by the Communist Party to the death of Hu Yaobang, a reformist official backed by Deng but ousted by conservative elements in the Party. The demonstration grew and evolved into a call for democratic reform. Ultimately, the Communist Party hardliners prevailed. Martial law was declared in May 1989. After an initial military advance against the city was blocked by residents, the

Party sent over 200,000 soldiers with tanks and helicopters to force-fully remove the protesters from the square, resulting in an unknown number of deaths and casualties. Western nations voiced their objections to the treatment of the protesters, but the status quo in terms of economic integration remained unchanged.

While tectonic shifts were occurring in Earth's political and economic landscape, computer scientists were making steady progress toward Earth's entry into the digital age. The seeds of the digital age had already been planted when Josh departed Earth for Senia in 1977. Scientists had concluded in the 1940s that binary switches of ones and zeros were the best way to develop the logic circuits necessary to perform mathematical and other calculations. What started out as large machines full of thousands of mechanical switches then became electronic circuits with thousands of vacuum tubes, then transistors, and finally the microchip, first developed by Intel in the early 1970s. Personal computers hit the market in the mid 1970s, but there were many who could hardly conceive of the personal computer becoming a household appliance that would be considered necessary for everyday life. Apple Computers was formed in 1976 with the rollout of the Apple I, and then the Apple II in 1977. Word processing, the first widely useful application for computers, came into being in 1979. In 1981, IBM released its first personal computer running the Microsoft MS-DOS operating system. In 1983, Apple released Lisa, the first computer with a graphical user interface, which was then followed by Microsoft Windows in 1985.

The personal computer engendered a revolution in communications. In 1978, the first computer bulletin board system, Ward and Randy's CBBS, Chicago, came into being, and the first unsolicited bulk spam e-mail was sent by Digital Equipment Corporation to every APRANET address on the west coast. In 1979, Compuserve began operation as a computer information service. By 1982, common protocols were developed for the APRANET, which would evolve into the internet. The ".com" system for domain names was developed in 1983, and by 1987 there were over 20,000 internet sites. The internet was still in its infancy in 1989, getting ready to explode in the next decade.

In the Middle East, the hope and promise of the Camp David Accord and the Egypt-Israel Peace Treaty gave way to the radical elements, stirred up and supported by the new regime in Iran, who refused any compromise with Israel. The new Islamic Republic was consumed by a bloody war with Saddam Hussein's Iraq during most of the 1980s, but this did not prevent Iran from fomenting trouble for peace efforts in the Middle East.

Lebanon was the primary battlefront between countervailing forces in the 1980s. In 1982, Israel invaded Lebanon, installing a pro-Israeli Christian government. This led to the formation of an anti-Israeli Shiite militia group known as Hezbollah, founded, trained, and equipped as a proxy army for Iran, which had established an Islamic Revolutionary Guard base in the Syria-controlled Bekaa Valley. In 1983, Hezbollah set off a suicide truck bomb at the U.S. Embassy in Beirut, killing 63 people. Later that year, Hezbollah set off two truck bombs at the barracks of U.S. and French peacekeeping forces, killing 299 American and French servicemen. This led to the withdrawal of American and French peacekeeping forces from Lebanon in 1984 and the subsequent rise of Hezbollah as a significant military force in Lebanon.

CHAPTER 7 - RETURN TO SENIA

November 14, 1994. President Clinton has agreed to change his outdoor routine after a recent attack on the White House. Personal computers are flying off the shelves at big box stores, CompUSA, Best Buy, Egghead, and Computer City.

Zfar, Fedar, Banar, Josh and Fela are on the bridge. This is it! They are finally about to enter into orbit around Senia after over seventeen Earth years in space. Josh, now forty-four years old, and Fela grasped hands in anticipation. The rest of the crew is at their stations, eagerly listening in on the ship's monitor.

All of their communiqués have now reached Senia and everyone on the planet is aware of the success of the mission in obtaining an Earth human and learning an Earth language. The reverse is true as well. All of the communiqués from Senia have reached the ship and the crew is fully aware of events on Senia, including the almost completed preparations for the Corilian attack. They are now speaking in real time to mission control.

Zfar gave the word to mission control. "Permission requested to enter orbit."

Mission control responded. "Permission granted."

Banar, who had received and located the landing coordinates, inquired: "Just to confirm, we are to land at the Capitol Stadium."

Mission control: "Confirmed. The Supreme Council has decided that this will be a planetary event."

Fedar then inquired: "What about security?"

Mission control: "Practically every dignitary on the planet will be there. Security is very tight."

With that, Zfar entered the commands to direct the ship into orbit. The deceleration from near light speed was almost complete and the ship was traveling toward the planet at a speed of about 20,000 miles per hour. They would intersect Senia at about 125 miles above the planet and be drawn into orbit by Senia's gravitational field. Then, the orbit would be adjusted to bring the ship over the landing coordinates. When in position, the ship would decelerate as it lost altitude to match the speed of rotation of the planet and the gravitational field generators would land the ship. There would be no manual control unless a problem developed with the auto piloting mechanisms.

The deceleration from near light speed had been an incredible experience. Like those distant Rocky Mountains over the Great Plains, the Senian sun first became apparent with the naked eye when they were about three months from Senia and half-way through the deceleration. Its brightness grew as they approached until it was not possible to view it directly with the naked eye. At that point, it could only be viewed through head gear that filtered the light and made it very difficult to see anything on the bridge. Most of the time, translucent panels were placed over the section of the bridge through which the sun shined.

On occasion, the panels would be removed so they could view Senia in orbit around its sun, along with three other planets in the solar system, against the backdrop of the Milky Way. To say that it was an utterly spectacular view does not quite capture how awesome it was to Josh and the others. There in the infinite vastness of the universe was home to all but Josh. With each passing day as they approached, the spirits of the crew grew higher until they could hardly be constrained by the rigors of space travel.

About fifty minutes elapsed after Zfar entered the re-entry commands. Senia grew closer and closer until at last the ship was between the planet and the sun and about to enter orbit on the dark side of the planet. They could now see their beautiful planet illuminated by the sun as they entered orbit.

Zfar spoke into the monitor: "We have entered orbit. We will be landing at 6:75."

There was a cheer on the bridge and throughout the ship, somewhat subdued in the Senian sort of way. They didn't scream and shout like Josh would have expected on Earth, and as he was inclined to do. Still, there was no mistaking their joy as they were about to land, having successfully completed their mission.

Zfar spoke again: "Everyone except engineering is welcome on the bridge for the landing. Be sure you have your head gear."

They were now traveling over the night sky, rapidly decelerating through repeated movements of the outer rim casting momentum at 180 degrees to their flight path. They would soon be on the other side of Senia with the bridge directly exposed to the intense sunlight. It would become more diffuse as they descended through the atmosphere, but would be extremely dangerous when first encountered. It would take another trip around the planet to align the ship's orbit with the landing coordinates. And then it would be time to land, at about mid-afternoon.

Zofar, Bandar, and Rosilea entered the bridge. Rosilea was now a stunning young lady of a little over sixteen Earth years, seventeen Senian years. She came up to Josh and Fela and they all embraced and stood there holding hands with Rosilea between them. Her excitement was overwhelming. She would be seeing her homeland for the first time.

A moment of great decision was drawing ever closer for Rosilea. She knew that, if all went well, there would be a return voyage to Earth and that Josh and Fela would be on that voyage. For all of her life, Josh and Fela, the other members of the crew, the *Explorer*, and the universe were all she knew of life. The energies and desires of youth were starting to flow within her, and she did not want to spend the next eighteen Senian years of her life on a starship, not getting to know love or experience passion. Yet, she deeply loved her parents and could hardly imagine life without them, as they would not return to Senia after the Earth voyage. Of course, they wanted her to return to Earth with them, but would not impose that on her if she chose to remain on Senia.

Up to now, she did not know what life was like on Senia or Earth. Josh had told her about how beautiful Earth was, with its varied climates, wondrous landscapes, and abundant wildlife. He also told her of the dangers of living on Earth with the threat of nuclear weapons. She knew that Senia faced the same danger from the Corilians and was fully aware of the immediate threat of Corilian attack, having been told by Josh and Fela when she was fourteen.

There was still much time to decide. They would first have to survive the Corilian attack. It could be many months or even years before they would be ready to return to Earth and she would at least be able to spend some time on Senia. It was constantly on her mind.

Meanwhile, back on Senia, preparations for the landing were proceeding at a feverish pace. This would be the event of the year, if not the decade. The successful return of the Earth mission was not unlike the Earth landing of a man on the moon in 1969. Living under the threat of Corilian invasion for so many years had hardened the sensibilities of the Senian people. The successful completion of the Earth mission would help to renew Senian hopefulness for the future and determination to repel the Corilian attack. It was for this reason the Supreme Council had decided to make the landing a public event. To say the least, the curiosity and desire to see the Earth human and the Earth-Senia offspring in person was at a fever pitch.

The VIPs were starting to assemble at the Capitol Stadium. Although popular Senian sentiment was overwhelmingly in favor of the Earth mission, there were a few xenophobic Senians who opposed the mission for some unknown reason that they could not articulate with any rationality. There was also the very remote possibility that a deranged Senian would seek to harm the crew or the Earth human in an effort to gain the spotlight. In any case, the Supreme Council was not taking any chances and security was very tight.

Josh had no idea that he would be the center of attention when they landed on Senia. He expected that he would have to make some remarks and was intently thinking about what he would say. He was the ambassador from Earth and was now fluent in the Senian language. Of course, he would convey a message of peace and friendship. Many different ways of saying the same thing were running through his mind.

Zfar activated the gravitational field generator and the ship started to lose altitude. The outer rim continued the deceleration process. There was a tense excitement on the bridge.

Zfar and the other Senians thought about how their lives would change after they landed. Zfar was thinking that he would not return to Earth. He had left his life on Senia behind and was not sure whether there would be anything for him to return to. Still, he was now over 79 Senian years old and another mission to Earth meant that he would either die in space or on Earth.

The same was true for much of the crew. They would now have to put their lives back together on Senia. No one except Josh and Fela were thinking of someday returning to Earth. They expected to receive some commendations and then be on their own. Little did they know or contemplate what heroes they would be when they returned or how well they would be rewarded financially.

It took another thirty minutes for the *Explorer* to complete its descent. Avilia, the Capitol city, gradually came into view and grew larger as they approached. After a few minutes, they could see the stadium on the monitor. It was packed with people. Their excitement and anticipation became tinged with apprehension and nervousness as to what would be expected of them when they landed.

The ship slowly completed its final descent as the tripod legs extended from beneath the ship to the landing position. They would exit the ship from a small port on the second level. This way, there would be no reversal of the gravitational fields that would occur if they exited on the first level. The gravitational field generator for the first level would have to continue to operate while stationary on Senia in order to prevent chaos on that level.

The *Explorer* settled in on the pavement as the outer rim slowly came to a halt and rested in its cradle. They had arrived! Everyone breathed a sigh of relief. The incredibly long and difficult journey was finally over.

Zfar gave his last command of the voyage.

"Let's all assemble at the escape port."

Minar checked all of the ship's systems one last time to make sure that everything was in order. Zfar would emerge first. Fedar would be next, and then the rest of the crew. Fela, Josh and Rosilea would be last.

Minar climbed the ladder and opened the hatch. As it opened they could hear the excited hum in the stadium start to grow louder. Zfar climbed the ladder and emerged from the ship as the hum in the stadium grew to a near deafening roar of cheers and applause. The platform to carry them to ground level was being drawn into position. Zfar slowly walked down the sloped side of the ship toward the platform as the other crew members exited to the deafening roar of the crowd and took their position on the platform.

Josh was the last to emerge. Fela was first, and then Rosilea. The people knew about Rosilea from the reports to mission control, which included many photos, portions of which were shared with the public. It had greatly popularized the mission, as if it needed more popularization.

When Josh emerged, as if the roar of the crowd was not deafening enough, it became even louder. There he stood, the first human from Earth to contact alien life in another part of the galaxy. He wondered whether he would ever get back to Earth to tell of his experience. The thought occurred to him to raise his hands in the air as a gesture in response to the roaring crowd. He held back as he looked about at the other crew, who were calmly walking onto the platform, hardly acknowledging the excitement that surrounded them.

The stadium was remarkably similar to anything he would have expected to see on Earth. There must have been over fifty thousand people. They looked very much like Earth people, casually dressed in a variety of colors.

They all stood there on the platform for a few minutes. Zfar raised his hands to waive to the crowd as it continued to roar and everyone followed suit. Then, they descended the stairs to ground level and walked over to the platform that had been erected on the field for the welcoming ceremony.

The weather was very pleasant. The temperature was in the low 80s. The Senian sun shined brightly and a few clouds wafted across the sky. The air was fine to breathe, not at all polluted for being at the center of a large city.

The Chancellor was there to greet them as they stepped onto the platform. He was an elderly man, who appeared to Josh to be about sixty Earth years old. He was wearing a loosely fitting gray pullover long sleeve shirt and dark blue pants, similar to the type of clothes worn by the crew and the thousands of people in the stadium. There was nothing regal about his clothes or his demeanor.

Josh was surprised at the level of informality.

Have these people never heard of suits? he thought.

It was a traditional Senian greeting. He stood opposite each crew member and bowed his head at a slight angle, quickly picking it up. The crew members then did the same. When he came to Josh, he did the same and Josh followed suit. The stadium roared after each greeting.

Then Josh did something impetuous. He grasped Fela's and Rosilea's hands and began to move their hands up, looking over to the rest of the crew to follow. They quickly followed suit and together they all raised their clasped hands to the sky in a gesture of unity and triumph. The stadium roared again. Josh worried later as to whether he had upstaged or offended the Chancellor.

When the crowd died down, the Chancellor approached the podium for his welcoming speech.

"On behalf of the Supreme Council and my fellow Senians, I welcome you back to Senia after your long journey. You have all made a great sacrifice for the people of Senia. It is with the greatest of pleasure that I welcome you, Josh, the first human from Earth to visit our planet. I thank you for your courage in undertaking this journey and know that this will begin the bonds of friendship between Senia and Earth.

You return to Senia at a time of the greatest of challenges. We are locked in a struggle to maintain our way of life in the face of the imminent threat from Corilia, our brothers and sisters of the flesh, but not of the spirit. We have been most fortunate that there are still those on Corilia who continue to maintain the struggle against the forces of evil that now rule Corilia. Perhaps the day will come when Senia and Corilia can be reunited under the rule of law and respect for human dignity. We must all never lose hope that such a day will come.

I want to afford a special welcome to our newest Senian, Rosilea, who is a most special person. She represents our hope for the future and the ties to be developed between Senia and Earth. Through the painstaking effort of Fela and Josh, our new friend from Earth, we can now communicate with Earth and build these ties.

To Zfar and all of the members of the crew, I convey the greatest of appreciation for your dedication to this mission. Together, you have succeeded in opening a path to a future in which Senia and Earth will build ties that will be beneficial to humanity throughout our galaxy.

We will return to Earth after we repel the Corilian attack force. For now, we must all continue our steadfast effort to prepare our defenses.

Thank you again. I would like to afford Zfar, our mission commander, the opportunity to address you as well."

Zfar approached the podium, not quite knowing what he would say, but having given it considerable thought.

"Thank you, Chancellor. It was indeed an awful day six years ago when we received a communication from mission control telling us of the impending Corilian attack. We received each communication after that with great relief that this beautiful planet that we call home had not yet come under attack. We are most relieved to arrive in time to help participate in the effort to repel this most grievous effort to destroy our way of life."

Zfar then withdrew from the podium to thunderous cheers and applause.

The Chairman stepped up again. "Is there anyone else that would like to say something."

The crew looked about at each other. Fedar stepped forward.

"I just want to say how happy we are to be back on Senia. We are now part of your struggle and will do everything in our power to help defeat the Corilians."

Then Banar stepped forward:

"I can only echo what my other crewmates have said. It is good to be back on Senia."

Fela stepped forward.

"Thank you for your good wishes and for coming here today to welcome us back. I too cannot say how much it means to me to be back on Senia. I can tell you that the Earth human, Josh, is a kind and good person, and that, as our Chairman has said, we can look forward to a future in which Senia and Earth join together to oppose tyranny and oppression in our galaxy."

As Fela stepped back to more thunderous cheers and applause, the other crew members looked about at each other. No one appeared to be stepping forward. Josh didn't know what he should do. Then, the Chairman stepped to the podium.

"Let us have a few words from our new friend from Earth."

Josh stepped forward as the stadium again became filled with the sound of cheers and applause.

He thought to himself, *One small step for a man, one giant leap for mankind. No, that won't do.*

The crowd kept up its applause for what seemed like an eternity to Josh, giving him time to compose his thoughts.

"My name is Josh Rinaldi. For thousands of years, from the beginning of our recorded history, we on Earth have wondered whether there is any form of life in the galaxy other than on Earth. Now, I have come to learn that, not only is there other life in our galaxy, it is human life that closely resembles human life on Earth. I am eager to return to Earth to share this knowledge with everyone on Earth. I believe it will have a profound effect on my troubled planet.

What I have come to learn of the history of Senia and Corilia shows me that good and evil know no bounds. It is up to those of us who believe in doing what is right to never shirk away from our duty to live up to our beliefs and oppose those who would do evil.

I will join you in your struggle against the evil that now exists on Corilia. Such evil has existed on Earth many times during our history, but there have always been those who have fought for good and overcame evil. I am fortunate to come from a nation that fights to protect human dignity and freedom.

There is so much that we will be able to learn from you. Your technology is much more advanced than the technology on Earth. And perhaps there is something that you will be able to learn from us. Thank you."

Josh stepped back to his spot as the crown cheered and applauded. The Chancellor took the podium and thanked everyone for coming. With that, the ceremony was over.

The ceremony could not be transmitted live across the planet due to the continued need to maintain secrecy. Instead, there would be an official government press release, leaving out all of the discussion of the Corilian attack force. That and word of mouth would prove to be very effective in disseminating word of the new era in Senian history.

The Chancellor put his hands on Josh and Fela's shoulders.

"Come with me," he said. "You will be staying in the guest quarters at my official residence."

"Thank you," Fela quickly replied. She knew this to be a great honor.

Finding a place to stay on Senia would not be a problem for Josh and Fela. Fela was now a very wealthy person by Senian standards, along with the rest of the crew. She had accumulated over thirty-six Senian years of pay at twice the normal rate, along with accumulated leave that in and of itself amounted to a small fortune. If that was not enough, she would soon be flooded with very lucrative offers for product endorsements.

The Chancellor's security service guided them to a special exit not available to the general public. Once outside, Josh, Fela, and Rosilea were quickly shepherded into the back seat of a sleek, silver grey automobile. The Chancellor, his wife, and others in his party went into another similar vehicle.

Josh was all eyes as he gazed about him at the city and the electric powered car started to move, hardly making a sound. He had learned much about Senia during his many years in space and was hardly surprised by anything he saw. Still, he gazed about in amazement as the photos and videos he had seen for many years suddenly came to life.

It was a very well kept, beautiful city. There was an arid sense about it, but it was nevertheless full of carefully manicured vegetation along the medians of the roads, sidewalks and the park areas that he passed along the way to the Chancellor's residence. The road was not crowded and full of noisy, honking cars, as he was familiar with from his many trips to Manhattan. He could see that there were some vehicles that appeared to be like small buses traveling in the air about two hundred feet above him.

They passed under a monorail system. Josh looked up and could see that it appeared to extend for miles. A few monorail cars quickly flashed by, hardly making a sound as they were magnetically levitated above the base of the monorail. He saw one of the air buses dock at a landing station about twenty feet above the ground, with passengers departing down a stairway to ground level.

The architecture of the buildings was not at all ornate. There were design elements along the lines of Frank Lloyd Wright, with functionality the main consideration. Josh wondered how the Senians would react to seeing the U.S. Capitol Building or some of the ornate architecture in the cities of Europe.

It appeared that the main building material was light brown clay, molded into large bricks a little bit smaller than the standard concrete block used on Earth. There was very little wood that he could see. The buildings were not nearly as tall as buildings on Earth, the tallest building he could see being about ten stories high.

Iron ore was not nearly as prevalent on Senia as on Earth and was very limited in its use as a structural element for building construction. Instead, the Senians relied upon composite materials made from carbon fibers for key structural elements, along with the structural brick exterior and interior walls. As a consequence, the height of buildings was much more limited than on Earth. This had the beneficial effect of letting in light and allowing air to flow freely throughout the city.

After about fifteen minutes, they pulled into the Chancellor's residence. The Chancellor's car had arrived first. He was there with his wife, daughter, her husband, and his grandson.

"Welcome," he said with a smile. "This is my wife, Keala, my daughter, Salea, her husband, Nemar, and their son, Vinar."

Josh, being the head of the family, thought it was up to him to make the introductions.

"Very pleased to meet you," he said with a smile. "My name is Josh. This is our daughter, Rosilea, and of course you know my wife, Fela."

Rosilea looked over at Vinar, who was looking at her. He was a very handsome young man, with a strong jaw, soft brown eyes, and straight light brown hair that tossed about his head in the slight breeze. When their eyes made contact, she felt a sudden rush of excitement as she briefly smiled at him and then turned her eyes toward Josh and the Chancellor.

The Chancellor continued: "We are very pleased for you to stay with us as our guests until you can make arrangements for a place to stay on Senia. We have much to discuss, but we can save that for later. For now, let me show you around our residence."

"That would be great," Josh replied.

Fela added, "Yes, we are very honored."

Rosilea glanced over at Vinar as they departed. Their eyes met again. He smiled and she quickly smiled back as she turned her head to follow the Chancellor.

The Chancellor and his wife accompanied Josh, Fela, and Rosilea throughout the residence. It was smaller than the White House, as no official business was conducted there other than dinners and receptions for provincial leaders and other dignitaries and public figures. For official business, the Chancellor traveled through a secure underground facility to the Supreme Council Building, which housed his administrative staff and the meeting facilities for the Supreme Council. The residence was beautifully decorated with hand-crafted furniture from the rarest woods on the planet, large pictures on the walls showing scenes from the Alasia River and other beautiful areas of the planet, and, of course, many portraits of former Senian Chancellors. The floor in the grand reception area was a light grey marble, laced with fine hues of green. In the remainder of the residence, the floors were an eggshell colored tile, made from the planet's abundant supply of limestone. Beautifully crafted carpets covered many of the floors. Light streaked through the large windows throughout the residence, reflecting off the floors and casting shadows that accentuated the simple utilitarian designs throughout.

"We will see you for dinner tonight," the Chancellor said as they departed.

It would be an official state dinner, attended by all of the members of the Supreme Council, provincial leaders, business leaders, entertainers, and other people of great importance. The Chancellor's wife, Keala, was responsible for the guest list. It was a very difficult task, as the Capitol was flooded with dignitaries from all over the planet and there was not nearly enough room to accommodate all of those who wished to attend. There was no avoiding the fact that the guest list would amount to the top of a "who's who" in Senian society.

When the Chancellor left, they settled down in the very comfortable guest living area. The furniture was not lavish, most closely resembling mission style furniture on Earth, made from lightly finished tight-grained hardwoods.

"What a day," Josh said with a sigh of relief that they had successfully gotten through the stadium events and meeting the Chancellor and his family.

"It's not over yet," Fela replied, thinking of what lie ahead with the state dinner.

Rosilea's mind was somewhere else. She was still thinking about the handsome fellow she had just met.

Would he be at the dinner?, she wondered.

She hoped so. She knew better than to fall in love with the first guy she met that was her age, but, *he sure was nice*, she thought, as she tried to pretend she was keeping up with the conversation between Josh and Fela.

"I'm going to check out my room," she said, standing up.

Josh and Fela nodded with a smile, not having any idea of what was running through her mind.

"What am I going to wear?" Josh exclaimed, as the thought ran through his mind in a near panic.

Fela laughed. "We will have to get you some clothes. Let's go shopping. You wait here."

She left the room and went to the security guard standing near the entrance.

"Can you contact the Chancellor's wife for me? I would like to speak to her."

He made a few contacts and soon Keala appeared on the monitor in the living area of the guest quarters.

"What can I do for you, Fela?" she said.

"Josh is in a panic that he does not have anything to wear. Can you make arrangements so that we can go shopping?"

"Oh, yes. Would you like me to go with you?"

"If you like, that would be very nice."

"I'll meet you in the foyer in fifteen minutes."

"Thank you."

When Keala appeared at the foyer, she was accompanied by two security guards. Two cars then appeared, one for them and one for security. There was not a great concern about security, as it had been many years since there had been a security incident involving the Chancellor or his family. Still, they needed to take some precautions.

It was a joyful late afternoon as the four of them went to one of the finest stores in Avilia to buy clothes for Josh, Fela and Rosilea. The store agreed to charge the clothing to Fela, as her payment authorization had long since expired, although her bank account was loaded full of money.

Although the Senians were almost always very casual in their dress, for the most special and formal occasions the men did wear a suit without a lapel that would lie over the loose fitting pullover shirts they were accustomed to wearing. Josh quickly found a light brown suit, as the choices in his size were very limited, and the accoutrements to go with it, including a new pair of shoes.

They then shopped for Fela and Rosilea. Fela picked out a beautiful black evening dress that looked absolutely exquisite on her. Rosilea wanted something more colorful and picked out an emerald green evening dress with light grey trim that was also very stunning on her, almost matching the color of her eyes.

This was an evening to be remembered, especially for Rosilea. The room was almost full. The Chancellor and his wife were at their side as they entered. There were no formal introductions, but the room fell silent as everyone turned to see them and get a closer look at Josh and Rosilea.

Rosilea had only one thing on her mind.

Would Vinar be there?

She looked around and there he was, looking at her from across the large reception area. Their eyes met at a great distance and they acknowledged each other with a smile. Rosilea's heart was pounding as Vinar walked over to her.

"You look very, very lovely," he said, not at all shy.

"Thank you. I was hoping that you would be here."

"And I could not wait to see you again," he replied.

"This is all so new to me. My whole life has been aboard a starship."

"I know. Will you let me show you Avilia?"

"That would be wonderful," she said with an excited and eager voice, as she started to calm down inside.

He likes me, she thought, *and I like him.*

Vinar put out his hand for her to grasp, which she did.

"Let me show you around. I know a few people here."

As they wandered off to mingle with the crowd, Rosilea, arm in arm with Vinar, caught the attention of Josh, Fela, the Chancellor, Keala, and Vinar's parents, and Salea and Nimar. They stood in a circle conversing as everyone in the room cruised about, waiting for an opportunity to come over and be introduced.

"Well, look at them," the Chancellor said in an approving tone, not quite knowing what to make of it.

Fela quickly replied: "Vinar is a very fine young man."

Salea responded: "Thank you. He has completed his accreditation in mechanical engineering and will be starting his studies at the space academy this year."

Josh chimed in: "Rosilea has spent her whole life in space. She is very eager to see what life on Senian is like."

Salea replied: "I think Vinar will be seeing to that."

Josh, not sure whether she approved, asked: "Is that permissible?" not knowing a Senian word for "okay."

"Oh, yes" she replied. "They make a lovely couple."

Salea was fixed in the moment and not thinking about the potential implications of a romance between Vinar and Rosilea.

It was a whirlwind evening with endless introductions. Josh gave up on the handshaking gesture, as no one knew what it was, and went with the quick bow of the head until his neck started to creak. There was no dais. Everyone sat at tables, seven persons to a table. There were about two hundred people at the event.

It was a wonderful, sumptuous dinner of Senian fish, fresh vegetables sautéed in butter, wine and brandy. Josh, Fela, and Rosilea could not get enough of the food after so many years eating the regimented space menu. There were many jokes about space food and how good it was to be on Senia eating some real food and no protein wafers.

After dinner, the Chancellor went up to the podium and made a brief welcoming speech. Josh and the rest of the crew stood for a round of applause. Rosilea and Vinar sat together, becoming ever more comfortable with each other.

As the evening was winding up, Vinar turned to Rosilea while they stood in a corner of the room as people were leaving.

"Would tomorrow be too soon for me to take you on a tour of Avilia?"

"Oh, yes. That would be great," she replied.

As they parted they clasped hands again. Rosilea wanted him to kiss her, and he wanted to, but held back, not wanting to be too forward on their first meeting and fearful of what the Chancellor and his parents might think.

Later, as she lay in bed thinking about the evening, Rosilea could not deny herself. She felt as though she was in love and she knew it. He was so handsome, and had such a calm, nice manner about him. They had hardly had the opportunity to talk about anything important. She was looking forward to the chance to learn more about him, what he did and what his plans were for his life. The question of whether she would return to Earth with Josh and Fela was always somewhere on her mind. Now, perhaps there was a possibility that she would remain on Senia with Vinar.

That's a very remote possibility, she thought, *but it's still a possibility.*

She cautioned herself again not to fall in love with the first guy she met, but it was not doing any good. All she could think about was Vinar and the day she would spend with him tomorrow.

Josh and Fela settled down in a large queen size bed. It was such a luxury after years of being cramped together on the small bed in their quarters.

"Tonight is the night for love," he said.

Fela smiled and kissed him from above.

After Rosilea was born, their love life had taken a sudden turn for the worse. They knew there could be no more children while on the mission. There were no contraceptives or birth control pills on the ship, as Fela had started the mission with a firm belief that she would not be making love to anyone. This left them the rhythm method as their only means of birth control, which meant that they suffered through a two-week drought in the middle of every month, when Fela was most wanting of Josh and him of her. Fortunately, Fela was very regular in her period and she did not become pregnant again.

Josh put his arms around her and they rolled over, back and forth, exploring the full limits of the bed. They were in the quarantine zone of Fela's menstrual cycle, but that was not going to stop them tonight.

CHAPTER 8 - LIFE ON SENIA

Josh's communicator rang about an hour after sunrise. He was still sleeping off the evening and night of passion with Fela. It was Fedar. Wearily, he answered the phone.

"What's up?" he said in English. Fedar was now familiar with most of his English idiomatic expressions.

"Want to go for a ride?" Fedar said in Senian.

"Where to?" Josh replied.

"You will see." Fedar did not want to lose the element of surprise. He enjoyed seeing the expression of awe on Josh's face as he encountered new things.

"You bet," Josh said in English. Fedar knew that meant yes.

"I'll pick you up at 4:80 on the roof of the building."

Josh knew this was going to be exciting. *Roof of the building?*, he thought. *Must be a helicopter. No big deal.*

He only had about twenty minutes to get ready, so he jumped out of bed and took a luxurious shower *with no timer*. He put on his now precious pair of very well worn jeans and a Senian shirt.

Fela was still sound asleep. Not wanting to wake her, he wrote her a note: "Off with Fedar to see something. He would not tell me what or where. I'll call you later."

Fedar had obtained clearance to land on the building. At the precise time, Josh was standing by the landing area, expecting to hear the roar of an approaching helicopter. Instead he saw a saucer shaped vehicle that appeared to be about twenty-five feet in diameter silently approaching.

Wow! he thought. *They can't possibly have a nuclear reactor on that.*

He stood there in wonderment as Fedar slowly lowered the craft onto the landing area using the stabilizer jets that encircled the craft just inside the spinning outer rim.

It appeared to be almost identical in design to the starship, just on a much smaller scale. A rectangular opening across the mid section of the craft slid open, creating an entryway about five feet high. Then, a mechanical stairway unfolded to ground level and Fedar said, "Hop in" in English. He was in a very good mood, finally able to roam about Senia free from the confines of space travel.

Josh boarded the craft and took a front seat next to Fedar. There were eleven seats in total, two in the front and then three rows of three seats each. It appeared to be a commuter type vehicle. Everything was on one level. The propulsion system was at the rear of the craft, with the electrical wiring and other systems below the floor.

"Does this have a nuclear reactor?" Josh asked.

"No," Fedar replied. "It is powered by a combination of batteries and hydrogen fuel cells. It is good for short hops."

"Where are we going? Will you tell me now?"

"Buckle up. You will see."

They buckled up and slowly gained about one hundred feet altitude above the building through the gravitational field generator with the stabilizer jets hissing as the outer rim started to spin faster and faster.

Then Fedar said, "Hold on."

He hit a few touch screen controls and they were off with a jolt. The Capitol passed by below them as they continued to gain speed and altitude with the progressive jolts of the outer rim. Josh could see that the roads were laid out in concentric circles with lots of trees and carefully manicured greenery alongside. The monorail system was also visible along every other concentric circular avenue, with perpendicular links like the spokes of a wheel that connected the central core of the city with the beltway that encircled its perimeter.

Soon they were over open land. They appeared to have about 1,500 feet of altitude and were now moving very fast. The sky was crystal clear. There was an underside monitor, but it was not needed, as Josh had a good view through the transparent shell that encased the cockpit after the ship leveled off.

The Capitol was near the Senian Sea, the one large ocean that covered about one-quarter of the surface of the planet. It was a deep blue color, like the clear waters of the Bahamas on Earth. Josh could see the Alasia River, about 30 miles off in the distance, as it meandered toward the Senian Sea, the forests that lined the river, and the vast unspoiled wetlands that surrounded the mouth of the river before it opened to the sea.

As he looked around, he could see the highways emanating from the Capitol in all directions, extending at regular intervals from the circular beltway that surrounded the Capitol. It appeared to be an octagonal design, with the roads extending out from the Capitol at the eight points of the octagon. Then they were over the vast undisturbed savannah, covered with grasses and sparsely dotted with scraggly trees, where herds of animals ran free. Running through the savannah and encircling the Capitol about five files out was a vast array of wind turbines.

"Wow!" Josh exclaimed. "They are only beginning to discuss wind energy on Earth."

"The wind turbines supply over half of the energy consumed by the Capitol," Fedar replied.

"What about the other half?" Josh asked.

"It is mostly supplied by surplus solar energy from the residential areas that encircle the Capitol. There is also a system of hydrogen fuel cells that are used to meet peak demands."

"No nuclear power?" Josh asked.

"No," Fedar replied. "Uranium is far too scarce on Senia." "We need all the uranium we can find for the defense fleet. It is the same on Corilia. That's why the Corilians want to conquer Earth."

"Yes, I knew that," Josh replied.

After running at constant speed for about thirty minutes, Fedar started to decelerate. Now, instead of being yanked back in their seats, they were pulled forward. As they drew closer to their destination, the vast Sinarta military installation started to unfold before Josh. His eyes opened wide as he began to make out, spread across a large paved area, twenty starships that were in the final stage of assembly. They were upside down, with the first level facing toward the sky, held in place by large circular cradles that spread the weight of the ships over the majority of the second level. The bridge protruded from beneath the cradle. The base was a hub of activity, with workers moving about, entering and exiting the ships through ramps that carried them up the side of the ship and down through the shuttle bay door.

Fedar landed along the perimeter of the field. As he was landing, Josh could see the *Explorer* cradled in place with the bridge facing toward the sky. He wondered what they were doing about the first level.

After they had landed and exited, they started to walk toward the *Explorer*.

Josh asked Fedar: "What are they doing about gravity on the first level?"

Fedar replied: "They have to keep the gravitational generators on until the system is drained and everything is buttoned down. The nuclear reactor is being powered down. After that the gravitational field will be maintained with outside power until it can be deactivated."

"What are they going to do with the ship?" Josh asked.

"It will get a complete overall of all systems and be re-supplied for the return voyage to Earth, assuming we defeat the Corilians."

"How long do you think that will take?"

"A little over four homats," which was about six Earth months.

"That doesn't leave us much time to spend on Senia," Josh replied.

"Don't forget about the Corilians," Fedar quipped.

"Yeah," Josh said with a sigh. It was ridiculous to even think about returning to Earth when they still had to face the Corilians.

"What's that over there," Josh said, pointing to an immense black web of a structural frame in the shape of a huge waffle iron, about two hundred feet high and mounted on a flat bed vehicle with large wheels all around. It looked to Josh somewhat like the vehicle used at the Kennedy Space Center for moving rockets to the launch pad.

"That is what we use to flip the ships over," Fedar replied. "The second level and the bridge are constructed first. Then, the ships are flipped over to construct the first level. They are just about finished with installing the power and weapons systems and other equipment on the first level. Then the ships will be turned over again and the gravitational field generators will be activated. The ships will then be test flown, and if everything checks out, on board crew training will begin. The crews are being trained on the ships that we have operable, but they will need more training."

They started to walk over toward a large building near the center of the base.

"Are you going to be on one of those ships?" Josh asked.

"Yes. Zfar and I will each have a command."

"What about me? I want to do something too."

"No," Fedar quickly replied. "You are much more valuable to us alive for the return to Earth. Many of us are going to die even if we are fortunate enough to save Senia. You have a wife and child to think about too."

"Will you return to Earth?"

Fedar thought for a moment, as he didn't quite know how to put it. He didn't want to tell Josh how hard it had been for him to get used to Josh and Fela being together, and that he could hardly bear the thought of another long lonely voyage with Fela, but without her affections. He was now seventy-six Senian years old. Anther mission to Earth meant that, if he lived to survive the voyage, he would die on Earth. He very much wanted to see Earth, but also thought about trying to put some kind of a life together on Senia without Fela to remind him of how his hesitation had cost him her affections.

"I am too old for another mission to Earth," he replied with a sad ring to his voice.

They walked along silently for awhile and then Josh said: "Perhaps you will change your mind. I will miss you and I know Fela will too, and Rosilea, if she comes."

"Perhaps," Fedar replied.

"What about Rosilea? Do you think she will go with you?"

"It's her choice. But I don't think that she is going to come. Will you keep in touch with her? If she stays on Senia, she will stay with Fela's brother, Mishar."

"Of course I will. I'm her uncle, am I not?"

"You bet."

They arrived at the base command headquarters and took an elevator to the third floor after passing through security. Fedar had called ahead on his communicator and they were expected. They entered the Defense Command Center, a large circular room with many people buzzing about, filled with large monitors that encircled the entire room.

Fedar found Dakar, the Senior Defense Commander, who would be in charge of the ground control facilities and direct the Senian response to the attack in the atmosphere and space.

"Dakar, I want you to meet Josh," he said. "I don't know if you two had a change to meet last night."

"Very briefly," he replied.

Josh remembered his face, but that was all.

"It is a pleasure to meet you again," Josh said in Senian. "There were so many introductions last night that it was hard to keep up."

Dakar was impressed with Josh's fluent Senian.

"I hope that we will be able to return you safely to Earth," he said, trying to find something to say.

"I am confident that you will," Josh replied. "And if there is anything that I can do to assist with the defense, I want to help."

"Your job is to stay alive and in one piece."

Dakar then looked over to Fedar.

"The ships will be ready for test flights in two weeks. So far, we have not detected any sign of the Corilians."

"How far out do you think you will be able to detect them?" Josh asked.

"Somewhere between three and four weeks."

"Then we should at least be able to get the ships operational," Fedar added.

"Yes," Dakar replied, "but it would be good to have at least two months for training."

They briefly toured the facility, stopping in on some of the class-rooms and flight simulators where the crews were being trained. Each ship would have a seven-man crew. The Captain, Co-pilot, and Communications Officer would be on the bridge. Down below, there would be two weapons officers and two engineers to monitor the various systems and make emergency repairs if needed.

When the tour was over, Fedar flew Josh back to the Chancellor's residence and returned to the military base, where he would stay until becoming situated again on Senia. It was a little after mid-day. Josh had spoken to Fela and knew that she was at the bank getting her accounts in order, and that Rosilea was touring Avilia with Vinar. That evening, the three of them would have dinner with Fela's broth-er, his wife and two children. He settled back in the comfortable couch in the living area, turned on the monitor and started scanning the channels, thankful for some time to relax.

Rosilea was walking arm in arm with Vinar down along Veronia Street, the main tourist street with all of the fancy shops. It was a beautiful street with a tree-lined median and a wide walking area on both sides of the median. Vehicles were not permitted. She didn't have any money to spend, but it was wonderful to see all of the luxu-ries of Senian life for the first time. They were happy to be anony-mous, out of the sight of anyone that they knew.

They stopped at a small café to sit down and have something to eat. She wanted to try everything on the menu, but settled for a glass of wine and fresh grilled fish on crackers.

Vinar seemed to get handsomer every time she looked at him. This was their first opportunity to really talk to each other about their lives, as the morning had been devoted to living in the moment about the various sights she was seeing for the first time.

"I'm having such a wonderful day," she said with a smile.

"So am I," he replied, looking intently at her beautiful green eyes.

She opened up with what was always on her mind.

"I don't know what I'm going to do when my parents return to Earth. If I don't go with them, I will never see them again, but I don't want to spend another eighteen years in space. I want to have a life too."

Vinar thought for a moment.

"That must be really hard for you. Did you know that I am planning to start training at the Space Academy this year?"

"No, I didn't know that," she said with surprise, the thought starting to run through her brain that perhaps he could go with her to Earth.

"What will you do?"

"I'm not sure. I could go into space travel or I could say on Senia and work in design engineering and preparing the ships for space missions."

"What do your parents think about you going on space missions?" she asked, wondering how receptive they would be to Vinar going on a mission to Earth.

"They are hard to understand. They are proud of me going to the Space Academy, but they do not want me to go on long space voyages. They would prefer that I stay on Senia or confine myself to space travel within our solar system. It is mainly my mom who doesn't want me to travel very far."

"Would you like to see Earth?" she boldly inquired.

"With you, I might," he replied, hardly believing that the utterance had come out of his mouth.

He could see the earnest longing in her eyes. She was so sincere and so beautiful. He thought he could go anywhere in the galaxy to be with her.

"Rosilea, how old are you?" He had hesitated to ask that question, but now he needed to know.

"I'm seventeen. How old are you?"

"I'm twenty-three."

Their ages were not that far apart. Rosilea was a little young, but the age difference would melt away after not too long.

There was a long pause. Neither of them quite knew what to say next. They had touched upon what might become a lifelong commitment, but this was only their first time together. They needed more time together to see where things might lead them.

"Where would you like to go next?" Vinar said to break the silence.

"Wherever you would like to take me," Rosilea replied.

"Let's go for a walk in Veronia Park."

"Okay," Rosilea said in English.

"Okay?" Vinar repeated.

"That means yes," she replied in Senian. "It's an English word my dad uses a lot instead of 'yes.'"

"Why not just say 'yes'?"

"I don't know. It is more informal."

"Okay," Vinar said, happy to have learned an English word.

They took a short walk down Veronia Street over to Veronia Park. It was a beautiful setting, full of flowering desert-like vegetation that covered the ground, offset by very large trees with their meandering branches that looked like oaks. They had been there for hundreds of years and formed a canopy over the many meandering pathways through the park. It was now mid-afternoon, and the park was almost empty, with most people in the government offices.

They settled down on a bench by a small pond in an area with no one else around. Vinar put his right arm over Rosilea's shoulder and looked over at her. She looked up at him and placed her hand over his left arm in a beckoning manner. She so wanted to kiss. This would be her first kiss.

Vinar looked in her eager, beautiful eyes as they started to close, awaiting his kiss. He drew her closer to him and they kissed a soft, gentle kiss.

"I wanted you to do that," she said.

"And I so wanted to do that," he replied, boosted by her display of affection toward him.

They kissed again and again as the excitement built between them. Then, Rosilea slowly pulled away, laying her head against his chest. She did not know how to deal with the surge of passion she was feeling.

"I really like you," she said.

"I feel the same way about you," Vinar replied. "I hope that we will be able to spend a lot more time together."

"Me too."

"I guess it is time to start heading back."

"Okay," Rosilea replied, not wanting to go.

Rosilea turned her head up and they kissed again.

Josh was dozing off as Fela entered the room. She put down several bags of clothes she had purchased with her new account authorization on the way back from the bank and sat down next to him on the sofa. Excited to tell Josh how rich she was, she gently shook his shoulder.

"I have a surprise for you."

"What could that be?" he said, as he began to get his bearings.

"I'm rich!"

"We knew that," Josh replied.

"No we didn't," she retorted. "Not this rich. I have over three million rinads in my account. I didn't try to calculate the interest that would accrue. And I made Mishar trustee of my account and he invested some of the money in the stock market and did very well."

Josh did not know how to equate the sum that Fela had told him to wealth on Senia.

"How much money is that on Senia?" he asked.

"It's enough money to buy a beautiful home and live here for the rest of our lives without working another day."

"We have to return to Earth. Don't we?" Josh said with a tinge of concern.

"Yes, I know. This will provide well for Rosilea if she decides to stay on Senia."

She stood up. "Come on. I'm going to get you some more clothes."

"What about Rosilea? When is she getting back?"

Fela called Rosilea. She was on her way back.

The three of them then went out for a joyful shopping trip on Veronia Street. Rosilea knew just what she wanted, having pined over many of the items in the store windows a short while ago.

When they returned from their shopping spree, it was time for them to head over to Mishar's house for dinner. Fela had spoken with Keala, who wanted them to have dinner with the Chancellor and his family. Keala understood that Fela needed to see her brother after so many years, and insisted that they be provided with a car and driver for the visit. There was a largely unspoken concern on the Chancellor's part about making sure that no harm came to Josh and Fela while they were on Senia.

It was shortly before dusk when a car similar to the car that had carried them to the Chancellor's residence arrived. They would be going to one of the satellite residential communities outside the central business core of the Capitol.

The design of the Capitol and ultimate build-out was planned from the laying of the very first block. The city was designed to accommodate about three and one-half million people, more than enough it was felt to meet the needs of the planetary government. It was laid out in a series of nine interconnected circles, each about ten miles in diameter. The core of the Capital included the Chancellor's residence and government and commercial multi-story buildings and residences. It stood at the center of the city and was known as the Central District.

The other eight development areas were primarily for single and small multi-family residences and light commercial activity, except that the development area immediately north of the Central District, known as Area 1, contained the airport and some industrial development. These development areas branched out from the Central District along eight equidistant transportation corridors, forming an octagonal ring around the Central District. About ten miles of open space separated the Central District from the eight surrounding development areas.

The Chancellor's residence stood like a bulls-eye at the center of the Central District, surrounded by a large open space, and then the headquarters for the Supreme Council, various agencies and the Supreme Court. After that, in order to have a continuous monorail system along the major roads, the city was laid out in concentric circles until reaching the perimeter beltway. The outermost edge of the city was ringed with multistory apartments and condominiums outside the perimeter beltway and overlooking the open savannah that separated the development modules.

All of the surrounding modules were developed along the same basic design, but the major roads were perpendicular streets and avenues so that the residences could be oriented in the same direction toward the sun, maximizing the efficiency of the solar array on the roof of each residence. There was a traffic link between the perimeter beltways for each module. The maximum residential lot size was about one acre. These lots were for the wealthier Senians, lying outside the beltway along the perimeter of each module, also overlooking the open space of the savannah.

Mishar lived in Area 4, to the southeast of the Central District. They traveled in a clockwise direction on the six-lane road, called the Central Circle, around the core governmental area. What was so routine for the driver, and not new to Fela, was an awesome sight for Josh and Rosilea. They gazed to their right at the beautiful grayish brown government buildings and the many trees and other plantings around the road and walkways. To their left was the monorail along the outside edge of the Central Circle with a station at each intersection with a transportation corridor. At each station there was a pedestrian crossing over the highway to the government buildings. Above them, they could see an airborne bus setting down at the monorail station.

They reached the intersection with Transportation Corridor 4, pulled to the left and stopped, waiting for the light to change. Josh looked over to his left and at the huge intersection that connected the Central Circle to Transportation Corridor 4. There were four lanes in each direction in the Transportation Corridor, separated by a wide, tree-lined median that contained two tracks for the trains that ran back and forth in opposite directions along the median. People were departing from an incoming train stopped alongside the monorail station. Some were ascending the stairs to the monorail.

They turned left and began to speed away from the Central Circle. It was a limited access highway with entry and exit points about every mile and an overpass for intersecting roads. The road was full with people leaving the Central District, but the traffic flowed freely at about sixty miles per hour. Josh looked to his left and could see the commuter trains stacked up on the furthermost track leaving the city. He wondered how they turned around, as there was no place for them to turn around at the termination point by the Central Circle.

After a few minutes, they were outside the Central District of the Capitol. The sun was starting to set, created a beautiful yellow and orange backdrop for the open savannah. Then, the glistening array of wind turbines, as far as the eye could see, that Josh had briefly observed earlier that day, came into view. He recalled how, before he left Earth, there had been some discussion of wind energy during the energy crisis that afflicted President Carter. Now, as he stared in wonder at the turbines rotating in the sunset, he had a sense of what could be the future of energy supply on Earth.

After about fifteen minutes, the driver exited the highway at Area 4.

"Where to? he asked.

Fela replied: "The address is 21.14 Southeast, Unit 3.39."

Area 4 contained hundreds of small developments with a single point of entry and exit. The streets and avenues intersected, forming a block that contained four development areas. Each development area looked basically the same, with an access road through the area and houses on both sides oriented toward the sun. The number of residences depended upon the size of the lots, which ranged from about one-third acre to an acre.

The address told the driver a specific point where a numbered street and avenue met. He then knew to go to the development block to the southeast of that point. Within that development block, he would go to development Unit 3, and then to residence number 39. It was a colorless system without names for the streets, avenues, or development units, but it worked very well for locating a specific residence and applied throughout the Capitol, except for the Central District.

As they headed down Fourteenth Avenue, Josh could see roofs of the houses on both sides, all oriented in the same direction. They slowed down and made a left turn into an entranceway marked Unit 3. They made a quick right down the street and parked in the driveway to a house with the number 39 displayed by the entrance door and on the mailbox.

It was a pleasant looking, but very utilitarian development. There was a lot of open space, filled with well manicured ground cover, shrubs, trees, and some tall grasses like those that grew naturally on the open savannah that surrounded the city. Mishar's house was modest in size, a single story, built from the same grayish-brown brick that Josh had seen throughout the Central District. He could now clearly see the solar panels that covered the right side of the roof.

Mishar and his family rushed out of the house as soon as the car pulled up. There was his wife, Elara, and two children, Kenar and Rilesa. Fela ran to him and they embraced. Fela only knew of Mishar's family through the video communiqués she had very belatedly received from Senia during the mission to Earth. After a round of introductions by Mishar, it was Fela's turn.

"I want you to meet my Earthman, Josh," she said, with a hint of humor in her voice.

"I'm so happy to meet all of you," Josh said in fluent Senian.

He then clasped hands, one at a time, with all of them, not wanting to be relegated to the more formal Senian bow of the head. They were a little mystified at first, but followed suit.

Mishar showed Josh and Fela the house while Elara went back to the kitchen to finish dinner preparations. It was a nicely designed house of about 2,500 square feet, not unlike a house Josh would expect to see in any middle class community on Earth. It was built about nine years ago, after they had learned of the impending Corilian attack. Mishar explained that there was a design requirement that the house contain not less than about 600 square feet of solar panels.

Mishar opened a door in the master bedroom at the rear of the house that led down a stairway to another door. He swung open the heavy door and they entered an underground room about twenty feet square, stocked with cans along the walls, a computer monitor and a variety of other equipment, and a small bathroom with a door in the corner, about four foot square.

"Most of the houses in Area 3 have bomb shelters," he explained. "Some people decided to rely upon the public shelter at the center of Area 3, but I wanted us to have our own shelter."

For the first time since they arrived, Josh and Fela got a sense of the fear that the Senians had been living under since first learning of the Corilian attack. That sense became more apparent as they sat through dinner. It hung over the room. Everyone tried to be joyful about the occasion of Fela and Mishar being reunited after so many years, but they still could not escape from the foreboding sense of what was to come. Virtually everyone on Senia was determined to resist Corilian domination, even if it meant having to endure an attack with nuclear weapons and then rebuild from whatever was left afterwards.

Elara made a fine dinner of Senian moslan, a game fish imported from Vilarian Province several thousand miles north of the Capitol. After dinner, they settled back in their chairs for some Senian brandy, a coffee-like drink called bukart, and some after dinner conversation.

There had been some dinner discussion of preparations for the Corilians attack, but that was shoved aside in favor of more trivial conversation about Josh's new surroundings and many comparisons between life on Senia and Earth. Mishar was an engineer, employed by the Capitol Transportation Authority. Elara was a lawyer for the Water Development Authority, which coordinated water issues between the provinces and engaged in a few large-scale water projects.

Josh was full of many questions for both of them, but the big question on Josh's mind was related to the Corilians. Feeling a bit provocative, he asked Mishar somewhat rhetorically:

"How is it that you people are more intelligent than Earth humans, so much more technologically advanced, and have such advanced social and governmental systems, and yet, Corilia is ruled by a regime that resembles the Nazi regime on Earth and some of the dictatorships that have followed since the Nazis?"

Mishar was lost for words as he did not have a good answer. "I don't know the answer to your question," he said. "From what little we know from the Corilian underground, all of the people on Corilia live in fear of the regime, except for those that are in the regime."

"It shows you how long a regime built on fear can last," Josh replied. "The Roman Empire on Earth lasted for over five hundred years."

"But they eventually were overthrown?" Mishar inquired.

"No," Josh quickly replied. "They just fell apart from their own weight and corruption."

"How is it then that the Earth has not become like Corilia?" Mishar asked.

"Just luck," Josh replied. "It came very close to being dominated by tyrannical regimes during the Second World War. If a few things had gone the other way, it could have happened. The most important thing is that the good guys, the Americans, were the first to develop a nuclear weapon. If the countries the Americans were fighting or the Soviets had been first, things would have turned out very differently."

Josh explained the geopolitical situation between the U.S. and its allies, the Soviet Union and the Chinese communist regime, as he knew it seventeen years ago, and how the doctrine of "mutual assured destruction" with nuclear weapons had resulted in a geopolitical stalemate between the major powers.

Becoming tired of all the weighty discussion, he asked Mishar:

"How do the trains turn around? I could see trains going in both directions coming here, but I didn't see any place for the trains to turn around when they reached the last stop at the Capitol?"

Mishar laughed. He had never thought of that as a mystery.

"They don't turn around. The incoming track at the Central Circle slides over to the outgoing track and the train leaves."

"But then the train is going in the opposite direction. Is there a locomotive on the other side? What about the seats? They would all be facing backwards."

Mishar laughed again. *Locomotive*, he thought. *That's ancient.*

"No," he replied. "The magnetic field that levitates the train is reversed to propel the train in the opposite direction. As to the seats, after everyone exits at the station, they automatically rotate to the opposite direction. That way, we minimized the amount of track at the center of the city."

"Wow!" Josh said. "How simple a solution can be to what appears to be a complex problem."

Josh went on. "Elara, I have a question for you. How is it that there are so many trees and so much nice vegetation? I thought water is scarce on Senia."

"There is a simple answer to that too. Our city is designed just like the *Explorer*. There is a dual piping system everywhere, including this house. Water from the bathrooms is treated and used for irrigation. Water from the kitchen is treated and recycled for drinking."

"Don't you have to bring any water to the city?" Josh asked.

"Yes. We bring water in from the Sefara Mountains over three hundred terrats away. The prevailing winds are from the Senian Sea toward the mountains, so most of the precipitation occurs on our side of the mountain. There is a large reservoir near the base of the mountain. From there, the water is piped, mostly by gravity, to the city through an underground system."

"Why not draw water from the Senian Sea?" Josh asked.

"Because it consumes too much energy to remove the salt and other minerals," she replied. "We used up most of our available stores of fossil fuel energy thousands of years ago and now rely mainly on solar and wind energy. All of the uranium we can find is needed for planetary defenses and space travel."

Rosilea was adrift. She had been adrift ever since Vinar had walked her to the door at the Chancellor's residence and they said goodbye. Her cousin Kenar was also very attractive, but he was her cousin, so that was that. She smiled at him across the table and had the feeling that they would become friends. Her other cousin, Rilesa, who was younger than Kenar, also seemed welcoming. She knew that if she stayed on Senia, it would be with Mishar and his family, so this visit was important to her. As the after dinner conversation dragged on, Kenar and Rilesa became bored and asked to be excused. Rosilea followed suit, and they went to the video room to play the latest games and get to know each other.

After Rosilea left, Mishar turned to Fela.

"She is a lovely child. We would be very happy to welcome her to our family."

"Thank you so much," Fela replied. "It will be very hard for me to leave Senia knowing that I will probably never get to see her again. But I feel much better about it knowing that she will be with all of you."

"Has she decided yet?"

"No," Fela said with a sad ring to her voice, "but I think she is going to want to stay on Senia."

Fela did not know that Rosilea was hatching a new plan to return to Earth with Vinar.

"Where are you going to live while you are on Senia?" Mishar asked.

"We're not sure yet," Fela replied. "We want to get an apartment in the Central District, but the Chancellor told me that he wants us to stay on the Sinarta military base where it is more secure."

"Rosilea can stay with us if you like," Elara chimed in.

"That probably would be good. I don't have the heart to drag her to a military base if that is where we end up."

Josh shook his head in agreement.

They chatted on for about an hour and it was time to leave. The driver had left with instructions to call him when they were ready to return, but Mishar decided to drive them back to the Chancellor's residence. They called the driver and he arranged for them to get clearance to enter the residence.

As they departed Mishar's car, he asked Fela: "When will I see you again."

"When we drop off Rosilea," she replied.

Fela knew deep down that she could not disregard the Chancellor's wishes regarding their security.

Rosilea looked up in disappointment. *Would she be able to see Vinar if they did not stay in the Central District?* she wondered.

The next day Rosilea awakened with excitement. They had the entire day to themselves to explore the Central District and its many museums. And then there would be a private dinner with the Chancellor and his family.

Surely, Vinar would be there, she thought.

Perhaps he will call.

Josh knew just where he wanted to go first, the Museum of Earth Exploration. But first there was breakfast with Keala, their gracious host whom they could not refuse. The Chancellor had left much earlier for the Supreme Council Building.

It was a sumptuous breakfast in a small dining area set aside for just the Chancellor's family. There were delicious fruits and fruit juices, plenty of smoked moslan, and an assortment of crackers, rolls and bread made from various Senian grains. To Josh's surprise, there were no eggs.

Keala brought up the subject of how to respond to the news media and talk shows.

"My office is receiving many requests to interview all of you. What should we do?"

"What do you recommend?" Fela replied.

"You know that we are concerned that no harm come to you. You are free to do as you wish, but I suggest that we arrange a round of interviews with the major news outlets and some of the talk shows just before we move you to Base Sinarta. That way, you will have some degree of privacy while you are still in the Capitol."

Fela looked at Josh. Their response would not only involve the news media. It also involved living at a military base.

"What do you think?" she asked.

Josh didn't like the idea of losing his anonymity and being hounded by the news media. He also did not like the idea of spending the majority of his time on Senia cooped up on a military base. Still, he wanted to do whatever he could to help the war effort and being on a military base would allow him to at least see the war preparations if not somehow participate.

"That sounds fine to me," he replied. "But we don't want to overstay our welcome here and were planning to rent an apartment in the Central District."

Keala smiled, pleased with Josh's manners.

"It would be better for you to stay with us while you are in the Capitol, and do not worry about overstaying your welcome. We enjoy having you with us."

"When would you set up the interviews?" Fela asked.

"How much time would you like to have to yourselves?"

"It would be nice to have about a week to see the Central District and catch up with some friends."

"That will be perfect. I'll have my staff start arranging the interviews."

Rosilea listened to the conversation and wanted some assurance that she would not be staying with them at the base.

"Mom, will I be able to stay with uncle Mishar?" she asked with some concern.

"Yes," Fela replied. "We are not going to drag you out there."

They thanked Keala for the wonderful breakfast and went back to their suite, ready to depart for the day's events. At Keala's insistence, two security personnel would accompany them on their walk to the Museum of Earth Exploration.

As they were descending down the long stairway to the reception area, Rosilea's communicator rang. It was Vinar. She beamed with excitement as she answered.

"Hi!" she said in English, forgetting that Vinar would not know what she was saying.

Vinar understood by the happy and welcoming tone of her voice.

"Hi!" he replied in English. And then in Senian: "Would you like to go for a boat ride on the Alasia River today?"

"Oh, yes! When would you like to leave?"

"We should get started as soon as possible. It will take over an hour to get to the river."

Rosilea turned to Josh and Fela. "It's Vinar. He wants to take me for a boat ride on the Alasia River. Can I go?" she asked most earnestly.

Josh was a little surprised, but not Fela, who had sensed that something was brewing between them.

"Of course you can go. Be careful!" Fela replied, trying with the tome of her voice to hint that she should watch herself sexually.

"I can go!" she told Vinar.

"I'll be by to pick you up in thirty quarseks."

Rosilea waved goodbye to Josh and Fela, deciding to wait for Vinar in the reception area.

"What's up with them?" Josh asked Fela as they walked away.

"Your guess is as good as mine. I'll talk to her later."

"Well, if you can't trust the Chancellor's grandson, who can you trust."

"Right!"

With that, they decided to let go of their worry and focus on what would be for Josh another truly amazing experience.

It was about a twenty minute walk from the Chancellor's residence to the museum. The museum was along the Capitol Circle on the side of the street opposite all of the government buildings. They walked along, hand in hand, with the security guards following about twenty feet behind them. The bright Senian sun had now risen above the many buildings and it was starting to get warm, but still very pleasant. The many passersby took immediate notice of Josh. They smiled and Josh and Fela smiled back. Some asked if they could take a picture, and Josh and Fela graciously complied. As they stopped to pose, a small crowd would gather and more communicators would come out for a picture. This happened several times before they finally made it to the museum.

The museum was a magnificent looking building, two stories tall, with five large pillars along the front, characteristic of a museum one might find on Earth. The Senians had intentionally copied from some of the Earth architecture they had observed during their most recent visit. As one entered the lobby, there was a holographic replica of the Earth on display, about fifteen feet in diameter. They stood there for several minutes as Josh tried to regain his memories of his life on Earth, which now seemed so distant.

He thought he was fully prepared for what he would see at the museum, having exhausted the *Explorer*'s database from the Senians' two prior visits to Earth during the many years of the voyage to Senia. Now it was time to actually see the objects and photographs gathered from Earth's early exploration up close and he was brimming with anticipation. This would be a historical record unlike anything on Earth.

The Senians did not know how to date their Earth voyages in terms of Earth years until after Josh explained the zeroing out of years before and after the birth of Christ. The first Senian voyage had occurred 4,764 Senian years ago, which amounted to 4526 Earth years. They now knew that this voyage had occurred in the Earth year 2532 B.C. The second Earth voyage had occurred 507 Senian years ago, or 482 Earth years ago, during Earth year 1512 A.D.

Josh had studied the complete photographic record of both Earth voyages. Still, he looked about in awe when they passed through the door from the first floor lobby to the remainder of the first floor, which was entirely devoted to the first Earth voyage. It was a large area, over two hundred feet wide and several hundred feet deep. He was immediately struck by an animated holographic display showing an Egyptian pyramid under construction. Hundreds of workers hauled large blocks of stone along rolling flats where they could then be hoisted into place on the pyramid. As he drew closer, he had the feeling that he was there watching the actual construction of what would be later known as the second pyramid at Gizeh. There were holographic images of members of the Senian crew standing in the foreground, joined by two Egyptian overlords.

As one wandered the remainder of the first floor, the Earth as it existed over 4500 years ago came to life. There were holographic displays of life as it existed in civilized areas across the planet, including the Sumerian city of Ur along the south side of the Persian Gulf in what is now Iraq, the civilizations that had developed along the Indus valley in what is now Pakistan, and the Neolithic agrarian communities that had developed without large cities along the Mediterranean, Europe, China, Asia, Africa, and the Americas. Farmers tilled their fields around the small villages with oxen drawn plows. The displays were arranged on the floor in a similar pattern to a flat rendition of the globe.

The second floor was more like one might expect to see on a visit to the Museum of Natural History on Earth. It contained three dimensional photos and videos of the vast unspoiled areas of the planet from the first visit, a variety of bronze-age weapons and other implements, and many photos of the indigenous people of Earth, who treated the Senians as though they were Gods that had descended from the heavens.

There were also many photos from the second visit in Earth year 1512 A.D. The great cities that had developed across the globe were photographed in great detail. The battle of Valeggio between French and Venetian forces was photographed in a video from above, as was the Battle of Ravenna, when the French defeated the Holy League in a major battle of the Italian Wars. Earth having now developed armaments that could destroy the ship if it landed, the Senians decided not to land, instead circling the planet for about ninety Earth days before returning to Senia.

Josh left the museum exhilarated by his experience. He had a keen sense of how much humanity had progressed over a relatively short period of time, when viewed from the perspective of the Senians, who were so far advanced.

If only Earth could continue this progress to achieve what the Senians have achieved, he thought.

Rosilea did not have to wait long for Vinar. He pulled up to the Chancellor's residence in a shiny silver grey, two seat convertible that would have been the envy of anyone on Earth. It was another beautiful sunny day, starting to get a little warm. Rosilea could see him pull up. She flew out of the reception area.

"Hop in," he said, startled by how beautiful she was in her new summer dress of gently flowing light green cotton-like fabric that fell just below her knees and revealed a little bit of her breasts.

"This is so nice," she said, as she leaned over to give him a little kiss, knowing her mom and dad were not there to see.

Vinar loved getting the kiss.

"Where are we going?" she said.

"There is a place on the Alasia River where we can rent a boat and ride down the river to the Senian Sea."

"I would love to see that! I have only seen it in pictures and videos."

The Alasia River flowed from west to east from the Sefara Mountains to the Senian Sea. It was surrounded by a natural floodplain that extended for about ten miles on both sides of the river as it drew closer to the sea. The construction of the reservoir at the base of the Sefara Mountains to supply water to the Capitol had somewhat diminished the river's flow and reduced the frequency at which the floodplain was fully inundated, but it still remained a viable and pristine ecosystem full of a variety of abundant avian and other wildlife.

The Capitol was laid out about thirty miles north of the river and twenty miles west of the Senian Sea coastline so that there would be a buffer between the Capitol and the riverine and coastal ecosystems, which were not nearly as abundant as on Earth.

As they drove happily along the Capitol beltway, Rosilea's soft brown hair tossing about her face, they chatted about Rosilea's life growing up on a starship and Vinar's life as the privileged grandson of the Chancellor. Vinar wanted to find something meaningful to do with his life. He was not content to rest upon his fortunate birth for his lot in life. For that reason, politics did not interest him. Instead, he wanted to make some sort of a contribution that would better Senian life, although it felt like everything that could possibly be done had already been accomplished. He had focused on the Space Academy because it might lead him to a meaningful space discovery and was definitely intrigued by the thought of being on the *Explorer* when it journeyed back to Earth. Rosilea bared her deepest thoughts about her dilemma regarding whether she should return to Earth with her parents or remain on Senia.

The car whirred away and they headed off the beltway for the Area 5 Transportation Corridor. The road was almost clear and they breezed to the highway around Area 5. Rosilea loved the new found feeling of freedom. When they reached the southernmost point of Area 5, Vinar exited the highway for a four lane road that would take them to the river.

The ride across the savannah to the river was enchanting. Large herds of different species of fleet-footed animals rambled about them on both sides. The road was elevated about five feet above the surrounding land, with excavated areas on both sides where fill material had been taken to elevate the road. Every mile or so, the road returned to ground level so that there would be a place for the wildlife to cross the road. They had to go very slow at times and paused several times to view the many creatures up close as they crossed the road.

After about fifty minutes, Vinar pulled into a recharging spot in the parking lot of the recreation area. It was a long corridor of cars parked under a roof covered with solar panels. Vinar swiped his communicator by the device mounted at the front of the parking spot and plugged the car into the charger. It would take about two hours to fully recharge.

They rented a boat about sixteen feet long, powered by an electric motor that was fitted under the rear seat. Vinar sat at the rear, operating the steering wheel and controls that were mounted in front of him. Rosilea had the whole second seat that stretched across the boat in front of the steering column. She soon found a comfortable position to spread out, gazing up at Vinar with adoring eyes as he continued to marvel at how beautiful she was laying there in front of him.

Vinar had to be careful to conserve his limited store of electricity so that he would avoid the embarrassment of having to call for help. He let the river slowly take them to the mouth at the Senian Sea. They didn't say much, looking about in wonder at the tree-lined shores and the abundant wildlife flying over them. Rosilea took some pictures with her communicator.

When they reached the opening to the sea, Vinar stopped the boat and threw over the anchor. He climbed over the seat and sat next to Rosilea, reaching for the cooler he had brought. They snacked and drank a bit, and then it was time for them to sit back and take it all in.

What a sight it was! Thousands upon thousands of birds of many different species flew in large flocks above and around them. They looked over the side of the boat at the clear water about ten feet deep and could see the many fishes scurrying around.

Vinar put his arm around Rosilea.

"This is so amazing," she said. "I have seen the Alasia River many times in videos aboard the *Explorer*, but even the virtual reality videos cannot compare with this."

"Just think, this can be yours forever if you stay on Senia," he replied, his mind only on her.

"I want to," Rosilea wistfully replied. "But I still cannot imagine never seeing mom and dad again."

"What if I went with you to Earth? Would that make a difference?"

Again, he could hardly believe what came out of his mouth. The thought had been there, but he had hardly articulated it, even to himself. And now, he was saying it to Rosilea. Did he really mean it? He did not know. He only knew that he was absolutely crazy about Rosilea and wanted to be with her, whatever it took.

"Yes!" she almost shouted in an excited and happy voice.

"That is what I was so hoping you would say."

After she responded with such enthusiasm, he knew that he did really mean it.

They looked longingly into each other's eyes. There was nothing else to do but kiss - a long, sweet kiss.

As her eyes opened, she looked at Vinar and said "I love you."

"I love you too," he responded.

Suddenly, the fearful thought hit her. "What are your parents going to say? And what about the Chancellor?"

"My mom will say that I'm being too hasty and that I've only known you for three days."

"And what about your dad."

"He'll go along with whatever my mom says."

"Are you being too hasty?" Rosilea asked, worried about what the answer might be.

"No! I am not."

"Are you sure?"

"I am sure. Are you sure?"

"Yes. My mom will say the same thing. And that I should not fall in love with the first guy that I meet."

Vinar was a little hurt. He had not thought of that. Was it that he was just the first guy she met?

"Are you sure that it is not because I'm the first guy you met?" he asked, wanting to be reassured.

Rosilea wanted to say something funny that they could laugh about.

"You are not the first guy. I met the driver of the car and the security guards at the Chancellor's residence and I didn't fall in love with them."

They laughed as she had hoped. Then she wrapped her arms around him and said: "You are the first guy I've met and I don't want to meet any other guys. I want you."

Vinar was reassured. He held her in his arms and let the boat rock them like they were two babies in their cradle, ready to fall asleep.

After thinking awhile, he said: "We should not tell them right away. We can wait a month. Then, when we tell them, they will not be able to say that we are being too hasty."

"Yes, that is what we should do. And if you cannot go, I will stay here with you."

They kissed again to seal their plan.

Josh had no idea that the evening with the Chancellor would turn out to be as significant as it ended up being. It would ultimately determine how they would survive when they returned to Earth and how the enormous Senian technological advances would be developed on Earth.

The evening started out innocuous enough. Everyone gathered for a pleasant round of drinks and before-dinner conversation in the parlor next to the dining area. It was just the Chancellor and Keala, Josh, Fela and Rosilea, the Chancellor's daughter, Salea, her husband, Nemar, and Vinar.

Rosilea lit up in eagerness as Vinar entered the room - something that did not go unnoticed by both Fela and Salea. Their eyes only met for an instant in an exchange of their love before turning about the room.

The Senians, especially those of high intelligence, although not telepathic, were very perceptive of emotions and what other people were thinking and feeling. It did not take long for Fela and Salea to sense that there was something more between Vinar and Rosilea than a pleasant boat ride on the Alasia River. Rosilea and Vinar tried to keep straight faces throughout the conversation, but it was a lost cause, as anyone who has tried to cover up an office romance will probably agree.

After sipping on Senian brandy and other condiments, they adjourned to the dining room for a dinner of fresh moslan prepared by the chef and his staff. Josh, as usual, was full of questions about Senian life.

"One thing I've never asked Fela over all these years is why all female names end in "a" and all male names end in "ar?" I didn't notice it while on the *Explorer* because there was just Fela. And it seems that no one uses their last name when they are being introduced. Why is that?"

They all looked toward the Chancellor to give him the opportunity to reply.

"It is part of our language that male names end in "ar" and female names end in "a." This goes back to before Senia was settled. As to surnames, there are only eight different surnames on Senia, going back to the original eight families that settled Senia. So we try to be distinctive with our first name. Anything goes as long as female names end in "a" and male names end in "ar."

They talked about Josh's many comparisons between life on Senia and Earth, and how Josh was so impressed with how there were no traffic jams and everything in the Capitol moved with a quiet hum, as opposed to the near chaos of American cities.

"Is there any crime on Senia?" Josh asked.

"Yes, there is some crime," the Chancellor replied. "But not very much."

"What kind of crime?"

"Theft, embezzlement, that sort of crime."

"What about murder and other types of violent crime."

"No, we are not a violent people," the Chancellor replied. "And murder is very rare. All murderers are put to death."

Josh was embarrassed to tell the Chancellor what it was like on Earth. He did not want the Senians to know how violent it could be on Earth, although they had a good sense of that from observing the wars occurring on Earth during their last visit in the sixteenth century.

Fela interrupted: "Let us talk about something more pleasant. Tell us about your ride on the Alasia River today," she said, looking at Rosilea and Vinar. She also made eye contact with Salea, who knew exactly what she was thinking.

"It was great," Rosilea gushed, trying to sound nonchalant, before Vinar could say anything. "We went down the river to the Senian Sea. It was so beautiful."

She looked over at Vinar with an unmistakable sparkle in her eye. Vinar smiled.

"Yes, it was very nice" he said, also trying to be nonchalant while not hurting Rosilea's feeling by sounding too dismissive.

Fela and Salea felt confirmed in their suspicion that something was happening between the two of them. Looking at each other, their eyes told the story. They would dig deeper later.

After dinner was over, Rosilea, looking over at Vinar, asked if it would be permissible for them to take a walk outside within the grounds of the Chancellor's residence. Permission was granted and they departed. Keala invited Salea and Fela to her private "woman's cave," where she showed them her art work, completed and in progress, and they settled down for more quiet conversation. That left the Chancellor, Nemar and Josh to adjourn to the Chancellor's study, where the Chancellor broke out some of his best brandy.

They talked about the preparations for the Corilians.

"I want to be able to do something to help," Josh said emphatically.

"What you can best do is help us prepare for the return trip to Earth after we defeat the Corilians," the Chancellor replied.

This was the entrée that Josh, in the back of his mind, was looking for. He had given much thought on the voyage to Senia about what they might be able to do on return to Earth with the Senian technology. Knowing something about patent law, he thought about obtaining patent rights and licensing the technology to control its use. He knew that some of the technologies would have military value on a par with the atom bomb and would have to be turned over or licensed to the government. Still, there were many technologies that would have commercial applications, such as the incredible communications systems he had observed, which reminded him of Dick Tracy's wrist watch, only much better.

"Have you given any thought to how Senian technology could be used on Earth?" Josh asked.

"No, I have not," the Chancellor replied. "Most of the technology we have on Senia was originally developed on Corilia under our system where the developer of the invention has a property right in the invention but is required to license the technology to others at no more than certain percentages. Since we can no longer be a part of that licensing system, the Corilian technology is licensed by the Central Authority at certain rates that help to fund our government. New inventions are licensed under the Corilian system."

"We have a similar system on Earth," Josh replied. "Many of these technologies would be a great benefit on Earth. I hope you will consider making them available."

"Yes, I want them to be used to benefit Earth," he quickly replied. "We want nothing from Earth except some of its uranium and for Earth to be our ally against the Corilians."

"We will need a source of income to survive on Earth," Josh slowly replied, not quite knowing how to approach the subject.

"Earth is more violent than Senia and there are many more people, some of whom are mentally unstable. We will be an oddity and very famous and will need to protect ourselves from intruders."

"Do you have something in mind?" the Chancellor asked.

"No, not specifically," Josh replied. "I have given this some thought, but I would like to give it more thought before I propose something to you."

"That will be fine. I will need to discuss whatever you propose with the Supreme Council, which will have to approve."

As soon as Vinar and Rosilea were out of sight of the Chancellor's residence, they embraced and kissed a very long kiss that stirred their passion for each other.

"Do you think they know about us?" Rosilea asked as they slowly broke away from each other.

"I don't know," Vinar replied, "but it doesn't matter anyway. I want to go with you no matter what they say."

"But they have to give you permission. And you are just starting at the Space Academy."

"Right! What am I thinking! I'm not qualified yet to go on a space mission."

"We can still try," Rosilea quickly replied.

"Yes. When the time is right, I will talk to my mother. She is the only one who would maybe say no."

"What about the Chancellor?"

"Maybe him too, but maybe he will let you go so you can be with your mom and dad when they return to Earth."

"Maybe," she said with a sigh, hugging Vinar closely as they swayed back and forth in the gentle evening breeze.

It did not take long after they returned to their guest quarters for Fela to decide that the time was right for her to ask Rosilea about what was going on between her and Vinar. Josh had quickly showered and gone to bed, anxious to clear his mind so that he could concentrate on what he would propose to the Chancellor about managing the transfer of Senian technology to Earth.

Fela prepared for bed next, but then sat down in the living area instead of going to the bedroom. When Rosilea finished in the bathroom, she found Fela there waiting for her with a sincere motherly look on her face.

"Come sit down. I want to talk to you," Fela said, with a blend of seriousness and sincerity in her smile.

"Tell me how you feel about Vinar."

In that instant, Rosilea had to decide whether she would lie to Fela and play down her feelings or tell her how she really felt.

"I love him," burst out of her. "And he loves me."

Fela could think of only one thing. "Does this mean that you have decided to stay on Senia?" she said, trying to conceal her disappointment.

"No, mom. Vinar wants to go back to Earth with me. We want to get married."

Fela's quick mind could hardly process the implications of what Rosilea was saying, but from somewhere in the depths came forth a feeling of great relief. She would not have to say goodbye to her only child, likely to never see her again.

Her mind caught up after a few moments of being absolutely

stunned. "What about Salea and Nemar? Do they know of your plans?"

"No, not yet. We were planning to wait a month before we said anything so that you and Salea would not say that we hardly know each other, and you would not say that I am falling in love with the first man I met."

"Well," Fela said. "Are you not falling in love with the first man you have met?"

"Yes I am," Rosilea said, with a determined ring to her voice. "And he is really wonderful. I really do love him."

Rosilea leaned toward Fela on the couch. "Please don't tell his mom and dad. We both promised not to say anything yet."

Fela sat back, looking toward the ceiling. She sensed Rosilea's determination and knew better than to challenge her decision any further. Still, not telling Salea was another matter.

"I don't see how I can not tell Salea. She will be losing her only son like I would have lost you. I cannot have her learn that I held this from her."

"Please wait until I talk to Vinar," Rosilea begged.

"Okay. But you will need to talk to Vinar tomorrow."

"Come here," Fela said, holding out her arms.

Rosilea slid over on the couch and they hugged.

"I want whatever will make you happy," Fela said. "If you are sure that Vinar is someone you want to spend the rest of your life with, that is fine with me."

Then it popped out. "I've also promised Vinar that if he is not allowed to go back to Earth with me, I will stay here with him on Senia."

Fela continued to hold her in her arms. "I don't want to lose you," she said, as the tears started to well up in her eyes.

Rosilea started to cry, not knowing what to say. They sat there holding each other closely as the tears died down.

"Let's go to bed," Fela finally said.

She repeated: "What is most important to me is that you are happy."

"I love you, mom," Rosilea replied, as she wiped the tears from her eyes with her hands.

Fela found Josh in bed, wide awake, intently staring up at the ceiling.

"I have something to tell you," she said as she settled in bed beside him.

Josh rolled over toward Fela, putting his arm around her.

"You're pregnant," Josh quipped, sensing from her voice that it was going to be something serious.

"No, no, no! Rosilea says that she and Vinar are in love and that Vinar wants to return to Earth with her."

"What! So fast! How can they be in love? They have only known each other for a few days."

"She also says that she has promised Vinar that if he is not allowed to travel to Earth, she will stay with him on Senia."

Josh's mind, which had been embroiled in questions about patent law, slowly grasped the situation. However it went, either Fela or Salea would lose their only child. He could see the concern in Fela's eyes.

"Let's sleep on it," he said. "We knew that it would eventually come to this."

He drew Fela close to him for a kiss. There would be no sex tonight. Face down on the bed, he laid his arm around her as she slowly settled to sleep.

Josh could not sleep. After Fela was asleep, he rolled over and started to stare at the ceiling again, trying to recapture his thoughts about what to propose to the Chancellor. Now he would also have to try to sort out the situation with Rosilea. It would be a long night.

In the many hours of lonely space travel, Josh's thoughts had often wandered to thinking about the unfathomable wealth that could be generated by the transfer of Senian technology to Earth. Initially, he thought there would have to be some type of a government to government transfer. But then, what would the U.S. Government do with all of this technology? Would it be made freely available to all comers? Would it try to license the technology through some type of bidding process? How bureaucratic would the process become? How much delay would there be? Would it become subject to political influence, or even worse, corruption? Would inventions be suppressed in order to protect vested interests?

The more Josh thought about it, the more he became distrustful of a government to government transfer, even with the U.S. Government. He wanted to maintain control over the process so that bureaucratic incompetence and political wheeling and dealing could be avoided. Two alternatives came to mind. He could set up a non-profit corporation to license the technology and use the proceeds for beneficial purposes, including developing closer ties between Senia and Earth. That might involve a lot of government restrictions on how the profits could be used and who knows how much oversight by the IRS. The other alternative was to simply set up a for-profit corporation, pay taxes, and have the freedom to conduct itself like a normal business.

Josh had never come to a conclusion as to the best approach. He did not know enough to decide. A final decision would require consultation with tax and patent lawyers and whomever else they might lead him to. Now he had to come up with something and it boggled his mind.

He now realized that any arrangement would need to be in the form of some type of official document, signed by the Chancellor and approved by the Supreme Council. It would have to be something that would be recognized as legally binding in the U.S.

Keep it simple, he thought. *What about a simple assignment of rights?* The Senian government owned the rights to most of the Senian technology. This would be in keeping with their usual practice.

The more he thought about it, the more he liked that idea.

But who would the Chancellor assign the rights to? he wondered. There was no legal entity existing in the U.S. to accept an assignment of the rights. They would have to charter an entity on Senia with its own governance mechanism to take the assignment, and then create another entity when they returned to Earth to manage the technology consistent with the authorization in the original Senian charter. The Senian entity would have the authority to establish whatever form of business organization on Earth most suitable to accomplishing its objectives.

Josh breathed a sigh of relief. He knew what he would propose to the Chancellor. Now Rosilea loomed heavy on his mind.

Would Salea allow Vinar to return to Earth with Rosilea?

Would she agree to lose her only child forever?

Would the Chancellor allow it?

The more he thought about it, the more he realized that the outcome was not under his control, or even influence. They had long since decided that Rosilea could stay on Senia if she so decided. So, it was actually a "no lose" situation for them. If Vinar was allowed to go, they would not lose Rosilea. If not, they would not be any worse off than what they had originally decided.

Was Vinar a good mate for Rosilea?

He could not say, but he seemed all right. Time would tell. At peace with the day's events, he rolled over and went to sleep.

When Vinar left the Chancellor's residence with Nemar and Salea, he faced the same situation as Rosilea. Salea did not hide her concern about his new romance. Rosilea was adorable and she had no objection to her, but what did this mean for Vinar, she wondered.

"It looks to me as though you and Rosilea have become quite attached to each other," she said, wondering what type of response she would receive.

"Yes, mom, I really like her a lot."

"Is she going to return to Earth?"

"Yes, she is planning to return," Vinar replied, fearful of what the next question would be.

"Well, then you should not become too attached to her."

"Yes, mom, I know," he replied.

Vinar was not comfortable with misleading his parents in this manner. He decided to test the waters.

"How would you feel about me going on the return mission to Earth? I would have wanted to do this even if I had not met Rosilea."

Salea's heart sank. This is what she most feared.

"If you go on the Earth mission, I would most likely be dead and buried by the time you return to Senia."

"I would not return to Senia," Vinar replied. "Rosilea and I would settle and raise a family on Earth."

"Is that supposed to make me feel any better?" Salea exclaimed, raising her voice.

"No, mom. I know it will be hard for you, but I want to live my own life," Vinar replied, putting his hand on her shoulder from the back seat of the car.

"What does your father have to say about this?" she said, slightly lowering her voice.

Nemar was sympathetic with his son's desire to live his own life. He recalled his own transition into manhood and how much it had meant to him to assert his independence. Still, he questioned whether Vinar was making a rash decision, as he had barely met Rosilea, and despite how beautiful she was, he really did not know very much about her and how compatible they would be in the long run.

"I think you should take some time to get to know Rosilea better, and if that is still what you want, then you are entitled to live your own life."

Vinar was relieved. He had taken it as far as he thought he could for the moment.

"Yes, dad, I will do that," he said, glad to bring the conversation to an end.

Salea did not say any more. She stared blankly forward, trying to digest the thought of losing Vinar forever. There was still time. Perhaps it would not work out between them.

When they awoke the next day, there was much for everyone to do. Rosilea needed to speak to Vinar. Fela needed to speak to Salea. And Josh needed to speak to the Chancellor. As usual, the Chancellor was at the Supreme Council building when they met Keala for breakfast in the dining room.

After breakfast, Keala arranged a meeting for Josh with the Chancellor at the Supreme Council Building, who arranged for the Director of the office that licensed Senian technology and other key staff to attend.

Rosilea found a quiet place to call Vinar. When her face appeared on the screen of his communicator, he could see that she was very upset.

"What's the matter?"

"I had to tell my mom yesterday about our plans. She says that Salea would never forgive her if she kept this from her."

"Oh, don't worry," he said with a smile. "I ended up telling my mom and dad too. But I didn't tell them that you said you would stay with me on Senia if I was not allowed to go with you."

"What did they say?" she asked with some urgency.

"My dad says that I can go, but we should take some time to be sure that we are right for each other."

"What about your mom?"

"I don't know. She was not very happy about it. It will take some time for her."

"My mom is going to call her today."

"I'll tell her to expect the call."

"I love you. I'm sure about you," Rosilea earnestly replied.

"And I'm sure about you. I have some classes today. I will call you later."

Fela called Salea, telling her that she wanted to discuss the budding romance between Rosilea and Vinar. They decided to meet for lunch at a café on Veronia Street. Fela was the first to arrive, waiting anxiously for Salea, not quite knowing how to begin their discussion.

Salea arrived a few minutes later in an awful mood, thinking about losing Vinar forever. They greeted each other with a brief hug and sat down at a small table in the corner where they could talk quietly.

Fela started the conversation.

"Rosilea told me last night that she is in love with Vinar and that they want to get married. They are discussing Vinar returning to Earth with her on the next mission. Do you know this?"

"Yes," Salea replied, with unmistakable sadness in her voice. "It is hard for me to think about losing Vinar forever."

"I understand," Fela said. "We decided long ago that we would provide for Rosilea to stay on Senia if that is what she wants, so I know how you feel. According to Rosilea, Vinar says that he wants to go on the Earth mission."

"Yes, I know. I've tried to discourage him, but he is set on making his mark somewhere in space and I do not seem to be able to talk him out of it."

"Apparently, they are very much in love. Rosilea told me that if Vinar is not allowed to go on the Earth mission, she will stay with him on Senia."

Salea was shocked. Vinar had not told her that! She suddenly found herself holding all of the cards, or at least most of them.

"Vinar did not tell me that," she quickly replied.

"Yes," Fela replied. "So it is really up to you."

"I don't know what to say," Salea replied. "I will need to think about this, but I thank you for being so forthcoming and telling me all of this."

"Whatever you decide will be fine with Josh and me. We have been prepared for many years for the possibility that Rosilea would stay on Senia."

They ultimately decided that it was first up to Vinar and Rosilea to spend more time together and make sure that they wanted to spend their lives together. There was much yet to come with the impending Corilian attack and the times were far too uncertain to dwell excessively on something that might never come to pass.

During lunch they chit chatted about whatever they could think of that did not involve Vinar and Rosilea, and departed with another hug. Fela was glad that she had spoken with Salea, although she felt almost certain that Salea would nix Vinar returning to Earth with Rosilea.

Walking back to her residence, Salea was totally oblivious to her surroundings, thinking intently about what she should do. Fela had been most gracious and forthcoming in telling her everything. Nemar would not approve if she stood in the way. And then there was Vinar and what he would think. He might never forgive her. She would have to think much more about it.

Josh attended a late afternoon meeting at the Supreme Council Building where he presented his proposal. It was favorably received. They decided to turn the matter over to the Office of Legal Affairs to draft the charter for a new entity that would be known as the "Senia – Earth Technology Transfer Authority." It would be governed by a three-member board consisting of the Chancellor and the directors of the Technology Licensing Office and the Office of Legal Affairs. As there could be no effective communication between the board and the Earth mission, the yet-to-be determined Captain for the Earth mission would have full authority over all decisions pertaining to the form of business entity to be established on Earth and the transfer of specific technologies in accordance with the charter. Josh would assist in developing all of the key documents and translating them into English so that there would be no doubt on Earth as to their legal authority and ownership of the proprietary rights to the technology. At Josh's suggestion, technology transfer would be authorized only under U.S. law and only if the U.S. remained under democratic government and the rule of law.

The rest of the week went by uneventfully as the tension mounted toward the meetings with the press. Fela and Josh visited some of Fela's old friends throughout the city. Rosilea and Vinar spent more time together, becoming ever more convinced that they were right for each other. All too soon, it was the evening before the press meetings as Fela and Josh awaited the arrival of Fedar and the others.

Fedar was at the controls as the saucer jolted itself forward toward the Capitol at about 400 miles per hour. This time the craft was full. Zfar, Banar, Zofar, Elar and Minar were aboard, as well as several others from the base. They had finished shutting down the *Explorer*'s nuclear reactor, removing the fuel rods, draining water from the horticultural and recycling systems, removing all of the plants, and inspecting all systems. The gravitational field generator for the first level continued to operate under supplemental power. Most of the plumbing on the ship would be replaced in order to guard against a failure during the next voyage. For now, however, there would be no further activity until after dealing with the Corilians.

This was the first time after over thirty-six Senian years that the crew was actually free from their duties to the Earth mission, except for meeting the press tomorrow. They were both joyful and apprehensive, like someone released from prison, not knowing how to adapt to civilian life. Zfar would visit with his daughter, who would host the whole family. Fedar would visit with his brother. Banar, Elar and Minar would stay with their parents, at least one of which was still alive.

First, however, before meeting with the press and disbursing from the Capitol, they would have their long anticipated celebration of completing the mission. Money was no object as they were now very wealthy. They would go to the finest restaurant at the Capitol, and afterwards, Bandar and Minar were pushing for them to continue the celebration at the Sonora Club, where there was entertainment and plenty of sexy women. Due to the media interviews the next day, they could not get too wasted. For that reason, Zfar and Fedar had some reservations about continuing to the Sonora Club.

The sun was starting to set as they began to decelerate for a landing at Area 1. The sky turned a blend or orange and red against the deep blue background that drifted into soft shades of purple, illuminating the savannah around the Capitol in brilliant color. Wind turbines as far as they could see slowly turned as they flew by. It was a peaceful moment for all as they reflected on their long journey and the sense that it was finally coming to an end.

They landed in an area reserved for the military and walked together across the pavement toward the depot where they would rent cars and go their separate ways.

Fedar went over the plan one last time.

"I'll pick up Fela, Josh and Rosilea and we will meet at the restaurant at 8:50."

That left all but Fedar with about forty minutes to kill.

Fela, Josh and Rosilea eagerly awaited Fedar's call. Up to now, they had been sheltered by the Chancellor and had not had any unrestricted contact with the Senian people. Tonight, they would be going to a very exclusive restaurant.

Would they be recognized? Josh wondered.

Perhaps not Fela and Rosilea, but he would stick out like a sore thumb.

How would the people behave? Would they be friendly or hostile?

Josh recalled an experience he had when his van broke down in Calahan, Florida, and he was confronted that night in a bar by someone trying to pick a fight because he was a stranger with long hair. That time he was with some of the locals, who backed the punk down.

Fela's communicator buzzed. It was Fedar.

"I'll be there in fifteen quarseks. Where should I pick you up?"

"We will be at the main gate."

They all looked very elegant in their newly purchased Senian clothes. Josh abandoned his denim jeans for loose fitting tan slacks and a colorful long sleeve pullover shirt that blended shades of grey, forest green, brown, and yellow. Fela looked absolutely gorgeous in a black evening dress that showed part of her bosom and lay gently over the rest of her shapely body. Rosilea loved the dress she had worn to the Chancellor's reception and was wearing it again.

With security guards in tow, they hurried to the gate. Soon Fedar pulled up in a silver blue sedan. Fela sat in front. Josh and Rosilea sat in the back. Fedar looked over at Fela, the blood starting to flow more rapidly in his lower regions.

"It is good to see you. How have you been?" he said, as he hit the pedal, trying to draw his energy away from his emerging desire for her.

"We have been well. The Chancellor and Keala have been very hospitable. We have decided to stay at Base Sinarta for now."

Fedar was glad that Fela would be near him, but concerned for her safety from the Corilians.

"That base is going to be the prime target for the Corilian attack. Should you not be someplace safer?"

"We will move to the shelter in the Sefara Mountains before the attack, but Josh and I want to be where we can help with the preparations as long as possible. And the Chancellor wants us to stay at a secure facility."

"I don't know that there is much you can do to help," he replied. "Right now, the focus is on flight checks for the fleet and training the crews."

"There must be something we can do."

Recognizing that their minds were made up, he said: "We will find something. There is always a need for extra hands."

They met the others at the restaurant and settled down at their table after many hugs and expressions of the absolutely stunning appearance of Fela and Rosilea. All eyes were on them as they were guided to their table. It was a cozy, exquisitely decorated and quiet restaurant that seated about fifty people with plenty of room. They were seated at a large table in a corner section that was somewhat isolated from the main seating area.

Josh looked about and everywhere he looked the people were looking back at him.

I knew it! I need a hat. Or perhaps I can have something made up to go over the top of my head to give me that bulbous look, he thought with a subdued smile.

The women were absolutely lovely, and of all ages. He felt like he was somewhere in Scandinavia, where all of the women were beautiful. They were all very slender.

Perhaps that's just because we are in an exclusive restaurant where all of the people are rich and beautiful, he thought.

Then came the dinner menu. Fish, fish, and more fish!

I've had enough fish, he cried to himself. Josh would have given the whole dinner menu for a hot dog and some French fries at Nathans in Coney Island, as he used to enjoy after returning from a day working with his father at his garment factory.

"Don't you folks ever eat anything besides fish and vegetables?" he exclaimed for all to hear.

They all were stunned. This was the first time Josh had ever complained about the food, and now in one of the best Senian restaurants, of all places.

"What do you want?" Fela asked.

"Meat," Josh replied.

"Do you mean animal meat?" she said, raising her voice somewhat in an exasperated tone.

"Yes, I was looking forward to a good steak."

"Steak?" Fela asked.

"Don't you raise cattle for their meat?"

"Oh, no," she replied. "The only meet that we eat is when the government culls the talepeon herds and makes some meat available for consumption. It is very expensive and I don't like it."

She pointed to an item on the menu where Josh could order talepeon if he wished. Josh decided to skip it and ordered moslan, something he was familiar with and liked. It was exquisitely prepared with various herbs and a creamy sauce derived from the milk of a gaton, which resembled a very large goat.

Now it was making sense to Josh why all of the people on Senia were so slim. All they ate were fish and vegetables. He wondered what it would be like for them if they returned to Earth and were exposed to all of the decadent eating habits that prevailed in the U.S. and elsewhere. Would they love it or be repulsed? He could not imagine them not liking a pastrami sandwich at Katz's Deli on the lower east side of Manhattan.

After they got over Josh's bout with the menu, it was a very enjoyable dinner. Word spread through the tables that they were the crew from the *Explorer*, including the Earthman, but no one disturbed them. People eventually stopped staring and went about their business.

As they were settling back for an after-dinner sip of Senian brandy and other condiments, Minar brought up the subject of where to go next.

"Are we ready to head over to the Sonora Club?" he asked with a mischievous smile.

Josh's eyes lit up. *What's this about?* he wondered.

Zfar looked at Fedar. They were both thinking about whether it would be wise to expose Josh to the less sophisticated people that inhabited the Sonora Club. They would have hell to pay if anything bad happened to Josh.

"Sound's good to me," Josh eagerly replied, thinking it must be some sort of place where the Senian people loosened up and had some fun.

Zfar and Fedar non-verbally communicated their reluctant approval to each other with a slight movement of their heads and their facial expressions.

"All right, let's go," Fedar replied. "But Rosilea is not old enough to go."

Rosilea was overjoyed. She was anxiously waiting for the dinner to be over so she could call Vinar.

"That's okay," she said. "Vinar and I were planning to go for a walk in Veronia Park after dinner."

Fela wasn't sure what to do. Josh looked so eager to go. She decided to go along to help keep him out of trouble.

After Vinar picked up Rosilea, they departed for the Sonora Club. It was a short hop to the entertainment area of the Capitol, where Senian night life was in full display. The entertainment area was like a large shopping mall. There were large parking areas at both ends of the strip, with no vehicular traffic along the tree lined street that ran the length of the strip. The street was full of people gaily walking along in their evening dress to their club of choice.

Josh hoped that he would not be noticed as he quickly walked along with Fela close beside him in the center of their group. After a short walk, they entered the Sonora Club. A new world opened up as they passed through the door. It was very much like a high end bar in lower Manhattan near the financial district. The people were very well dressed and for the most part appeared to be near the upper end of their youth.

All heads turned toward them as they entered. There was no escaping. Josh would have his first real mingle with the Senian people. He smiled and nodded as he entered and everyone nodded back. Minar placed his hand on Josh's shoulder, as if to say to everyone, "He's with us."

Everywhere Josh turned there was a beautiful lady smiling back at him.

Now, this is more like it, he thought, as he smiled back. Fela drew closer as she sensed all the attention Josh was receiving.

They walked past the bar to the main room. Almost all of the tables were taken, but they managed to put together a table near the wall farthest from the stage. On stage a four piece band was playing and a very sexy lady with light blonde hair and a sleek dark blue dress was singing what can best be described as a sultry blend of blues and an Indian mantra. Her voice lofted up and down through a wide vocal range as she entranced her audience with her gently swaying hips.

A beautiful young female server quickly came to their table and introduced herself.

"So you are the Earthman," she said, looking at Josh.

"That would be me," Josh replied with a smile.

"Are you enjoying yourself on our fair planet?"

"Could not be better, especially tonight."

She took their orders and rushed to tell everyone she worked with about her conversation with the Earthman.

They sat there for awhile listing to the music and sipping on their drinks. Josh stuck with a brand of Senian brandy that he was starting to like. Fela ordered wine. Fedar and the others ordered a Senian brew that tasted like a somewhat bitter ale.

As he looked around at the relatively sedate crowd, Josh wondered: *Is this it? Is this what they call getting wild and crazy on Senia? I'll have something to show them when we get back to Earth,* thinking about the last Grateful Dead concert he had been to.

Slowly, as he sipped more and more brandy, Josh began to feel the rhythm of the Senian music. It was not a rock and roll rhythm that hit you over the head with an unmistakable beat. Rather, it was a very subtle and intricate rhythm.

He looked over at Fela. "Let's dance," he said in English.

"Dance?" she replied. "I don't know that word."

It then occurred to him that in all of the time they had spent together they had never danced.

"Come, I'll show you."

She took his hand and he led her to the open floor area by the bar. Everyone was watching. Then he took her in his arms and started to move back and forth to the rhythm of the music. Fela followed and quickly got the sense of what Josh was doing.

"Don't you dance on Senia?" Josh asked.

"No," she replied. "Not like this. There are some traditional dances that dance groups do for entertainment."

Fela got into the mood of Josh's dance moves and rested her head on his shoulder as they slowly moved about the small area that opened up for them. Then, to Fela's surprise, another couple started to dance beside them, copying Josh and Fela. Before long, there were several more couples dancing beside them with the people seated at their tables looking over at the Earthman and this new Earth custom. Lila, the singer, did not like everyone being distracted in that way and signaled for a break.

The club broke into applause as she left the stage, both for her and the dancing couples. She walked over to Josh and Fela.

"What are you doing here?" she asked in a somewhat irritated tone.

"We are dancing," Josh replied in a mixture of Senian and English, not knowing the Senian word for dancing.

"It is an Earth custom," Fela interjected.

"Well, nobody is paying attention to me while you are dancing over here."

"Then, why don't we dance over by you," Josh replied, knowing how it is typically done in a club on Earth.

Everyone around them was listening. There was a collective decision to compress some of the tables to clear some space for a dance floor by the band. Then, the band started again with Lila happily casting a melody over the crowd dancing in front of her. Before long, half of the couples in the club were dancing with the tables and chairs being pushed further back over each other.

Zfar, Fedar, and the others watched from the back of the room with great interest and amusement. People were snapping pictures with their communicators and they did the same. The news media would soon find out. This was sure to create a sensation on Senia.

While Josh and Fela were dancing at the Sonora Club, Rosilea and Vinar were sitting on a bench in Veronia Park cementing their love for each other with many more kisses. Their passions were aroused, but Vinar was keeping a lid on it. It would ruin everything if he, the Chancellor's grandson, were to make her pregnant. Rosilea would have made love to Vinar if he wanted.

It turned into a most memorable evening for all. Josh got more relaxed as the evening wore on, joking with everyone about how they were learning something new from Earth. After much smiling, bowing, and friendly pats on the shoulder, it was finally time to leave. Fedar wanted so much to dance with Fela, but it seemed far too intimate a custom for him to ask and he never did.

Josh and Fela said goodbye to the crew and Fedar dropped them off at the Chancellor's residence. Tomorrow would be the media interviews. Everyone was in good spirits and felt relaxed and ready for the media.

Sure enough, photos of Josh and Fela's escapade at the Sonora Club had gone viral over the global communication system, and virtually everyone on the planet had seen photos of Josh and Fela dancing, posing with Lila and other Senians, and generally whooping it up when the media came to call at the Chancellor's residence the next morning. It was a completely unplanned circumstance that turned out to be a great media introduction of the "Earthman," as Josh was becoming known, to the Senian people, somewhat scooping his media introduction, but they had no choice but to go along with it.

Fedar and the others gathered at the Chancellor's residence in the press room. Zfar, as Captain of the mission, made the opening statement. There was a bevy of questions about the mission. Then the questions turned to Josh and Fela.

How do you like it on Senia?

Did you have fun last night?

What is life like on Earth?

When did you fall in love?

Will Rosilea be returning to Earth with you?

How did you learn to speak Senian so well?

Fela and Josh weathered the storm of questions in good spirits. They did not know it, but they were well on their way to becoming the newest celebrities on Senia.

After the press conference, the crew broke up for individual interviews. Everyone was interviewed at least once, sometimes only by the home town media. They would all become heroes in their home town and across the planet. There was no discussion of the impending Corilian attack, as everyone was well drilled in that regard.

When it was all over, the crew scattered to their separate destinations, due to return to Base Sinarta in twelve days. Only Fedar would remain in the Capitol with his brother, Tufar, who worked in one of the ministries.

Fela and Josh had twelve days to kill. They didn't want to impose on the Chancellor any further, but they also did not want to travel to the base until the crew was due back. They knew they needed at least a few days to set up their residence at the base and decided to stay at the Chancellor's residence for another week before heading to the base.

It was mid-afternoon when Fedar finished with the press, had lunch with Josh, Fela, Rosilea and Keala at the Chancellor's residence, and was ready to meet Tufar at Area 1 to return the car and travel to Tufar's house in Area 6. When he last saw his brother, they were young men in their thirties. Now, he was seventy-six years old, with graying hair that was starting to recede up the sides of his forehead.

Tufar's entire family was there to greet Fedar when he arrived. There was his wife, Amora, their two children and four grandchildren. Some of Fedar's old friends and their wives were also there. He was overjoyed at first to see everyone, but as the day wore on he started to feel more and more out of place. Once the subject of the Earthman was exhausted, there was not much else of interest that he had to talk about – just thirty-six uneventful years of traveling through space. Tufar's family was consumed with events in their lives that he knew nothing about, and the conversation with his friends about their families and lives on Senia just made him feel more out of place.

When the evening was over, he felt lonelier than ever. He would stay with Tufar until it was time to return to base. Perhaps, he thought, he just needed more time to adjust to Senian life. The image of Fela in her sleek black evening dress was still running through his mind.

Zfar's reaction to being with his family was entirely different. He was now the patriarch of a very large family and he rejoiced in every moment of being with them. His wife, Kala, was still alive and had gathered the entire family for his homecoming. The family stayed for several days and then slowly drifted off. They spent many hours recounting the events of their lives and Zfar intently lived with them through every moment. As the days passed, he felt more and more comfortable with his decision that he would not be a part of the return mission to Earth.

Minar went to stay with his parents in Monorian Province, far south of the Capitol. All he could think about was trying to make up for lost time. He was a celebrity in his home town and reveled in every minute of it, especially with the ladies. He bedded several women during the first few days, but word of his exploits quickly spread among the ladies until he found himself getting nowhere toward the end of his stay. He very quickly became bored with the stay with his parents and started to look forward to returning to Base Sinarta.

Banar's experience was similar to Fedar's. Both of his parents were gone, so he went to stay with his sister, Mavala, in Falidia Province. Her husband, Gondar, a wealthy owner of a chain of sporting goods stores, sponsored a reception and dinner at an exclusive club. They invited a number of local officials and business leaders and everyone they could think of that was a member of the family or a friend of Banar. It was a downright harrowing experience for Banar, as he did not know virtually anyone and was very uneasy with all of the commotion after so many years in the quiet calm of space. He too was looking forward to returning to base.

Zofar's wife, Sonora, had died during the voyage, so he went to stay with his son, Elkar, who had followed in his father's footsteps and had a thriving practice in internal medicine. There was a small reception for friends and family. Elkar asked Zofar to join with him in his medical practice and Zofar felt that he would have no trouble adapting to life on Senia. Still, there was this lingering feeling about perhaps returning to Earth with the next mission instead of trying to start a new life on Senia.

Bandar was an only child and both of his parents had long since passed. He rented a hotel room in Monorian Province and visited with a few friends, but was already starting to sorely miss his life aboard the *Explorer*, where he was involved every day in growing and preparing food for the crew. After all the commotion that surrounded their return died down, he started to feel useless. It was as though he had walked off a cliff into an abyss of nothingness. He would not even play a significant part in preparing for the Corilians. A life of useless leisure on Senia did not appeal to him. He could open a nursery business, but that also had no appeal when compared with his role aboard the *Explorer*.

Elar returned to Senia to find his wife, Verona, gravely ill. The years of loneliness had taken their toll and she had lost the will to live. Their son, Tefar, had done all that he could, but she had slowly progressed toward dementia, along with her failing health. There were no celebrations for Elar's return. He was immediately consumed with caring for Verona, who barely recognized him.

One week later, it was time for Josh, Fela and Rosilea to leave the Chancellor's residence. Fela had purchased a new silver grey Rovecta, a sporty sedan that she would give to her nephew, Kenar, when they left Senia. She also rented a small apartment at the Capitol so that Josh would have a place to stay when he worked with the Senia – Earth Technology Transfer Authority, which had been quickly approved by the Supreme Council that week. They had a very pleasant farewell dinner with the Chancellor and Keala the night before leaving, at which the conversation was light and business was not discussed.

First, they would drop Rosilea off at Mishar's. Then, they would drive Fela's new car to Base Sinarta, northwest of the Capitol at the base of the Sefara Mountains. But Josh wanted to first see the Senian Sea, so they decided to detour to the coast before traveling inland.

Rosilea was all smiles when they parted, thinking of all the time she would have to spend with Vinar.

"Can I come see you?" she said, knowing what Fela's reply would be.

"No," Fela said. "We will come and see you. Josh will be coming back to the Capitol and I will go with him once I have the house set up."

Fela pulled Rosilea to her. She knew that from here on, Rosilea would be living her own life. One way or the other, she was going to stay with Vinar.

"I love you so much. I am really going to miss you," she said, her eyes starting to tear.

After a long hug, Rosilea backed slightly away so she could see Fela's face beginning to sprout tears.

"Oh, mom. Don't cry. It's not like I'm never going to see you again."

Josh chimed in, trying to lighten things up, "With these communicators, you can't get away from us, even if you try."

"Yes," Rosilea replied. "I'll call you every day."

After many more goodbyes, they were off for an exhilarating ride around the Capitol beltway to the highway that would take them to Nolimar, a tourist town that overlooked the Senian Sea. Fela drove and Josh looked at the surroundings. Here he was, driving in a car somewhere sixteen light years away from Earth, and it did not seem much different than when he traveled to work with his dad on the Southern Parkway in Long Island. The road had virtually no one on it, and the surroundings were infinitely more beautiful, but still, he was driving in a car trying to get somewhere, just like on Earth. Somehow, it made him think of home and the family he left behind – something he did not often think about. He wondered who would be left if he ever returned to Earth.

They pulled into a recharging facility at a nice restaurant overlooking the Senian Sea and went in for a bite. Fish it was again, and, *holy cow, they actually know how to fry fish!* It was absolutely delicious. Josh forgot for a little while his longing for a Nathan's hot dog.

After eating, they found a walking path along the coast from a vantage point about fifty feet above the sea. It was an awesome view in all directions, as Nolimar had been built on the highest ground for miles around. Sea birds flew overhead in great abundance. The land was pristine as far as the eye could see. Ocean waves gently rolled onto the shore.

There were some people walking along the shore and they decided to venture down the walkway to the beach. Now, Josh was really starting to feel like he felt many years ago on Earth. He was taken back to his last day on Earth, walking along the shore at Crescent Beach. It was even more beautiful.

"We have places like this on Earth," he said, holding Fela's hand as they walked along the water. "One day I will show them to you."

Fela suddenly stopped. She wanted a kiss, a very long and romantic kiss, and pulled Josh to her. Josh was most willing to oblige. It might have been the longest and most romantic kiss of all their time together. There was nothing to say after that. They walked along quietly together, content with their own thoughts about where life had brought them.

They quietly walked down the beach, hand in hand, knowing that, as far as they walked, that was how far as they would have to walk back. Still, they kept walking, not wanting to turn back. Fela's soft dirty blonde hair tossed about her head in the gentle ocean breeze. The sun was starting to set, filling the sky with color.

After walking several miles, Josh finally felt they had walked far enough, but he still did not want to turn back. Nothing was more important at that moment then taking in the beautiful sunset. They sat down on the sand, looking over the ocean, with Fela cradled in front of him between his legs, swaying back and forth.

How was it, Josh thought, *that this beautiful planet could be so threatened. They had to survive the Corilian attack!*

Not being a religious person, he nevertheless said a quiet prayer to himself for their survival.

It was almost dark when they finally got up and started back. Now they would have to change their plans. The trip to base was about 350 miles, and it was far too dangerous to drive across the savannah after dark, when one could easily collide with one of the many animals that roamed the plain. They booked a room overlooking the ocean at a small hotel and spent the rest of the evening on the balcony staring out at the stars and talking about the next phase of their life together.

Earth is out there somewhere, Josh thought, wondering what might have happened during the last sixteen years since he left Crescent Beach. Josh had long since given up on trying to keep track of the passage of time on Earth.

On that day, as Josh sat on the beach looking at the setting Senian sun, it was December 7, 1994, on Earth. The U.S. space probe Galileo began its orbit of Jupiter.

Rapid change continued on Earth while Josh and the Senians

completed their journey back to Senia. The transition to the digital age proceeded at an accelerating pace. In 1990, HTML language was developed by a Swiss researcher, giving rise to the World Wide Web and the creation of a means of communications similar to Senia's global communications system. By 1993 there were 600 websites and the White House went online. Microprocessors steadily increased in computing power, with the Pentium microprocessor introduced by Intel in 1993. In 1994, personal computers came into widespread use as gaming machines, with many powerful new games hitting the market. Netscape came into being in 1994 as the first major Web browser program.

In the geopolitical world, the most noteworthy event was the breakup of the Soviet Union and the outlawing of the Communist Party in what became the Russian Federation. Mr. Gorbachev had become convinced in his early years as General Secretary of the Communist Party that fixing the ailing Soviet economy would not be possible without reforming the political and social structure of the Soviet Union. But the new freedoms presented by Glasnost and Perestroika unleashed repressed forces and desires among the populace that he did not anticipate. The fall of the Berlin Wall late in 1989 was the culmination of a process that had spread across all of the Eastern European satellite nations of the Soviet empire. One by one, the Communist Party dictatorships fell to popular democratic regimes.

Then the Soviet Union itself began to fragment. It began with the Baltic Republics of Lithuania, Latvia and Estonia, which had been annexed into the Soviet Union by Joseph Stalin in 1940. By 1991, all three had declared their independence from the Soviet Union, which was recognized by the Soviets under Gorbachev later that year. The independence movement did not end there, as many of the Soviet republics were actually brought into the Soviet Union over many years of conquest. In 1991, the republics of Georgia, Ukraine and White-Russia also declared their independence from the Soviet Union.

As if this was not enough for Gorbachev, the creation of a freely

189

elected Congress of People's Deputies in 1989 led to a power struggle between the Communist Party apparatus of the Soviet Union, over which Gorbachev presided, and the newly created democratic institutions of Russia, over which Boris Yeltsin obtained a leadership role, including being elected President of the Russian Federation in 1991. Gorbachev sought to keep the Soviet Union together through a new treaty of union that would create a voluntary federation in a more democratic Soviet Union. Yeltsin and other radical reformists, who were convinced that the Soviet Union needed a rapid transition to a market economy, opposed the new treaty. The treaty was approved by a majority of the electorate, but was overtaken by other events.

In August 1991, hard-liners within the Communist Party of the Soviet Union and some of the military staged a coup against Gorbachev to prevent the signing of the new union treaty. Gorbachev was placed under house arrest, but Yeltsin saved the day. He raced to the White House of Russia in Moscow and defied the coup by making a speech from atop the turret of a tank, mobilizing popular support and causing the troops to defect and the coup attempt to crumble.

Gorbachev was restored to his position, but destroyed politically. The mantle of leadership had de facto passed to Yeltsin. Yeltsin began a formal takeover of various ministries of the Soviet Union and issued a decree in November 1991 banning all Communist Party activities in Russia. One month later he announced the dissolution of the Soviet Union in favor of a voluntary Commonwealth of Independent States. Gorbachev then accepted the dissolution of the Soviet Union as a *fait accompli* and resigned his position. The Russian Federation then took over the Soviet Union's seat at the United Nations.

The ailing economy of the former Soviet Union continued its downward plunge during Yeltsin's leadership. He implemented a rapid privatization program that ultimately resulted in selling of the former Soviet state's valuable assets in oil, gas and other natural resources to a handful of very wealthy "oligarchs," as they became known, for a fraction of the actual value. Productive capacity rapidly declined as outdated factories that could not compete with western technology shut down, leading to widespread inflation. Yeltsin's popularity in Russia plummeted, but he remained popular with western leaders due to a shift in foreign policy to be more accommodating of western interests. At the end of 1994 the former Soviet Union remained in dire economic straits despite billions of western economic aid.

In the Middle East, Saddam Hussein, the brutal leader of Iraq, was the main focus of the Earth's attention. The U.S. had provided Saddam with some military support in its war against Iran, which ended in a stalemate in 1988. Heavily indebted as a result of this war, Saddam sought to increase Iraq's oil export revenues. He accused Iraq's neighbor, Kuwait, of exceeding OPEC oil production quotas, which, in combination with other producers, had lowered the price of oil to $10.00 per barrel, and refused to pay back its debt to Kuwait for loans made during the war. Ultimately, after peace negotiations failed, Iraq invaded and quickly took over Kuwait in August 1990. President George H.W. Bush refused to make any concessions to Iraq as a result of its invasion and organized a coalition of nations to remove Iraqi forces through military means. There was much trepidation in advance of the assault that the coalition would suffer heavy casualties in opposing Iraq's army, which at the time was the Earth's fourth largest with over one million men. As it turned out, the Iraqi resistance collapsed under the superior armaments and tactics of the U.S. coalition forces, and the war ended with Kuwait's liberation four days after the ground forces invaded. President Bush called the ground invasion to a halt before reaching Baghdad and Saddam Hussein remained in power at the close of 1994.

The following day Josh and Fela were well rested, the car was fully charged, and they were ready to meet the challenges that lay ahead. They left at first light and arrived at Base Sinarta in the early afternoon. Fela drove and Josh enjoyed every minute, looking at the wide open Senian landscape.

They had been assigned a residence in an area normally reserved for senior military officers. It was about six miles from the base, surrounded by a perimeter fence with a secure entrance. Josh was not prepared for what he saw when they passed through the gate. The entire development was underground, with only the roads through the compound and the solar paneled roofs of the dwellings and some parked cars visible above ground. There were no trees – just a continuation of the natural savannah vegetation.

"I didn't expect this," he said.

"This area has been designed to withstand a nuclear attack on the base," Fela replied.

She pulled up to their residence. They walked down the entrance walkway stairs about ten feet to the front door, made of a heavy composite material that creaked on its stainless steel hinges as they entered. To their surprise, the interior space was very pleasant and well lit with the sunlight that streaked through the skylights and the long narrow windows just below the ceiling.

The unit had two bedrooms and two baths and was fully furnished with mid-grade furniture. Fela could have afforded much better, but it was adequate. They had about 1,200 square feet of living space and the rooms were fairly large. The interior was poured concrete all around with pleasant flowing designs built into the molds that made the walls. They were painted an earthy light grey. The stained concrete floors had large tan mats, woven from a flexible synthetic material. All in all, they were very pleased. It was certainly much better than their cramped quarters aboard the *Explorer*.

They unpacked what they had in the car and there was little else to do. Josh decided to explore further outside.

What happened when it rained?, he wondered.

It appeared that water would flow down the walkway and the driveway next to the walkway into the house and garage. Then he noticed the drains at his feet covered with a screen made from composite material. Apparently, there was an underground drain system. Still, he had many questions.

Where did the water go?

How did they get electrical power?

Was there a supplemental supply, and where did it come from?

Would that be capable of withstanding a nuclear attack?

Would the solar panels survive a nuclear attack? They looked very sturdy, but he thought not.

They decided to travel to the base and introduce themselves to the Deputy Base Commander, who would be looking after their affairs while they were on base. Perhaps he could answer some of Josh's questions.

The base was a beehive of activity when they arrived. Josh had one up on Fela, as he had already seen it, but Fela now looked in awe at the sight of twenty starships stretched across the vast pavement. They had been rotated since Josh last saw them so that the bridge was now upright. Supplemental power operated the rotational elevator and gravitational field generator for the first level.

Deputy Base Commander Levar greeted them after a short wait. After some chit chat, Josh asked, "How are the preparations going?"

"Very well," he replied. "The ships will be ready for test flights the week after next. We have trained the crews as much as we can on the simulators and it is now time for them to get the feel of what it is really like to fly one of these starships."

Fela interjected, "Do you have anything for me to do?"

"Yes," he replied. "The crews have expressed interest in the Earth mission. Could you prepare a presentation about the mission and how you went about learning the Earth language and teaching Josh the Senian language. We would not require that they attend, but I think you will have a great response."

"I would like that," Fela said with some enthusiasm. It was certainly more interesting than continuing her sporadic work on the Senian - English dictionary, which was, for all intents and purposes, largely complete.

"And for you, Josh," the Commander continued, "you will be able to freely roam over the base. Just be careful not to get hurt. I'm sure you will find much that will interest you."

"That will be very interesting," Josh replied. "There is so much for me to learn, and I am constantly amazed by Senian technology. I will do my best to stay out of the way of the preparations."

"Very well," the Commander replied. "Feel free to see me if you have any questions or I can help you with anything."

Questions? Josh thought. He had almost forgotten to ask about the water and electrical supply for their residence.

"Do you have time for a few questions about our residential unit?" Josh cautiously asked.

"What would you like to know?"

"How is the water supplied? I noticed the drains at our unit. Is the water recycled? Is there a supplemental supply?"

The Commander had heard of Josh's inquisitive nature and was glad to respond.

"All of the water treatment facilities are underground. There is a 200,000 gallon storage tank for rainwater and a 200,000 gallon tank for the sinks and showers. This water is treated and recycled. There is a deep well to provide supplemental water if needed."

"What do you do with the human waste?"

"There is a septic system for the development. We don't recycle that water."

"What about electrical power?" Josh asked.

"There is an underground battery storage system for the entire development. Supplemental power is brought in underground from the base."

"And if there is a nuclear attack on the base?"

"There would not be any supplemental electric power. But the solar systems are designed to withstand a two hundred mile per hour wind blast."

The Commander continued: "The residences are secondary to surviving an attack. If we have enough warning, everyone except those needed for our defense will be evacuated to shelters in the Sefara Mountains. They are supplied for two months. After that, there will hopefully be enough safe residences for people to return to. That is the best we could do."

"It sounds like you have done much better than we on Earth have done to prepare for nuclear war."

The Commander had read a few classified military briefing documents that provided the basic elements of Earth history and current world affairs as Josh had relayed them onboard the *Explorer*. He knew that Earth had not experienced a nuclear war, at least as of Josh's knowledge, which was now seventeen Earth years past.

"But you have not had a nuclear war on Earth," he replied.

"No, but we have come very close," Josh said, thinking of the Cuban missile crisis of 1962.

"So have we," said the Commander, thinking of ancient Corilian history when nuclear energy was first discovered.

Josh thanked the Commander for taking the time to meet with them and they returned to their new home. Fela called Rosilea and they saw her smiling face, larger than life, on the monitor hanging on the wall of the living area. Josh wished for a moment that he could call home, but this was his home now.

The weekend passed slowly for Fela and Josh. Fedar, Zfar, and the others began to arrive. They would be sharing three residences in the same development.

One evening, after everyone except Banar had returned to base, they gathered at the watering hole in the town of Nimalia, about twelve miles from the base, where most of the base personnel lived. It contained a mixture of underground housing, mostly built after the Corilian attack threat became known, and above-ground housing built before it was known.

The evening started out on a happy, carefree note, but as it wore on and their thoughts turned to what lay ahead, their mood became very somber. Their fun, such as it was, was now over. The enormity of what they were soon to face became prevalent in their minds. They adjourned with a renewed sense of the strong comradery built up over many years.

Outside the restaurant, Josh got the brilliant idea that they should form a huddle. He pulled Fela and Minar to his side with his hands on their shoulders and motioned for the others to do the same.

"Come on," he said, "let's form a huddle."

They looked at him with quizzical expressions.

"Oh, another Earth custom," Zfar thought.

"Alright," he said, joining up with Minar.

Fedar fell into place next to Fela and the rest followed suit to form a circle.

"We will make it through this," Josh said with emphasis.

He grabbed Fela's and Minar's hands and, raising his hands towards the stars, began to chant, "make it through, make it through."

The others joined in and after a little while they understood what Josh was doing. They would calmly do whatever they had to do and did not need to get riled up. Yet, there was an overpowering feeling of determination and unity that ran through them as they continued to chant. It was a good thing that Josh had done.

CHAPTER 9 - THE BATTLE FOR SENIA

Sunday, March 19, 1995, a day for prayer, rest and recreation on Earth. This was also the day that a battle would be fought sixteen light years from Earth that would determine Earth's destiny, as well as the destiny of Senia and Corilia.

A little over three months had passed since Fela and Josh first visited with the Deputy Base Commander. Preparations had gone well and the crews had about three weeks of flight training aboard the starships. Zfar had command of a starship, with Banar, Elar and Minar among the crew. Fedar was assigned command of a starship with a crew that had never been tested in battle. Zofar and Bandar would have to sit out the battle, as there was no need during the battle for a medical officer or a horticulturalist. If a ship was compromised and went down, there would be no survivors.

The base was evacuated, as it would be a likely target if the Corilians were able to penetrate Senian defenses. Command and control had been turned over to Commander Dakar at the Central Command facilities buried deep in the Sefara Mountains.

The civilian populations of all major Senian cities had been evacuated and were gathered around the monitors in their underground shelters throughout the planet. Rosilea, Vinar, Salea, Nemar and Mishar's family were together in a shelter in the Sefara Mountains. The Chancellor and Keala were at Central Command.

The Corilian fleet had been detected when it was about two weeks away from Senia. The Supreme Council and the military decided that it was time to abandon the need to maintain secrecy over the Global Communications System about Senian knowledge of the impending attack, as the Corilians would have expected the Senians to have detected their presence at that point. But there was still an absolute need for secrecy about the Senian war preparations, so the mili-

197

tary tightly controlled all broadcast communications necessary to conduct the evacuation.

Josh, Fela, Zofar and Bandar decided to stay at their off-base residences. Zofar would likely be needed on base immediately after the battle. Josh, Fela and Bandar also wanted to be there to help if needed. They stayed in their separate residences, as it might be impossible for them to leave for many days if the base was attacked.

Starships were deployed in formation on the side of the planet opposite the approaching attack fleet, just out of view on both sides of the planet, and ready to move on command.

As the Corilian fleet approached within visual range of Senia, Zenar, the Corilian Commander, was becoming suspicious. He expected the Senian defensive force to be in view, ready to intercept them.

What are they up to? he thought.

The Senians had considered sending in a small force of ten ships to initially engage the Corilians, with the remainder of the force then joining the battle from behind the planet. After numerous simulations, it was concluded that this would not work because, in order to force the Corilians to commit to a head-on attack, the remainder of the force would not have enough time to join the battle and the decoy force would likely be destroyed.

They also considered using ten ships to lure the Corilians to the other side of the planet, where the remainder of the force would attack. This was ruled out because there was no reason why the Corilians would follow the decoy force. They would just continue with the attack.

The Corilian fleet was now in rapid deceleration. It would only be a matter of hours before they would be in position to deploy around the planet and commence the attack. Still, there were no Senian defense forces in position to intercept the attackers.

Zenar began to smell a trap. Then it occurred to him.

The Senian ships might be on the other side of the planet!

He quickly realized that if he continued toward the planet and the

Senians were on the other side, he would not be able to maneuver his ships fast enough to avoid being outflanked. And he had no way of knowing in advance the size of the Senian defense force. There was no choice but to delay the attack to make sure there were no ships poised on the other side of the planet.

He spoke to Viskar, second in command aboard his ship.

"Something is up. There are no ships. They must have detected us by now."

Viskar replied: "They must be waiting on the other side of the planet."

"Yes," he said. "Let's split and circle the planet."

Zenar spoke to the rest of the fleet over a secure channel. There was no need at this point to continue to maintain radio silence.

"It looks like the Senians are laying in wait on the other side of the planet. On my command, split formation. We will swing as wide as possible but not so wide that we lose orbit. I'm sending you the coordinates now. Prepare for combat."

The Corilian approach was being closely monitored at Senian Central Command. Soon it would be time for Dakar to give the order for the starships to move. He did not know how the Corilians would disperse. They could scatter in multiple directions for the attack after coming close enough to achieve orbit, or possibly, if they anticipated the Senian defense plan, split before reaching orbital distance and meet the Senian force head on.

Zenar was waiting until the last possible moment to give the command to split the Corilian force. He wanted the Senians to think that he was falling for their ambush. They had decelerated down to a speed of about 25,000 miles per hour and were about 2000 miles from the planet.

Dakar was ready to give the command for the fleet to move. He had to be careful not to expose his ships to the Corilians until they were inside the ambush zone.

Zenar moved first. "Split formation now. Fire at will on contact," he calmly spoke into his communicator, expecting that the Senian force would be greatly outnumbered.

The Corilian force split off with great precision into two for-mations, swinging as wide as the outer rim would take them against their forward momentum.

Dakar's heart fell to the floor. There would be no ambush. They would have to meet the Corilians head on.

He quickly radioed to Fratar, Commander of the intercept force: "They have split up. Move out. Beta formation"

"Acknowledged," Fratar replied. He could also see the Corilian force splitting up on his monitor.

He then radioed to his commanders: "They have split up and are coming around. Beta formation. Let's go!"

Beta formation was plan B. If the Corilian force came around the planet, they would go for the high ground, so to speak, trying to gain as much vertical distance from the planet as possible so that they would be able to shoot down at the Corilian ships as they ap-proached. This would enable them to target the bridge area, which was the most vulnerable part of the ship.

The vertical thrusters of the Senian fleet rotated the ships until almost perpendicular to the planet. Then, the outer rim rapidly accel-erated the ships away from the planet.

The Senian ships were fitted with two powerful lasers, one on the second level above the outer rim, and one on the first level below. This afforded the capability to fire over a wide range. They had au-tomatic targeting mechanisms and needed seven seconds to recharge. In order to simultaneously fire both lasers, the ship would have to be pointed almost directly at the target. They would have to achieve enough altitude so that the vertical thrusters could then tilt the ship down before firing.

Zenar was also looking for the high ground. He had the ad-vantage because he was approaching from a great distance and could set the angle of approach as far away from the planet as he desired, limited only by the need to stay close enough to Senia to stay within the pull of its gravity. If the angle of attack was too wide, their ships would not be pulled in by Senia's gravity and would go off into space, having to circle around and double back. This would give the Senians great advantage because they could fire at will at the Corilian ships before they turned around and they would not have any means of returning fire.

The Senians were also limited by the need to stay within the planet's gravitational field or also risk being highly vulnerable as they attempted to circle back.

Zenar radioed to his commanders: "Set your approach to come in 150 terrats above the planet," which was about two-hundred Earth miles. This was at the limit of Senia's gravitational attraction for the Corilian ships, considering their forward momentum.

The one advantage that the Senians still had was that the Corilians did not know the position of their forces, while they knew the precise position of the Corilian forces. Dakar looked at the monitor that projected the trajectory of the Corilian and Senian forces. It showed the ships splitting wide away from Senia. They would not be able to calculate a trajectory for the attack until the ships turned toward Senia. He anxiously watched the monitor for the first sign of their trajectory.

For many intense moments Dakar waited as the Senian fleet continued to gain distance from the planet. At last, the Corilian ships turned toward Senia. His monitor flashed their trajectory. They would come in at the limit of Senia's gravitational field for maintaining orbit – the same distance from the planet his ships were headed.

He quickly concluded that Beta formation would not work. The Senian forces would not be able to gain the high ground. They would meet the Corilians head on, giving them no advantage.

Dakar had to think fast. There was no plan C. He decided to position the ships to attack from below. If they could get off the first rounds before the Corilians were able to respond, they would still have some advantage.

He shouted into his headphone: "We have got to abandon Beta formation. Get your forces down as quickly as possible. We'll go for a shot at them from below as they come around the planet."

Fratar barked the command into his communicator: "Head down, down! We have got to try to get at them from below. Use the gravitational field generators."

The vertical thrusters reversed the orientation of the Senian ships so they were pointed toward the planet and the outer rims now quickly reversed the direction of acceleration toward Senia. The gravitational generators were slammed on full force to pull the ships down as quickly as possible. They would need to lose altitude very rapidly so there would be enough time to stop the deceleration and reorient the ships for an upward shot at the Corilians.

Dakar kept shouting into his communicator: "Down, get down."

Fratar repeated this command to his commanders.

Dakar anxiously watched on his monitor as the Senian ships rapidly lost altitude. Thankfully, the Corilians did not change course. He projected that they would have a good shot at 6:74:16.

He spoke to Fratar: "You are going to get a shot at 6:74:16. Make the best of it. It's the only good shot you are going to get."

Fratar replied, "Acknowledged."

He shouted in into his communicator to his commanders: "They will be coming around in 1.3 quarsecs at 6:74:16. You are going to get one shot. Make it a good one."

Dakar and Fratar could see the forces moving together on their monitors. It looked good.

Fratar gave the command: "Reverse gravitational field and get ready."

With a strong jolt that threw everyone back in their seats, the Senian fleet reversed its gravitational field and decelerated to a stationary position as the vertical thrusters reoriented the ships in an upward direction toward the rapidly approaching Corilian fleet. The Corilians would come around the planet into view in about ten seconds.

Fratar gave the command: "Let's go. Forward thrust."

The outer rims kicked in to jolt the Senian fleet toward the approaching Corilians. They would get their shot, but had to be very fast so that the Corilians would not have time to respond. They were now more vulnerable to a strike if they were hit.

Zenar did not know what to expect when the other side of the planet came into view. And then there it was. The Senians were beneath him and approaching rapidly.

There are so many ships! he thought.

"Fire!" he shouted into his communicator, "Fire at will!" but it was too late. The Senians had discharged their lasers and the Corilian fleet was being decimated by numerous hits.

His ship took a jolt from a Senian laser.

"Damage?" he shouted.

Engineering replied: "We're hit. They have pierced the hull."

Atmospheric pressure was rapidly being lost on the first level. In a matter of a few minutes, everyone on that level would be dead.

"We're going down," he shouted into his headset to Engineering. "We have got to get into the atmosphere."

He turned the ship toward Senia and hit the gravitational field generator. With a rapid thrust of the outer rim, the ship was headed toward the planet.

As the Senian ships were circling around to give pursuit, he shouted to the fleet. "All ships continue the attack toward the planet."

The Corilian fleet was in complete disarray. Seventeen ships had been hit. Twelve had imploded and were drifting in space, starting to break up, all crew dead. Four were like Zenar's, still functional but needing to get into the Senian atmosphere. They still constituted a force that could inflict incalculable damage on Senia.

The Corilians had no time to go after the planet's global communications satellites. They needed to discharge their bombs. Those that were still able would return to Corilia. For the disabled ships, it was now a suicide mission. They could not return to Corilia.

The Senian ships had circled around and were coming on fast as the Corilians descended toward Senia. Dakar was watching the Corilians approach on his monitor. Fratar and the others did not need their monitors. They could see the ships.

"We got them! we got them!" he repeated. "Maintain pursuit. They are in for another surprise."

Indeed they were. Zenar thought he had now seen the entire Senian fleet. He gasped in fear as he could now see on his visual display that there were an additional ten ships rapidly approaching from below in two directions to form a pincer movement.

They were ruined and would be lucky if a single ship got through. There was no other alternative than to try to defend against the additional attackers.

"More ships approaching from below," he shouted. "Fire at will! Fire at will!"

They were still in the upper atmosphere, beyond the reach of Senian jets. Sandwiched between laser fire from all sides, it was a rout as the ships jolted about in all directions in an aerial dogfight unlike anything that could have been imagined by the military planners.

The Corilians got off many shots and inflicted some damage to the Senian fleet. Because they were now in the upper atmosphere, the damage was not fatal.

The same applied to the Corilians. The laser fire would only inflict fatal damage if it destroyed the bridge or was able to hit the nuclear generator that powered the ship. Some of the Corilian ships went careening toward the planet, but many were operable and still constituted a great threat.

Dakar spoke to Fratar: "Maintain pursuit. The air fleet is on its way."

Zenar could see the jets approaching. They would be cut to ribbons by the missiles fired by the jets as soon as they descended within range. It was now every man for himself as they battled to the death.

He shouted into his communicator one last time. "Jets approaching from below. Take evasive action."

He could not bring it upon himself to give the command to continue the attack. Nor could he order his ships to abandon the attack.

The Corilian ships that were still operational flashed off in all directions with the Senian starships in hot pursuit and the Senian jets waiting to fire their missiles. Zenar could hear the screams of his commanders and the sound of the explosions on his monitor as he careened out of the area with two Senian jets in hot pursuit.

He was now descending rapidly through the atmosphere. Avilia, the Senian Capitol city, was in sight. It would only be a matter of about fifty seconds before the city would be in range for him to fire his guided nuclear weapon.

He placed his hand over the control to release the weapon. The Senian jets fired their missiles. He maneuvered the ship with a sudden jolt of the outer rim at the last possible moment and the missiles streaked by. Now, he had a clear shot at the Senian capitol city.

It was time to release the weapon. His hand moved toward the button and stopped. Something inside him would not let him cause so much destruction in what amounted to a futile cause.

Dakar was watching in horror on his monitor as the Corilian ship approached the Capitol. When the missiles streaked by the Corilian ship, he thought it was all but over for the Capitol.

With another quick jolt of the outer rim, Zenar veered his ship off to the right away from the Capitol. He shouted to his Communications Officer, who was watching the events unfold in disbelief.

"Open up a channel to the Senians."

"Channel open," the officer replied.

"Request permission to land! Request permission to land!" Zenar repeated with great urgency.

Dakar had to decide fast. The Senian jets were moving around for another shot. The Corilian commander could have destroyed the Capitol and didn't. He would take a chance.

"Permission granted," he quickly replied. "Follow the jets."

Dakar then opened his channel to the pilots. "Hold your fire," he said, just as they were about to discharge their missiles.

"Acknowledged," the lead pilot replied.

"The ship has been given permission to land. Maintain one position in front and one behind. Take him to Base Pendelar," a small military base where the Corilian ship could not do very much damage if it were to take hostile action.

"Acknowledged," the pilot again replied.

Dakar then got on the open channel to Zenar. "We are holding our fire. Follow the jets to landing location."

Zenar replied: "Will do."

As Zenar was following the jets to base, the remainder of the Corilian fleet was being destroyed by the Senian starships and jets. One by one the Corilian ships careened downward toward the planet and disintegrated upon hitting the ground. Some of the ships fell into the Senian Sea and would be later recovered. Fortunately, none of the nuclear weapons were discharged.

For the ships that fell to ground, the ceramic nuclear reactors broke up without exploding, creating a zone of radioactivity that made the ships unapproachable. In most cases they fell over uninhabited areas, but in some instances, the populations would need to be evacuated.

Zenar and the men aboard his ship were the only Corilians to survive the assault. Zenar safely landed his ship and was taken to meet Dakar. As he entered the room at Central Command, the two men stared at each other intently.

Why had he not discharged his weapon? Dakar wondered.

"What is your rank," Dakar inquired.

Zenar could not see any point in concealing his true identity.

"I am the commander of the Corilian fleet," he replied.

"Why did you not discharge your weapon over the Capitol?"

"I could not see any point in it. We had lost the battle."

"You saved our Capitol city. For that I am grateful."

"I know. We have had too much destruction," Zenar replied. "It is very unfortunate that we cannot be brothers again as we once were."

"We cannot be brothers again until the Tskar is overthrown and democracy is restored to Corilia."

After some thought, Zenar replied: "I am afraid that day will not come soon. The Tskar is still very strong. There is still some resistance, but they are being crushed."

Dakar looked at Zenar. He seemed sincere.

Could it be that this Corilian really meant what he was saying, or was this just a ruse to placate his captors?

"Sometimes," Dakar said, "a regime that is built on fear and intimidation can collapse very quickly. We have learned much from the male human that we recently obtained from Earth."

Zenar was shocked. "You have obtained a human from Earth?" he said with astonishment.

"Yes. Our mission to Earth was successful."

"Perhaps one day I will have the opportunity to meet him."

"Perhaps," Dakar replied. "We will have to figure out what to do with you and your crew."

"The crew was just following their orders. We were all following orders on pain of death to ourselves and our families."

"Yes, I understand," Dakar replied. "But some on Corilia have joined the resistance."

"I did not support this mission, but I did my duty. I am a military officer," Zenar said, his voice shaking.

"And a good one at that. You almost had us," Dakar replied.

"Almost does not count in our business," Zenar said with a slight smile. "I will do all I can to help you. They may one day think of me as a traitor on Corilia, or perhaps, you are right and one day democracy will be restored and then I will be a hero."

"We will give you that chance," Dakar replied. "For now, you and your crew will be kept in confinement for questioning."

"They do not know very much. I will tell you what you need to know. If you need their cooperation, I will instruct them to cooperate."

"We will want to disarm your weapons and repair the ship."

"Understood."

With that, their meeting was over. Dakar and his crew were kept at Base Pendelar for questioning by the Senian Intelligence Service and the military. The installation was evacuated, with only a few brave souls remaining to disarm the nuclear weapons with the assistance of the Corilian weapons officer.

Once the weapons were disarmed, the Corilian starship was flown back to Base Sinarta, where it would be carefully studied and repaired, again with the assistance of the Corilian engineers. It was not that much different in its technology from the Senian starships, but there were some things to be learned, both to improve the capabilities of the Senian starships and to help defend against another Corilian attack.

On Corilia, it would be almost sixteen Earth years before the Tskar would learn that the attack had failed. He would assume that no one had survived the attack. By that time, too much time had passed for the Tskar to think about taking revenge against what remained of Zenar's family.

When the battle was over, a wave of joy and relief swept over Senia that can hardly be described. The Senian people were normally rather sedate about things, but this was different. Eleven years of anxiety and tension that had slowly built up to the climax of the battle was now relieved.

Josh was one guy who knew how to celebrate. He could hardly wait to see Rosilea and hold her in his arms. The global communications system had not been impacted at all, and Josh and Fela soon had Rosilea's happy face on their monitor. People were milling about behind her, singing, shouting, and just talking. The noise level was so loud they could hardly hear her.

"We are coming to see you," Fela shouted at the monitor.

"The buses will be coming soon to take us back to the Capitol," Rosilea shouted in reply.

"When will you be back?" Josh asked.

"I don't know. They say it will take three days to evacuate."

"You stay there," Josh replied, knowing that the elderly and infirm would need to be evacuated first. "We will come and get you."

Rosilea turned to Vinar beside her. "They want me to stay here until they come to get me."

Vinar knew that the Chancellor's family would be among the first to be returned in a vehicle driven by the Chancellor's protective service. Rosilea could have returned with him, but she wanted to stay with Mishar and his family.

"I will stay with you," he said.

"We will leave now and should be there by late tonight," Josh replied.

The car was fully charged and Josh and Fela were quickly on their way. When they hit the four-lane highway at the base of the Sefara Mountains, it was full of slow moving traffic. Many others had the same idea.

It would be an arduous journey. They needed to recharge twice instead of once and the recharging stations had long delays. They were in constant communication with Rosilea and finally arrived at the shelter early the next morning. The crowds were still teeming about, but amidst all the confusion, there was an overwhelming sense of joy and compassion.

They drove the rest of the night and, after dropping Vinar off, arrived at Josh's apartment the following morning. They went to bed and slept most of the day.

Mishar and his family would not be back until the next day. They all decided to go to the Capitol to take part in the celebration. Josh was mindful of the fact that he was still a stranger in a strange land, but there was no way that he could not be a part of this event.

The street celebration in the Capitol that night made the New Orleans Mardi Gras look like a Sunday prayer meeting, in a Senian sort of way. The people were not taking off their clothes or running around in strange costumes, but their joy was pure and genuine. The compassion everyone felt for each other was palpable and sincere. Vinar joined up with them, and they moved easily through the streets, with no one seeming to notice Josh. Solo musicians and combos played everywhere you walked, adding their tunes to the celebration. The restaurants stayed open and there was free food and drink to be had wherever they wandered.

Late that night, they settled in at Josh's apartment. Before they went to bed, Josh said to Rosilea:

"It looks like we will be returning to Earth. Pretty soon it will be time for you to decide."

"I know, dad," she replied, not wanting to think any further about it on this, the happiest of nights.

CHAPTER 10 - AFTER THE BATTLE

The new Senian starship, *Foralawa*, which meant "friendship" in Senian, stood upright on the pavement at Base Sinarta, almost ready to begin the journey back to Earth. Over five Earth years had passed since the Corilians were defeated. The celebrations continued for over two weeks as people slowly returned to the Capital and other cities. With the threat of a Corilian attack removed, they hardly knew how to get back to going about their lives, but eventually things returned to the peaceful existence Senia had known before the Corilian threat.

As it turned out, radioactive debris from the Corilian attack fleet ended up causing considerable damage and occupied the highest priority attention of the Supreme Council for many years after the attack, diverting attention and resources from preparing for the return mission to Earth. The attack ships that had been destroyed in orbit, ultimately disintegrated into many thousands of pieces of space debris, which over a period of years fell from orbit. Each attack ship was equipped with five nuclear weapons. Although none of them exploded upon hitting the ground, many broke up and scattered in large fragments, exposing a large surrounding area to radioactivity, in several cases in or near inhabited areas. This required a Herculean effort by the authorities to deal with the displaced people and the widespread radioactivity. Missiles that fell into the Senian Sea also had to be recovered. The Senian defense forces attempted to destroy the debris in orbit using the laser weapons, but this proved impossible as the debris field began to spread, endangering the ships. It was decided that it would be best to wait until the debris field had dissipated sufficiently to make it reasonably safe to launch the next Earth mission.

Josh and Fela spent these years exploring Senia while continuing to be a part of the space program. Although not interested in fame or fortune, it had been thrust upon them. Josh felt that it was his duty as the ambassador from Earth to give interviews as they toured Senia. Still, they tried their best to keep out of the limelight and stay anonymous most of the time.

Vinar finished his coursework at the Space Academy and was admitted to the Senian Interstellar Space Command. He took part in a mission to explore one of the moons of Cenaria – a planet in their solar system.

After about a year, he and Rosilea were married. About fifty people attended the ceremony at the Chancellor's residence, including Fedar, Zfar and the rest of the crew from the *Explorer*. Rosilea was almost their child as much as Fela and Josh. She looked as beautiful as ever in a new sleek white gown that was prepared for her at great expense. The news outlets had a field day with the story of their romance and pictures of the wedding.

Vinar remained determined to go on the Earth mission with Rosilea, but Salea continued to try to discourage him from going and would not give her definite consent.

The Corilian attack ship piloted by Zenar had been converted for the Earth mission. It was about fifty percent larger than the *Explorer* and could accommodate twelve crew members. There was room for Rosilea and Vinar, with some extra room to accommodate a child or two if that were to happen. Josh and Fela had thought about having another child, but Fela was at the end of her child-bearing years and they decided it would be better to hope to become grandparents.

Fedar would captain the ship. He had focused his attention almost exclusively on preparing for the Corilian attack and dealing with its aftermath. The little time that he spent with his brother and his family only made him feel lonely and out of place. Space travel was his life and there was no one better qualified than he to lead the mission back to Earth, so long as his health held out. He was now eighty-one Senian years old, and would be reaching the end of a normal Senian lifespan by the time they returned to Earth. Fela was and would remain the love of his life, and at least he could be with her in their loving, non-physical relationship.

Zfar had no choice but to stay on Senia. He was now too old to contemplate another Earth mission, and was fully settled into his new life as the patriarch of his large family.

The rest of the crew, Banar, Zofar, Bandar, Elar, and to everyone's surprise, Minar, would be on the mission. Minar had dogged around Monorian Province for several years after the Senian victory, but he eventually realized that the life of a rich playboy did not suit him. He was torn between wanting to do something useful with the rest of his life by being a part of the Earth mission, and the thought that he could not bear another eighteen Senian years in space without a female companion.

The situation resolved itself when Minar struck up a sexual relationship with Vilaria, who would take Fedar's former position as second in command. She was a vivacious woman a few years older than he, with deep black hair, soft olive skin, and sultry brown eyes that could stop a man dead in his tracks. He had courted her very carefully, abandoning the macho bravado for the intellectual side of his nature. Vilaria also wanted a sex partner for the voyage, so she went along with Minar's advances, finding him attractive and pleasant enough to be with. It was not the deep love that Josh and Fela or Rosilea and Vinar felt for each other, but it would do for them. This time, the ship would be adequately stocked with birth control medications and devices.

There would be another crew member aboard ship, who was no longer subject to suspicion and doubt - Zenar, the Corilian commander. He was intimately familiar with the ship's many systems and would be an invaluable member of the crew. Time and time again since the Corilian defeat he had proven his willingness to assist the Senians in preparing the ship for the mission. He had also provided invaluable intelligence about the political situation on Corilia, what the Tskar knew about the Corilian underground, and Corilia's military capability to mount an additional attack. None of his information could be verified, but much of it conformed with what they knew about Corilia from the Corilian underground.

There had been a heated debate at the Supreme Council as to whether he should be allowed to go on the mission. Fedar and Vilaria were present. He would have the ability to endanger the mission if that was his desire. Perhaps all of his cooperation was a ruse to get on the mission, it was argued, and his loyalties still rested with Corilia. It was not in Corilia's best interest for Senia and Earth to form an alliance. On the other side of the argument was the benefit he could provide to the mission and the fact that he had spared the Capitol from destruction.

After much debate the Chancellor turned to Fedar, who had been quiet throughout the discussion.

"You're the Captain," he said. "Tell us what you think."

Fedar went with his gut. "I think he will be a valuable member of the crew."

That decided it in favor of Zenar going on the mission. He would be part of the engineering crew under Elar with the same status as Minar. Minar was happy about it, as he had grown to like Zenar despite his early suspicions.

Josh would have official status on the mission as Bandar's assistant in the horticultural area. With the larger crew, there would be more work needed to supply the ship with food. Rosilea would help in preparing the meals if Salea and Nemar ultimately decided that Vinar could go.

Josh's role would really kick in when they returned to Earth. He would be responsible for making contact and providing for a peaceful entry. If that went well, he would help the Senians navigate through life on Earth, including the transfer of Senian technology to Earth and establishing the Senia – Earth Foundation, which was chartered to provide for peaceful cooperation between Senia and Earth, preparing a return mission from Earth to Senia with as much refined uranium as the ship could carry, benefiting the human condition on Earth, and preserving and expanding democratic institutions on Earth.

It was a tall order, and Josh could only guess at what Earth would be like when they arrived in the year 2017. He now felt a great loyalty to the Senian people. They were his family. He thought about the Watergate scandal, and how close the U.S. had come to losing its democracy. And there was the Soviet Union with its militaristic expansionism in the name of communism. He wondered about many things.

Would they find a planet where the U.S. was not longer democratic?
Or worse, perhaps the Soviets now rule half the planet.
Or even worse, perhaps there has been a nuclear war!

Now that Vinar had graduated with honors from the Space Academy, he was really needed for the mission, so that there would be some young blood in case any of the older crew did not survive the voyage. And then, there was also the possibility of a return voyage to Senia. If he went on the mission, he would be third in line for command after Fedar and Vilaria.

Vinar desperately wanted to be a part of the mission. As it turned out, it was no longer about being with Rosilea, as they were now married and she would stay with him on Senia if he did not go. It was all about Salea, and whether she would consent to losing her only child for the rest of her life. Nemar was still of the mind to let Vinar go if that was what he wanted. Ultimately, it was up to Vinar, as he was now well of age and did not need Salea's consent. Still, he could not bear the thought of going against her in that way.

Salea thought of nothing else in the weeks leading up to the departure date. She could not decide, constantly flipping back and forth.

What if he were to perish during the mission? she thought. *It was for his own good that he not go. Rosilea will stay with him on Senia, so why should he go? But he will hate me for the rest of his life if I stand in the way. Perhaps one day he will thank me. Am I being selfish? This is what he really wants to do.*

Am I only thinking of myself?

On and on it went in her mind until they were sitting down for lunch nine days before the departure date. Rosilea was visiting with Fela and Josh in their apartment at the Capitol. Vinar could wait no longer for an answer. They were starting to provision the ship and needed to know whether it would be supplied for him and Rosilea, and any possible new arrivals.

"They are starting to bring supplies on board the *Friendship*," he said, looking over at Salea. "I need to tell them whether I am going."

Salea, her eyes buried in her plate, looked up to see his earnest expression, pleading with her to say that it would be alright.

"Do you really want to do this?" she said, hoping against hope that he would express some doubt.

"More than anything that I have ever wanted in my life," he replied.

"Why?" she said in reply. "Why are you not content to stay on Senia with Rosilea?"

"It is not about Rosilea, mom. Space travel is something I have always wanted to do. I want to do something meaningful with my life."

Salea looked over at Nemar, who, as usual, was silent. She knew better than to ask him what he thought, as she knew what the answer would be.

Tears started to flow. "I will be losing my only child. I will never see you again."

"Mom, I love you. If you don't want me to go, I won't go."

The tears started to dry up. She needed to calm down. After all of the thought she had given it, she knew that she could not stand in the way of what he wanted to do with his life.

"I will miss you so," she said. "But I can't stand in your way if that is what you really want to do."

"It is what I really want to do. And I will miss you and dad more than I can say."

Vinar looked over at Nemar. His normally somewhat stoic facial expression had given way to sadness and loss.

"Son, we all must find our own way in life. You will be doing something very important for the people of Senia. I will miss you very much, but I will be proud of you."

"And I will be proud of you too," Salea chimed in.

Vinar walked around the table to where Salea was sitting and put his arms out. She stood up and they embraced as her tears again began to flow. Then, he walked over to Nemar and they embraced as well.

Vinar wanted to tell Rosilea and thought of calling her, but this was something he wanted to tell her in person. He cleaned up the dishes as Salea continued to sit at the table with her head in her hands, trying to contain her tears.

Nemar leaned over the table and took her hand.

"You did the right thing."

"I know," she replied, "but it's hard."

Vinar went outside to call Rosilea. He didn't want Salea to hear his excitement.

"Got to see you. I have something important to tell you. Meet me at the apartment."

He maintained an even tone, concealing his excitement, as he wanted her to be truly surprised when he told her the news.

"Okay," she replied. I will be there in 50 quarseks."

He dashed off in his car. Salea settled into Nemar's arms on the couch. They listened to a recording of a quartet playing light, soulful music, not saying much as they thought about their soon to be new reality without Vinar as a part of their lives.

Rosilea beat him back to their apartment, waiting anxiously as he walked through the door.

"What is it?" she said, her eyes filled with nervous anticipation, not knowing whether her life would continue on the Earth mission or Senia.

"My mom has said that I can go on the Earth mission."

He watched as Rosilea's facial expression went from anxious concern to sheer joy.

"Why didn't you tell me when you called?" she said with a slight touch of disapproval. "I was so afraid you were not going to be able to go."

"I wanted to be here when I told you. I'm sorry. I should have told you right away."

She reached up with both arms around his shoulders to kiss him.

"I forgive you."

With that, they kissed a nice long kiss.

Rosilea broke it off.

"I have to call my mom and dad."

Josh and Fela were sitting in their living room watching a fantasy about the Corilian underground when the call came. There was a smiling, very happy Rosilea with Vinar's also smiling face right behind her. It could mean only one thing.

"Why are you two so happy?" Fela said, trying not to steal their thunder.

Rosilea looked over to Vinar. He should break the news.

"My mom has agreed that I can go on the Earth mission," he said, in a somewhat serious tone.

Fela could hardly conceal her joy, but she knew that her joy was at Salea's expense, so she tried to do so.

"How is she?" Fela replied with genuine concern.

"She's sad."

"I'm so sorry. I have to call her."

Josh interjected, "Can I tell Fedar tomorrow?"

"Yes."

"He will be glad to know that you are going on the mission."

"I'm very excited about going," Vinar replied.

After they disconnected, Fela was confronted with the need to talk to Salea. She could hardly think of what to say, but knew that she had to call her.

Salea was still nestled in on the couch next to Nemar when the monitor signaled the incoming call. She hesitated for a moment before picking up, not knowing what she would say to Fela.

Fela spoke first. "Vinar has just told me that he will be going on the Earth mission. I want to thank you, but I know you did not do this for me. You did it for Vinar. I just want you to know that I will be whatever you want me to be for Vinar."

Salea was relieved. The words flowed easily. "I want you to love him like I do."

For Fela the words also flowed easily. "It is so wonderful for you to say that. I will love him just as I love Rosilea."

It was November 2, 2000, on Earth. On that day the first American-Russian crew arrived at the International Space Station.

On Senia, there was no question that this day would be an historic planetary event. The Chancellor and various other dignitaries were assembled at the Base Sinarta for the *Friendship*'s departure for Earth. The news media would broadcast the departure ceremony and the actual takeoff of the *Friendship* over the entire planet.

Friends and family of the crew had front row seats in the audience. Salea and Nemar were there, feeling both somber and proud as they saw Vinar standing on the platform with the other crew members.

The Chancellor reflected the joyful mood of the people and spoke vociferously about the events that had unfolded over the years that had elapsed since defeating the Corilian attack, remediating all of the damage, and preparing for the Earth mission. He talked about the courage and dedication of the crew and mentioned Zenar's participation in the Earth mission as perhaps signaling a better future in which Corilia and Senia would one day be again united in a common purpose.

When the ceremony was over, the crew departed from the platform for one last goodbye with their family and friends before entering the *Friendship*. Salea gave Vinar one last hug as Josh, Fela, Rosilea, the Chancellor and Keala watched.

She turned to Fela. "You will take good care of my boy," she said, tears flowing down her face.

Fela, hardly knowing what to say, went over to her and they embraced.

"He is my son too," she said. "I could not love him any more than I do now."

They smiled at each other and parted.

After many more goodbyes, the crew assembled again on the platform that would take them to the entry port on the second level. The Chancellor and a few other Senian dignitaries stood on the platform and gave them the traditional Senian farewell bow of the head as they passed by.

Their world changed when the entry port closed. Suddenly, the freedom of movement the *Explorer* crew had rejoiced in for many years was gone. But they had the advantage of being "space acclimated," as they would say.

For Vinar and the other crew going on their first space voyage, it was a different feeling. There was an eagerness and excitement about traveling into space that overshadowed any thought about being confined for the next eighteen Senian years to the narrow corridors and small rooms of the *Friendship* amidst the infinite reach of space. That would come later.

There was only room for seven on the bridge. Vinar and Rosilea were allowed on the bridge, along with Fedar, Vilaria, Banar, Zofar and Bandar. Josh and Fela strapped themselves to seats in the central area, while Elar, Minar, and Zenar strapped down in the engineering area. The monitors were split into two screens, showing the view from above and below.

Reporters and cameramen buzzed about below, getting into position to record the takeoff. The sky was crystal clear blue with the sun shining brightly near its apex for the day. Fedar hit the command sequence on his screen and the outer rim levitated from its stationary position and slowly and quietly began to turn. A cheer went out from the crowd. Then the stabilizer jets along the perimeter of the ship began to blow air toward the pavement as the outer rim accelerated and began to make a high pitched whirring sound.

Fedar activated the gravitational field generator and the ship gently lifted off as the crowd continued to cheer. The whole planet cheered along with them. Everyone on board was struck by the moment, but no one more than Zenar. The only time he could recall such cheering at an official event was when it was forced by the Tskar.

After the ship gained about 500 feet altitude, Fedar decided it was time to make their exit. He spoke into the monitor.

"This is it. Hold on. We are on our way."

After entering a few more commands, the magnetic fields turning the now rapidly rotating outer rim reversed and the *Friendship* lurched off to the east toward the Senian Sea, perhaps never to return. The cheering below slowly died down. Some felt the Earthman had brought them luck in defeating the Corilians. Hopefully, luck would stay with them on their journey back to Earth.

CHAPTER 11 - EARTH'S MANY CHALLENGES

While Josh and the Senians bolted through space for the next seventeen Earth years at near light speed, events on Earth continued to progress at a rapid pace. On the positive side, the digital revolution took hold in full swing, rapidly transforming Earth's technology across the full spectrum of scientific and artistic endeavors. On the negative side, the threat of Soviet expansionism that the Earth faced for many years was replaced by a major threat from extremist elements of Islam that would stop at nothing to impose their views on other Muslims. The United States fought two major wars in the Middle East. The promise presented by the breakup of the Soviet Union and democratization of Russia significantly deteriorated as Russia evolved into a political monopoly under the leadership of Vladimir Putin.

After the breakup of the Soviet Union in 1991, the new Russian Federation struggled under dire economic conditions for many years. Mr. Yeltsin was re-elected President in 1996, beating the candidate of the Communist Party, which had experienced a resurgence among a large part of the populace that sought a return to the financial security and domestic order under he former Soviet Union. Confusion and disarray continued to reign after Mr. Yeltsin's re-election, with repeated reshuffling of the cabinet and firing of the Prime Minister. In 1998, Russia defaulted on its international debt. The atmosphere in foreign affairs began to become more hostile toward western interests. Then, at the end of 1999, Mr. Yeltsin suddenly resigned from office, naming Vladimir Putin, his newest Prime Minister, to become the Acting President. Mr. Putin had resigned from the KGB in opposition to the 1991 coup attempt against Secretary Gorbachev and had been active on the liberal side of Russian politics.

Mr. Putin was elected President the following year. Under his leadership, the Russian economy began a period of vast improvement. The legal and tax systems were greatly improved through the implementation of new codes. The power of the oligarchs was reigned in, but forced to go along with Putin's leadership. Major industries were reorganized to be competitive on an international scale, while also being closely tied to Putin's influence and control. The economy greatly benefited from a substantial rise in oil prices.

The restoration of economic security and political stability was widely supported by the Russian people, and Mr. Putin maintained major popular support. He was re-elected President in 2004, and then appointed Prime Minister from 2008-2012, as he was prohibited from serving more than two consecutive terms as President. He was then re-elected President in 2012.

The year 2014 saw a major turn toward deteriorating relations with Western Europe and the U.S. as a result of a revolution in Ukraine, a former Soviet Republic. Relations had been in a downward trend over many years due to Putin's efforts to consolidate his control over Russian institutions, limit press freedoms, while being accused of using physical intimidation and murder against his political opponents. The Ukrainians threw out their Russia-leaning President in favor of leadership that favored closer economic and political cooperation with Western Europe and the satellite nations of the former Soviet Union. Separatist elements developed in Eastern Ukraine and Crimea, which Putin supported with arms and advisors. Russia then invaded the Crimea Peninsula. After a popular referendum approved seceding from Ukraine and becoming a part of Russia, the Crimea was annexed into the Russian Federation. Western nations refused to recognize the legitimacy of the election and secession from Ukraine. After annexing Crimea, Putin provided active military support for the separatists in Eastern Ukraine, resulting in a prolonged war with much destruction and many casualties.

Mr. Putin's policies toward Ukraine led to the imposition of an array of economic sanctions by the U.S. and Western Europe, which, along with a major drop in oil prices, significantly damaged the Russian economy. Years of economic progress with the benefit of western trade and investment wasted away under a steep decline in the ruble and a sharp rise in inflation. Putin's desire not to be seen as backing down over Ukraine led to an uneasy calm, with Russian separatists maintaining their control over the Donetsk region of eastern Ukraine. Large quantities of U.S. liquefied natural gas were being shipped to Ukraine and throughout Europe in order to reduce reliance upon Russian natural gas. The Russian natural gas pipeline to China was in service and Russia and China were growing ever closer in their geopolitical alliance against the United States and to some extent Europe.

As the Senians approached Earth, relations had grown steadily worse since the annexation of Crimea, with talk of a revival of the "Cold War" against the former Soviet Union. Russia actively opposed western interests in the Middle East. Its military became more aggressive at probing western air defenses. There began to be more talk among some of the more belligerent elements in the Russian command structure about the use of Russia's nuclear arsenal.

The many years the Senians spent quietly traveling toward Earth were also a tumultuous time for the Middle East, with the region in a state of near chaos as they approached Earth. Saddam Hussein remained in power after the 1991 Gulf War. Throughout the 1990s, he played a cat and mouse game with United Nations weapons inspectors seeking to determine if Iraq was engaged in development of nuclear weapons and other chemical or biological weapons of mass destruction.

Terrorist attacks against soft civilian targets proliferated. In 1993, a small group of terrorists, introduced to each other by a Muslim cleric, detonated a truck bomb in the parking garage of the World Trade Center in Manhattan, hoping to cause one building to collapse upon the other. They caused extensive damage, but their plan to collapse both buildings failed.

The second time around for the World Trade Center came on September 11, 2001, this time succeeding in destroying both structures and taking thousands of lives. The attack was eventually acknowledged to have been the work of al-Qaeda, a loosely knit terrorist organization led by Osama bin Laden. It was an offshoot of the Mujahideen who resisted the Soviet occupation of Afghanistan in the 1980s and now took shelter in Afghanistan, which was under the rule of the Taliban - a group that believed in strict adherence to Islamic Sharia law.

The September 11 attack, as it came to be known, precipitated a massive military response from the United States and other nations that took part in the coalition. President George W. Bush, with widespread public support, invaded Afghanistan less than one month after the September 11 attack, seeking to remove the Taliban from power and deny al-Qaeda its training camps and refuge in the country. They succeeded in removing the Taliban from power relatively quickly, but by 2003 the Taliban had reconstituted itself to begin a guerilla war against the Afghan government and coalition forces that was still ongoing as the Senians neared Earth in the year 2017.

In 2003, after much debate about whether Iraq was in possession of or developing weapons of mass destruction, President Bush ordered an invasion to remove Saddam Hussein from power and determine once and for all whether such weapons existed. Saddam was quickly removed from power, along with members of his Ba'ath Party, which was dominated by Sunni Muslims. The Sunni Muslims then formed an insurgency against the Shia-dominated government that was established after free elections. This insurgency grew as the new Shia-dominated government failed to be representative of Sunni interests throughout the country. The U.S. and coalition forces were largely successful in suppressing the insurgency after many long years of war. President Obama withdrew U.S. combat forces in August 2010 and then withdrew the remaining "advise and assist" forces in

December 2011 after the Iraqi government would not agree to grant U.S. troops immunity from criminal prosecution under Iraqi law.

U.S.-trained Iraqi forces ultimately proved not up to the task of defending their country against the Sunni-led insurgency. A new group, known as the Islamic State of Iraq, continued to carry out terrorist attacks against civilian and military targets, and in 2014 seized control of large portions of the country, including major cities. President Obama returned some forces to Iraq for training and aerial combat missions, as the country again descended into exchanges of terrorist attacks between Shia and Sunni fighters.

In what became known as the "Arab Spring," a movement toward democracy swept across many of the authoritarian regimes of the Middle East and North Africa, starting in Tunisia and including Egypt, Libya and Syria. Egypt ultimately returned to military control after its experiment in democracy failed to produce leadership that reflected the national interest. Libya descended into a war between competing forces seeking to control the country. Syria fell into a bloody civil war between the prior government, the Free Syrian Army, and other militant groups seeking to gain a foothold amongst the chaos. The Islamic State of Iraq ultimately gained a major foothold, controlling considerable territory and seeking to establish a Islamic caliphate across the region, including the territory it controlled in Iraq. As the Senians approached Earth, battles continued across the region.

China's economic miracle continued under the leadership of Deng Xiaoping's successors, such that it became the Earth's second largest economy. As the Senians approached Earth, China was projecting increased military power throughout the Asia-Pacific region and actively investing in the development of natural resources all over the planet in order to meet the needs of its rapidly expanding economy. It had assumed a major geopolitical role on the world stage, often neither directly opposing nor aligning with western interests.

The digital revolution was essentially complete, although there was no telling where it would continue to lead. The World Wide Web had many millions of websites. Electronic mail had largely replaced written office communications. Internet use was widespread for gaining information about just about anything. Televised entertainment was rapidly migrating to the internet. Personal computers penetrated most households in the industrialized nations and mobile computers, including phones and watches, were ubiquitous over much of the planet.

CHAPTER 12 - RETURN TO EARTH

November 7, 2017. The *Friendship* was still decelerating, about 35 million miles from Earth. The sun, about 120 million miles away, filled the bridge with intense light. Zenar, Vilaria, Banar, Vinar and Josh were on the bridge, wearing protective shielding over their eyes. In an hour or so, they would install the bridge shielding, but for now they wanted to see the full panorama of space. Earth was now coming clearly into view in an awesome panorama of the solar system that included Mercury, Venus, Mars, Saturn, Jupiter and Neptune in their orbits.

They were now measuring their speed in miles per hour instead of miles per second. In about five days they would be drawn into a wide elliptical orbit about 120 miles above the Earth at its closest point. This would allow them to gather data and make observations when close to the planet, then swinging as far away as possible from the planet to minimize the possibility of detection. Once within Earth's gravitational field, orbital adjustments could be made using the gravitational field generator.

Josh had spent countless hours thinking about how they should make themselves known to Earth. He knew they would be detected by the military, and probably university scientists. His greatest concern was that they not be sequestered off to a military base and held captive while the military or unscrupulous power brokers attempted to steal Senian technology. Not knowing the state of world affairs and governance in the United States in the year 2017 left him doubtful about what to do. Worst case scenario, although not likely, the United States had become a dictatorship like the Soviet Union. Best case scenario, things were pretty much the same as when he left. He did not imagine that the Soviet Union would have dissolved or that militant Islamists were now a major new threat to world order.

They would orbit for a few days and gather as much intelligence as possible. Everyone on the *Friendship* now knew how to speak English, so there would be no difficulty ascertaining the state of world affairs from news broadcasts. He thought all they would be doing is locating the major U.S. news media and the BBC and had no conception of the proliferation of the internet on Earth during his absence.

The key planning was done by Fedar, Vilaria, Zenar, Banar, Josh and Vinar. On the assumption that the United States was still a democracy, they decided to make their presence generally known over the news media before seeking permission to land from the military. This meant flying over a major American city in broad daylight, where their presence could not be covered up as just one more natural phenomenon mistaken for a UFO. New York City immediately came to mind to Josh and that became the plan. After that, they would make a video broadcast from the ship on a frequency that would be detected by the news media. Once their presence was generally known, the military would not be able to indefinitely sequester them away.

Any fear that Zenar would somehow sabotage the mission never materialized. As hard as he tried not to think about it, the thought of sabotaging the mission sometimes crossed through his mind during the early years. He would think about how he could redeem himself, unknown to anyone on Corilia, but in his mind, for his transgressions in failing to be loyal to the Tskar. Then he would quickly overrule that thought. The Tskar did not deserve any loyalty. He would probably murder his family when he learned of the failure of the attack.

And what was there to be loyal to?

Just a tyrannical regime. Now that he had experienced for the first time in his life a society that was not based upon tyranny, he knew that he could never betray his captors, who had treated him with kindness, despite the harm the Corilians attempted to inflict on Senia. Eventually, thoughts of betraying Senia faded from his mind.

In any case, it would not have been easy. Any attempt to cause the ship to deviate from its course would have been immediately detected. The nuclear power generation system had several layers of failsafe mechanisms to prevent an overload. This was Corilian technology that was designed with the Corilian underground in mind.

After the solar shield was deployed, Josh decided to check on Fela, Rosilea, and her two children, Josar and Misha. Josar, age fourteen, was the oldest, named after Josh. Misha, age eleven, was named after Fela's brother, Mishar. It was time to start preparing for the mid-day meal and they would all be in the central area.

Josar sort of looked like Josh. He had Josh's dark features and looked like he would be fairly tall, but with Vinar's Senian blood, his cranium was shaped like a Senian. He was very bright and spoke fluent English and Senian, as did Misha. Misha was beautiful, like her mother and grandmother, with dark green eyes and soft light brown hair. She too was Senian in her cranial appearance and very bright.

There was another child on board. Minar and Vilaria did not intend to have any children when they started the voyage. That changed after Josar was born and they decided, in the boredom of space, that a child would add something meaningful to their lives. They were married by Fedar, and with his consent, Vilaria gave birth to Valdar, now age twelve. He was a very rambunctious lad, full of energy, constantly running about the ship on the edge of getting into some kind of trouble. He certainly fulfilled their desire to help fill their empty days in space. Still, they had no second thoughts and loved him dearly.

Josh walked into the room and Josar and Misha immediately rushed to greet him. Josh, now sixty-seven, was starting to look like a grandfather with streaks of grey peppering his still thick head of wavy brown hair.

"What are you rascals up to?" he said in English.

"Nothing much," Josar replied, sounding somewhat bored.

"Do you want to go up to the bridge later? We can now see Earth and almost the entire solar system."

"Yes," they both eagerly shouted.

"Five more days and we will be orbiting Earth."

Valdar, who was helping Rosilea cut vegetables, heard Josh and quickly asked: "Can I go too?"

"Of course," Josh replied.

Fela got up from looking into space in her seat by the monitor to join the conversation. She was now most stately in appearance and still very beautiful. Her dirty blond hair was peppered throughout with fine shades of grey.

"Five more days," she said, with some trepidation in her voice. She knew that the Earth landing was subject to much uncertainty and could be dangerous.

"Yep," Josh replied. "Five more days and I'll be able to take you to Nathan's for a hot dog."

They laughed. He knew that it would be much longer than that.

November 12, 2017, 1:36 a.m., eastern U.S. time zone. Their speed was now about 17,000 miles per hour. In fifty-one minutes the *Friendship* would be entering orbit. The Earth loomed large ahead of them with the sun off to their left, filling the bridge with bright light as Fedar, Josh, Vilaria, Banar, Vinar and Fela, wearing their eye protection, anxiously awaited their entry into orbit. Elar, Minar and Zenar were in engineering, ready for whatever might arise. The rest of the crew, Rosilea, and the children were gathered in the central area, watching their approach on the monitor. They did not have any control over their path around the Earth for the initial orbit, as this was determined by their course from Senia and the Earth's position in its orbit as they approached.

They had detected the space station and the large number of satellites orbiting the planet and were concerned that Earth might have technologically advanced to the point where it could present a threat to their craft from below. The *Friendship* was equipped with two high powered lasers from the Senian defense fleet and could down an incoming missile if necessary.

For several days they had detected signals transmitted to the satellites that circled the planet. Fedar was astonished to realize that, in the relatively short time since their last visit, Earth had developed what appeared to be a global communications system similar to that on Senia. They were overwhelmed by the flood of transmissions and could not make much of it. Most of it was personal communications in a multitude of languages that did not tell them what they needed to know about the military or geopolitical situation. Hopefully, they would learn more as they orbited the planet.

They sat transfixed on the beautiful blue planet, covered with water, until it was time to enter orbit. As they anxiously clutched their seats, the command and control system placed them within reach of Earth's gravity and they began their course around the planet.

"It looks like it will be mostly ocean on this orbit," Fedar said.

"We're coming in over the Pacific Ocean," Josh replied.

Their orbit would take them at about a thirty degree angle to the poles.

The sun was shining brightly as they began their orbit in a northerly direction over the Southern Pacific.

"What is that below?" Josh said, looking at what appeared to be brownish clumps over the blue waters of the Pacific.

Fedar drew them into sharp focus on the monitor and they could now see that these were vast islands of trash that covered this portion of the Pacific.

"They were not here on our last mission," he said.

"It looks like we haven't stopped polluting our planet," Josh replied.

Fedar touched his controls a few times and their trajectory over the planet appeared in front of them on a holographic projection of the Earth. It would take them over the west coast of the United States and then over Canada and the northern Atlantic Ocean. The sun was rapidly dropping down over the ocean behind them as they approached the United States.

Josh could hardly wait to see his homeland. The abundance of satellites and ground communications had given him some assurance that there had apparently not been a nuclear war since he left. Still, this concern was paramount in his thoughts.

Soon they were over Southern California. It was 12:15 a.m., Pacific time. The dense patterns of light over Los Angeles and the other cities along the California coast became apparent and contributed to Josh's sense of relief that at least the Earth had managed to avoid a nuclear war in the many years that had passed since he last walked along the shore at Crescent Beach.

As they entered orbit over the United States, they were detected by US satellite defense systems. At first, there was alarm that it might be an incoming missile. That alarm soon gave way to the realization that the space object was in planetary orbit. General Florence, the duty officer at NORAD command, raised the alert level one notch. There was no known basis upon which an orbital satellite could suddenly appear without the launch first being detected by their satellite systems.

Are we dealing with a UFO? he thought.

A general alert was issued and the space station was notified to be on the lookout for the new space object. General Florence considered whether he should make contact with the Russians to try to confirm that they did not have anything to do with the new entry into Earth orbit. It was now 1:30 a.m., Mountain Standard Time. He decided that, as there appeared to be no immediate threat, he would continue to observe the object before contacting the Russians.

The *Friendship* was detected by the Russians as it passed over the northern Atlantic on its initial orbit. They too were initially alarmed, but soon came to the same conclusion as the Americans that a mysterious new object had suddenly appeared in orbit over the planet.

General Ruskoff considered whether he should contact his American counterpart to discuss what they had observed. Cooperation between the Russian and American military's had deteriorated significantly over the last few years as a result of the dispute over eastern Ukraine. Nevertheless, at 2:30 a.m., Mountain Standard Time, he decided that he needed to make contact.

The signal flashed on the hot line at NORAD Command that the Russians were seeking to make contact. General Florence, wearily sipping on a cup of coffee, was still on duty. He gave the okay and General Ruskoff appeared on the monitor.

General Ruskoff, speaking fairly good English, spoke first.

"We have detected an object orbiting the Earth that appears to have come from nowhere. Do you know anything about it?"

General Florence replied: "We have detected it too and are tracking it. It is not from us. We think it may be a UFO. If they come in range of one of our satellites and we can get a better look, we will let you know."

"We will do the same," General Ruskoff replied.

General Ruskoff was one of the generals within the command structure who was dismayed about the deterioration of cooperation between the Americans and Russians.

After passing over Greenland, Fader began to alter their course so they would be perpendicular to the equator. The gradual orbital adjustments meant that the next orbit over the United States would take them over the Rocky Mountains. It would take several orbits around the planet before they achieved the correct orbit.

After the *Friendship* achieved the desired orbital alignment, Fedar activated the photographic systems. Over the next twenty-seven hours they would survey the entire planet. The data would then be compared with the data they obtained in 1977 and they would decide how to proceed in making contact and entering U.S. airspace.

November 12, 2017; 2:30, p.m., Eastern Standard Time. Fader is now asleep in his quarters and Vilaria has the bridge. Josh is very weary, having been up for over twenty hours. Still, now that the Earth is illuminated by the sun, he cannot bring himself to stop looking out the bridge and at the monitor showing the lands and cities below in greater detail.

He was amazed to see all of the lights along the east coast of China and can hardly wait to see what it looks like during the day. They are now coming up over the east coast of Africa, which looks calm and peaceful. Banar was able to locate the broadcast frequencies for CNN and the BBC, and they know that is not the case on the ground, where the northern part of the continent is still being ravaged by the battle against Islamic militants in Nigeria, Mali, Libya and Sudan.

They have also learned about the group called ISIS and the war that is raging across the Middle East. Zooming in on the monitor, he can see the destruction across Syria and large portions of Iraq.

In addition to the many ongoing battles against ISIS and others of similar ilk, the Earth was also dealing with a rapidly spreading pandemic of the H5N1 virus, commonly known as "bird flu." The virus, with a sixty percent fatality rate in humans, had remained under relative control since it first infected humans in the early 2000s due to its lack of human to human transmission. This changed in 2016 when a new mutated form of the virus became airborne and readily transmissible between humans. It first appeared in Asia, killing hundreds of thousands, and then rapidly spread over the globe, killing many millions more. A vaccine was developed as rapidly as possible, but it proved to be largely ineffective. The virus, once having mutated in favor of airborne transmission, continued to mutate against various forms of vaccine. The world was gripped by this new fear. People avoided large gatherings and public places. About the only entities that could be said to have benefited economically from the pandemic were the makers of surgical masks.

Josh could not stay up any longer. As they began to circle over the North Pole, he retired to his quarters where Fela was sound asleep.

The *Friendship* was now being carefully tracked in a coordinated effort by the Americans, Russians, European Space Agency, China and India. General Florence had notified Air Force Colonel John Milsap, who was responsible for the group within the Pentagon that maintained records of purported UFO sightings and the Air Force investigations. It did not take long for them to locate the records of the June 15, 1977, incident, which was the only incident in the long history of purported UFO sightings that had been confirmed as involving a UFO. The report included reference to a person named Josh Rinaldi, whose disappearance from Crescent Beach, Florida, on the same day had been resolved by the local police as an unsolved murder. Knowledge of the incident had been initially suppressed from the news media, and when there were no further incidents, the matter faded from the consciousness of the military.

Colonel Milsap transmitted their file of the incident to General Florence, including close up photos of the craft.

We have got to get a picture of this thing, General Florence thought as he flipped through the file.

It is now 9:15 p.m. at the Pentagon, which is still buzzing with activity regarding the sighting. They determined that in a few hours, at 12:19 p.m., a Defense Intelligence Agency satellite would be in position to take photos of the UFO. Air Force Commander, General Ronkowski, and General Joseph Dunford, Chairman of the Joint Chiefs of Staff, had been fully briefed. President Trump would not be apprised of the matter until after they had obtained the photographic evidence.

President Donald Trump was the greatest change to occur in American politics since the third party candidacy of Ross Perot in 1992, the difference being that he had managed to get himself elected under the banner of the Republican Party. His campaign began in 2014 with the slogan, "Make America Great Again" - something had trademarked in 2012 after Barack Obama defeated the Republican Candidate, George Romney, to win another term in office. It was a brash, confrontational campaign, that began with the promise to build a wall along the southern border to stem the flow of illegal immigration and drugs from and through Mexico. To top it off, he promised that he would make Mexico pay for the wall.

The "Make America Great Again" theme also focused upon the people who had suffered in recent decades as a result of the expansion of global trade. This included many working class Democrats, who had become disenchanted with their lives and their economic conditions. He toured the many areas of the "rust belt" in the Midwest where countless factories had shut down due to low-wage foreign competition, and held large rallies where he railed against American businesses that had shifted production to Mexico and elsewhere in order to reduce costs of production.

There was also a racial element among the white working class, who were fed up with the "Black Lives Matter" movement that had become very vocal and disruptive in protesting against police shootings involving black males. The fact that a "black" President, had occupied the White House for eight years caused resentment among a segment of the white male population. President Trump portrayed himself as the "anti-Obama" on virtually every issue of national significance, including President Obama's most notable achievements in enacting a health care law known as "Obamacare," and leading the global community in adopting the Paris Climate Accord to deal with global warming as a result of burning fossil fuels.

The vast majority of political pundits counted Mr. Trump out from the beginning, but his poll numbers and support among a field of seventeen Republican candidates continued to grow. He made many intemperate and even outrageous statements during the campaign, but his base of support was unshaken. He ultimately won the nomination at a non-contested convention. As the election campaign proceeded, the pollsters continued to predict that the Democratic candidate, Hillary Clinton, would win the election. Virtually everyone was stunned on election night when he won several closely contested states in the Midwest that had formerly been considered part of the Democratic "Blue Wall," impenetrable by Republicans in a national election. That tipped the balance and he became the forty-fifth President of the United States.

November 13, 2017, 7:15 a.m., Eastern Standard Time. Lieuten-
ant General H. R. McMaster, President Trump's National Security
Advisor, called the meeting at the White House to order. The Defense Intelligence Agency had now obtained a series of photos of the
craft, confirming beyond any doubt that a starship from another
world was now circling the globe. When compared with the photos
from the 1977 incident, they could see that the craft was of the same
design, only larger. The photos had been shared with the Russians
and other governments around the globe.

The purpose of the emergency meeting was to brief the President, Vice-President and other key White House staff. The Joint
Chiefs of staff were also present. The intelligence regarding the 1977
incident was provided. After some discussion, President Trump concluded that it was not likely the aliens were hostile, as they had not
taken any hostile action during the 1977 incident. All agreed that they
needed to attempt to make contact with the craft.

After some subtle infighting as to who should take the lead, it
was decided that the President's National Security Advisor would be
the spokesperson, with a direct link to the President. The Defense
Intelligence Agency would be responsible for making contact in close
coordination with the Air Force and NORAD Command. The President gave a specific directive that hostile action should not be initiated if the craft entered U.S. airspace.

As they were discussing the situation at the Capitol, Fedar was at
the controls. They were approaching the Rocky Mountains in the last
of their twenty-four orbits around the planet. Josh was back on the
bridge.

National Security Advisor McMaster was in the special situation
room at the Pentagon, surrounded by military brass. With a professional calm masking his underlying sense of great excitement, he began to speak. His audio and video signal would be transmitted over a
variety of frequencies from numerous transmitters across the globe.

"This is a message to the commander of the starship presently in
Earth orbit. My name is H.R. McMaster. I am National Security Ad-

visor to the President of the United States. We wish to make contact and provide for a safe landing if that is your intention. Our President had directed that you may enter United States airspace and that no hostile action will be taken against you. Please contact us on this frequency."

Banar quickly intercepted the signals as they passed over the Mexican border and transmitted it to a monitor on the bridge.

Fedar looked at Josh. "Are we ready to make contact?" he said with some uncertainty, wondering whether they should deviate from their initial plan to first make visual contact over New York City before initiating contact with the military.

"I don't see where we have any choice," Josh replied. "I can still try to get them to agree to allow us to make visual contact over an American city before we land."

"All right," he said with some reluctance. "I will turn it over to you after I make the initial contact."

Josh was ready, having given much thought to what he would say.

"Okay," he replied.

"Banar, open up a channel," Fedar said in English. The moment of contact was at hand after a near lifetime of effort over his voyages to Earth and back in order to learn an Earth language. He was fully prepared to make contact.

Banar opened a channel for audio and video communication and, after some conversation with the communications officer at NORAD command, a secure channel was established.

Fedar appeared on the split screen of the monitor with Lt. Gen. McMaster appearing on the other side. Their signal was transmitted from NORAD Command to the Pentagon and the White House situation room, which was overloaded with the President's key staff and anyone else who thought they might be able to justify their being there for this historic moment.

"I am Commander Fedar Sonderia of the Senian starship *Friendship*."

Everyone on Earth looked in amazement at Fedar, who, although human, was clearly not of the Earth. They were suddenly transfixed by the enormity of the fact that they were actually making first contact with a being from another world. There before them was a stately looking, very elderly human with a somewhat bulbous head speaking in English from the bridge of a spacecraft.

Fedar continued: "We have just completed our survey of your planet and observed its many features and ongoing conflicts."

"Yes," McMaster replied. "It is a beautiful planet, and yes, you will come to find that it has many problems."

"We are here to help you solve those problems."

"We are very happy to hear that," he replied, not knowing whether he could truly trust the aliens who appeared to be so human.

"Where are you from?" he continued.

"We are from a planet we call Senia, which is over sixteen light years from Earth. I have someone I would like you to meet."

"Joshua Rinaldi?" McMaster replied.

"Yes," Fedar said with a smile.

Josh entered the field of view next to Fedar.

"I see you already know my name," he said, somewhat surprised, as his introductory remarks went out the window.

"I've reviewed the report on the 1977 incident. We have some fairly good photos of the spacecraft from that incident. Were you abducted?"

"No. I went voluntarily."

"Why have you returned to Earth?"

"It has always been the Senian's intention to make contact with Earth. They did not want to make contact until they were able to speak an Earth language and knew more about the geopolitical situation on Earth. The purpose of the 1977 mission was to obtain someone from Earth to accomplish those objectives. They knew that an abductee would not necessarily cooperate. They now know the geopolitical situation as it existed in 1977 and whatever we have been able to learn in the last day or so. I gather the United States is still a democracy?"

"More so than ever," McMaster replied. Much has changed since

1977."

"Is there still a cold war with the Soviets?"

"The Soviet Union fell apart in 1991, but we still have difficult relations with the Russians."

Fedar interjected: "We are prepared to share our technology with you. The Senian authorities have authorized me to license this technology and set up what we are calling the 'Senia – Earth Foundation' to promote betterment of the human condition on Earth and Senia."

"We now have a terrible problem now with the Avian Flu virus," McMaster replied. "It has ravaged many countries in Asia and Africa and tremendous resources are being devoted to containing outbreaks in the U.S. and all over the planet."

"I think we can help you with that," Fedar replied. "This ship has our very best bio-medical technology. We have to have that for the safety of the crew."

"How large is the crew?"

"We have fourteen people on board, including three children."

"What arrangement do you have in mind?" McMaster asked.

"We believe that we carry antibodies against all major Earth diseases and that we do not carry any viruses that would present a danger to Earth. Josh was assimilated into our crew without any medical issues. Still, we believe that a period of quarantine would be necessary so that we can be sure that we have all the immunities and will not present a danger to anyone on Earth."

"Yes," McMaster agreed. "Right now there is a lot of concern about the H5N1 virus, and someone is sure to question whether you could be carrying any dangerous organisms."

Josh interjected: "We would like to make our presence known to the general population before being sequestered."

"Why is that?" McMaster asked.

Josh had to think fast. He didn't want to ruin the constructive atmosphere around their discussions by suggesting that they were distrustful of the authorities and wanted the protection of public knowledge of their existence.

"We believe it would be a tremendous unifying event for the

Earth, like the landing of a man on the moon in 1969," he replied.

Fedar chimed in to help out: "It is part of our charter document that we establish friendship and cooperation between the people of Earth and Senia. We cannot do that if knowledge of our existence is kept from the people on Earth."

McMaster sensed that this was going to be a presidential decision.

"I'll have to discuss that with the President."

"Perhaps we could fly by the space station and have that be an introductory event before we land," Josh suggested.

"That might be a good idea," McMaster replied. "Would it be possible for our cosmonauts to board your craft?"

Fedar thought for a moment. The ship was not designed for anything to be accessed from the outside. The only airlock was on the first level for the shuttle bay. If they opened the shuttle bay door in space, the ship would lose some air that would have to be replaced from their pressurized emergency supply. It would be a great risk to the ship under ordinary circumstances, but considering that they were close to an Earth landing, Fedar was willing to take the risk.

"Yes," he replied. "They would need to access the ship from below. There is a shuttle bay door that we will have to open and will lose some of our air supply. They will need to enter the ship with their feet oriented toward the ship, as the gravitational field on that level is toward the center of the ship. Once inside the ship, they can remove their spacesuits and we will supply them with respirators for virus protection. They can then verify that we do not present a threat. The only weapons that we have on the ship are defensive laser systems."

Lt. Gen. McMaster and everyone in the room and at the White House became extremely excited about the prospect of what they were about to encounter. Suddenly, the idea of beings from another part of the galaxy had become very real. The intricacies about the ship's design gave them a sense that interstellar space travel was actually possible and not just a figment of some science fiction writer's imagination.

"That sounds like a good idea," McMaster said with some excitement. I am going to recommend it to the President."

"And then for the landing?" Fedar asked.

"We will have to come up with a plan for that. I will convene an emergency meeting of the National Security Council and the President."

"What about the Russians?" Josh asked. "Is there any chance that they could endanger our ship?"

"The Russians will know about it. There is a Russian cosmonaut aboard the space station. We don't think they have the capability to bring down a satellite and I don't see any reason why they would do that, but you should be on your guard."

"If we see a missile coming at us, we will shoot it down," Fedar replied.

The people in the room looked at each other, thinking about what that technology could mean on Earth.

Fedar began a series of steps to adjust their orbit so that they would be in parallel orbit with the space station. On Earth, while most people in the Capitol were having dinner, the President convened a meeting with the National Security Advisor, Vice-President, the Joint Chiefs of Staff, and the Secretary of Defense. Sandwiches were brought in.

Lt. Gen. McMaster gave a brief introduction and they played the video that was made of the conversation with the aliens and the missing person from Earth. It was quickly agreed that a rendezvous with the space station would be a spectacular event, and the best way to manage relations with the Russians. Virtually all of the major intelligence services were aware of the craft now orbiting the Earth and anxiously awaiting the next developments. There would not be any way to keep this matter secret, even if it was their desire.

Instead, President Trump decided that first contact with beings from another world would indeed be of historic proportions and could possibly serve to ease international tensions if the U.S. cooperated with other nations in the developing events. There was a shared concern about the military implications of the Senian technology falling into the wrong hands. Because there was an American on board the craft, and they would be landing in the U.S., they decided that those concerns could wait for another day.

It was also decided that an American and Russian cosmonaut should board the starship for the first greetings. Despite the tense relations, the U.S. and the Russians were still continuing their cooperation in space and leaving the Russian out would have surely exacerbated tensions and aroused suspicions.

Time was considered to be of the essence to ensure that the craft landed safely and as quickly as possible. President Trump would hold a news conference at 10:00 a.m. the following day in the East Room of the White House, joined by Lt. Gen. McMaster, who would provide the briefing. Assuming there were no security concerns after the inspection, the ship would land at Andrews Air Force Base as soon as it could be arranged. The meeting broke at 7:50 p.m.

For the time being, NORAD command would continue direct communication with the craft in order to maintain secret channels until the President's news conference. Communication would then be turned over to Houston mission control to arrange for the rendezvous with the space station.

At 8:10 p.m. McMaster and his key staff reopened communication with the aliens from the situation room. Fedar, Vilaria, Banar, Zofar, and Josh were on the bridge. The rest of the crew and the children were gathered in the central area watching on the monitor.

"I have discussed the situation with President Trump," McMaster said, trying to give the impression of calm amidst all of the excitement.

"He has decided to go along with your plan for a rendezvous with our space station. After that we want you to land at Andrews Air Force Base outside of the Capitol. We also plan on publicizing the landing, but will maintain very tight security. Preparations are being made to accommodate all of you at Andrews Air Force Base."

"Very good," Fedar replied. "We will stay aboard the craft until we determine that it is safe to leave."

Zofar interjected: "My name is Zofar. I am the Medical Officer. I will provide you with a description of all of the Earth pathogens for which we have developed immunities. I will need you to provide me with a list of all of the Earth pathogens that we are in danger of being exposed to, along with specimens of those pathogens. Can that be done?"

"Absolutely," McMaster replied. "It may take some time though. We have an agency called the Center for Disease Control that is the most medically advanced entity of its kind on Earth. After the landing, I will put you in contact with the Director of that agency."

Fedar spoke next. "We are adjusting our orbit to be in parallel orbit with the space station. It will take us about eleven hours, your time, to be in position. After that we can quickly move into position next to the space station."

McMaster replied. "We want you to land as quickly as possible for your safety. Let's plan on conducting the rendezvous at 2:00 p.m., tomorrow, Eastern Standard Time. We will prepare the landing area so that you can land at 10:00 a.m., Eastern Standard Time, the following day."

"How many do you wish to board our ship?" Fedar asked.

"Two. One American and one Russian. We believe that will help alleviate Russian suspicions and may improve our relations with them."

"We can accommodate two," Fedar replied.

"Very good! This will be quite the event."

McMaster could now hardly contain his excitement. This would be a "where were you when …" event, and he would be an integral part of it.

It was finally time to go home for the evening. McMaster thought about how he would notify the White House reporters about the Presidential press conference, and how they would be buzzing about something to do with the battle against ISIS or Avian Flu, or perhaps tax reform or the never ending effort to pass legislation on immigration. He could hardly wait to see their jaws drop when the President told them the planet was being orbited by beings from another world who would be sending live pictures of their craft from space in a few hours and were scheduled to land at Andrews Air Force Base the following day. Mission Control notified the space station to prepare for the space walk tomorrow. The Russians authorized their cosmonaut to participate.

November 13, 2017, 9:30 a.m., Eastern Standard Time. Banar will be using his communications link with NORAD to monitor the Presidential press conference. Fedar, Vilaria, Banar, Vinar, Josh and Fela are on the bridge. Rosilea is with Josar and Misha in the central area, along with Zofar and Bandar. The engineering crew is in engineering getting ready to receive the cosmonauts.

The East Room is abuzz with reporters and cameramen full of questions and hurriedly trying to get situated.

Why did they not use the press room?

The East Room was for special occasions.

Was this just to announce some new appointments?

Some had been assured that it was more important than that. The word was out that this would be something not to miss, but other than that, the White House was completely mum about it. CNN, the BBC and Al Jazeera would be in attendance, so there would be worldwide coverage.

At the appointed time President Trump and National Security Advisor McMaster took to the podium. The room quickly fell silent as anticipation filled the air. Seeing McMaster, many thought it would have something to do with the war against terrorism.

President Trump got right to it.

"I'm here to announce that we have made contact with human beings from another planet far off in the galaxy and that at 2:00 p.m. today an American and Russian cosmonaut will board their craft and send live video of the event back to Earth. This is a very auspicious moment for our planet Earth, one that I hope will help to bring us together to solve many of the problems that we face today. The space travelers are from a planet they call Senia that is over sixteen light years from Earth. It has taken them almost seventeen years to complete their journey. They come in peace. Aboard their craft is an American citizen who voluntarily left Earth with the Senians in 1977 and has taught them the English language, as well as learning their language. There is much more to tell, but events are moving very rapidly and I'm sure all of you will have much to do to prepare for their two o'clock rendezvous with the international space station, so I will turn this over to my National Security Advisor, Lt. Gen. McMaster, for a few additional questions."

President Trump left the room.

The room fell silent for a moment.

This is a hum dinger if there ever was one, McMaster thought as he looked across the room at the stunned faces of the seasoned reporters who could hardly be shocked by anything.

Hands flew up as the shock wore off. *This must be real*, many thought. *I'm in the East Room of the White House.*

The press conference went on for another fifteen minutes and then McMaster abruptly ended it, as he had much to do. There were many questions about their technology, which McMaster dodged, saying that they did not know very much yet about it. He focused upon their expressed willingness to make their technology available to improving the human condition on Earth, including helping to conquer the Avian Flu virus.

As expected, this precipitated questions about whether the aliens might carry any pathogens that could be dangerous to people on Earth. He explained that the Earth human had no difficulty being assimilated aboard their ship and that, if anything, the danger was that they would contact an Earth pathogen for which they had no immunity. Quarantine of the aliens aboard their ship had already been agreed to for their protection and to ensure that they would not spread any pathogens to Earth. Josh's name was not disclosed, so that he could quietly contact his brother, Bob, and other family members, and not have them swamped by the news media.

November 13, 2017, 1:30 p.m., Eastern Standard Time. The *Friendship* is now in orbit about two hundred feet away from the international space station. Rusty Carter, the American Commander of the mission, and Vladimir Danshov, the Russian cosmonaut, are being outfitted for the space walk. Video of the alien craft, which looks like a flying saucer from the movies of the early 1950's, is being transmitted to Earth, and billions of people are transfixed to their televisions, computers and mobile devices.

Guns fell silent in Syria and the various other war zones across the globe as the combatants huddled around their mobile devices to see the *Friendship* pull up alongside the space station, correcting its trajectory toward the station with a slight jerky movement that set it along a parallel course. For some, this was just another American hoax. Yet, they still watched.

The *Friendship* was now linked to Houston mission control, which would provide the audio and video signal back to Earth. Fedar, Vilaria, Vinar, Banar, and Josh were on the bridge. Josh could hardly stand the anticipation of once again being in close contact with someone from Earth. Elar and Zenar would welcome the space walkers in the shuttle bay and operate the video camera. It was decided that the cosmonauts would only remove their helmets, as it would take too much time for them to remove and then be refitted into their space suits. After their helmets were removed, they would be provided with respirators for their tour of the *Friendship*.

News anchors and commentators around the globe babbled on as Commanders Carter and Danshov exited the space station and slowly jetted over to the *Friendship*, remaining tethered to the space station in case of any mishap. The shuttle bay door slowly opened and released its pressurized air to gain equilibrium with the vacuum of space.

After several very tense minutes, the cosmonauts achieved their position beneath the underbelly of the *Friendship*. They could see the shuttle craft tightly fixed to its moorings. As they turned about to get into position to enter, their spacesuit video cameras beamed the image of the awaiting *Friendship* back to Earth. Even the most extreme doubters were now shaken in their belief that this was an American hoax.

The shuttle bay was just large enough to hold the shuttle craft, with only a few feet of free floor space around the craft. Elar minimized the gravitational field for the shuttle bay so that the cosmonauts would not fall rapidly as they came within its purview and possibly collide with the shuttle craft. Slowly, the cosmonauts descended into the shuttle bay, gently pushing off against the shuttle craft as they descended to the floor.

After they were lightly standing on the floor of the shuttle bay, they released their tethers, attaching them to a small fixture that was installed by Minar close to the shuttle bay door. Elar closed the shuttle bay doors and increased the force of the gravitational field. Carter and Danshov stared at each other in amazement as they slowly became heavier, realizing that the aliens had the technical ability to manipulate the force of gravity.

Air slowly entered the shuttle bay from the ship as the cosmonauts walked around the shuttle and wondered how it could fly. In a minute or two the shuttle bay was fully pressurized and the cosmonauts were given the signal by mission control that it was safe for them to remove their helmets. The door to the ship slid open and Elar and Zenar entered, wearing respiratory apparatus. Videos cameras in the shuttle bay transmitted their movements back to Earth and throughout the *Friendship* as Elar and Zenar assisted the cosmonauts in removing their helmets. At last, with their helmets lying on the floor of the shuttle bay, they were ready for first contact with the Senians.

"Welcome aboard our ship," Elar said in English as he bowed his head in the customary Senian fashion. Cater and Danshov did the same.

Rusty, who was very gregarious and never without something to say, was awestruck. He could now see up close that, although humanoid, the aliens were clearly not of the Earth. He carried the same burden that Neil Armstrong carried when he first set foot on the moon to try to say something meaningful. Yet, all he could think of to say was,

"It is a great honor for me to be the first person to welcome you to Earth."

For Vladimir's part, he offered the customary Russian greeting of friendship, "Nazdrovia."

Then, speaking in English, he said: "I too am honored on behalf of the Russian people to welcome you to Earth."

Elar and Zenar handed over the respirators and helped them get set up. It was now time to enter the ship. Elar opened the shuttle bay door. Once the door was closed, Elar and Zenar removed their respirators. Elar guided them to the elevator that would take them to the bridge while Zenar operated the video camera. Life on Earth virtually stood still watching the unfolding events.

When aboard the elevator, Elar grabbed the handrails and everyone followed suit.

"We are ascending to the bridge and will be reversing gravitational fields," Elar said.

As the elevator began its rotation, Carter and Danshov, who were seasoned space veterans, began to get the urge to vomit. It quickly passed as the gravitational field reversed and they again felt as through they were standing upright. Zenar kept the video camera rolling as people on Earth gasped in wonder at the swaying cosmonauts.

They quickly ascended to the bridge, where Fedar and the others were there to greet them, assembled in a line as the elevator door opened. Fedar came forward, with his strong countenance and head full of thinning grey hair. Banar switched the video feed over to the bridge cameras.

"I am Fedar, Commander of the Senian starship *Friendship*. I too welcome you aboard our ship."

Rusty spoke first. "My name is Rusty Carter. It is a great honor for me to be here to welcome you to Earth on behalf of the United States of America and all of the people of Earth."

Danshov joined in. "My name is Vladimir Danshov. I welcome you on behalf of the Russian Federation and all of the people of

Earth."

Fedar then introduced the other crew members, describing their positions and affording Josh no special preference. When they were through with the introductions, Josh stepped forward.

"I am Josh Rinaldi. I voluntarily left Earth on June 15, 1977. I did not know at the time where I was going or what would happen. Eventually, I learned that I was a part of the Senian mission to establish contact with Earth."

Josh's brother, Bob, now seventy-one years old, gasped in amazement. The brother he had long since given up for dead was alive and a part of the unbelievable unfolding events. Mom and dad were dead. If only they could have lived to see this.

For the next hour, Fedar took the cosmonauts and the people of Earth on a tour of the ship. When they entered the central area, all of the crew except engineering was there to greet them. Fela, Rosilea, and the three children presented an image that instantly endeared them to everyone watching, except perhaps those overcome by hatred for anyone that was not like themselves. Fedar was forthcoming in describing all of the ship's systems, including the laser defenses. It became apparent to everyone that the Senians did not present an offensive threat to Earth.

When the tour was over, they gathered again on the bridge. The bridge cameras transmitted video of the cosmonauts standing on the bridge with their respirators on while the international space station hurled along beside them. The beautiful Earth spread out beneath them with the Milky Way as the backdrop. They could see the vastness of the universe in all directions, a view the cosmonauts had only experienced when they left the station for a space walk, and then were too preoccupied to appreciate.

It was now 4:10 p.m. and time for the cosmonauts to return to the space station. Fedar and the others gathered on the bridge, said their farewells, and the cosmonauts departed with Elar and Zenar down the elevator back to the first level. The shuttle bay cameras transmitted the video signal as the cosmonauts donned their helmets with help from Elar and Zenar. Then, after Elar and Zenar left the shuttle bay, Minar opened the shuttle bay door very slowly to the vacuum of space. The gravitational field generator was turned down and the cosmonauts activated their propulsion mechanisms to leave the craft, reattached to their tethers. As the world continued to watch in amazement, they reentered the space station. Minar closed the shuttle bay door.

Fedar, Josh, and everyone else aboard the *Friendship* were relieved. It had gone well. They had accomplished their objective of paving the way for a safe landing, while at the same time ensuring that they would not be sequestered away to some secret military base, possibly never to be heard from again.

Unbeknown to them, they had also set the stage for a dramatic shift in the Earth's geopolitics. There was a noticeable drop in tension between the Russians and the Americans immediately after the spacewalk. The Americans had invited the Russians to take center stage alongside them in the dramatic events of epic proportions. This greatly increased the sense of pride of the Russian people and their feeling of good will toward America. President Putin could hardly deny or put a sour note on the cooperation that had ensued between their counties. Nor did he want to.

Suddenly, the tensions over Eastern Ukraine palled and elsewhere in comparison to the issues they would have to consider if the Americans were to gain access to the alien's technology. Should Russia respond with belligerency and threats, or cooperation? Belligerency and threats might not do any good if the Americans developed the superior technology. Perhaps it was time to make peace with the Americans. There was much to discuss.

At the White House, the events of the day brought an overwhelming sense of joy and accomplishment. Still, there was little time to contemplate these astounding events. They needed to prepare for the landing tomorrow. McMaster worked feverishly with the White House Press Secretary on what the President would say, while coordinating with the Joints Chiefs and the Air Force command to make sure that security was in place for the landing and Edwards Air Force Base would be able to accommodate the Senians' needs. Banar had communicated the dimensions of the ship and how they would disembark. There was not enough time to construct the platform they would need to disembark from the portal on the second level. Instead, the Senians would be lowered, one by one, from the shuttle bay, using specialized equipment they had developed to rotate between opposing gravitational fields.

What a sight that would be! McMaster thought, as it was explained to him by the Air Force Chief of Staff.

After the spacewalk was over, Josh and Vinar left the bridge to see Fela, Rosilea, Josar and Misha, who were still gathered in the central area. Everyone was watching the Earth coverage of the spacewalk on CNN, from which Banar had now managed to obtain an almost continuous signal as they circled the globe. They laughed as they watched CNN show footage of the spaceship in the 1950s classic movie, "Forbidden Planet," which turned out to be perhaps the most accurate portrayal of an interstellar spaceship.

"It looks like we will be going on that trip to Nathan's after all," Josh said to Fela as he sat down beside her and put his arm around her.

She looked over and smiled and gave him a kiss.

"I'll finally get to see what your Earth food is like."

"You probably won't like it. I don't know that I am going to like it anymore."

Josh was a changed person physically. He now looked like the Senians, very lean with wiry, strong muscles gained through the near daily routine of working out in the exercise room.

The news coverage and commentary was overwhelmingly positive, but there were some who expressed concern about the possible spread of contagions. The White House directed the Director of the Center for Disease Control to appear on multiple newscasts, including CNN, to discuss the measures that would be taken to ensure public safety. For the most part, public fears in the U.S. were calmed, but naturally there were some, not trusting the government, who went into a panic.

There were interviews with world leaders around the globe. The public discussion was uniformly about entering into a new era in human relations, in which the Earth would need to come together and find peaceful ways to solve its many problems with the help of the Senians. Privately, in the councils of Russia, China, and other nations that considered themselves to be adversaries of the United States, the discussion had already started about the Senian's anti-gravity technology becoming available to the United States and its military implications. Needless to say, the generals were alarmed about the implications for the balance of power.

November 14, 2017; 1:00 p.m., Eastern Standard Time. Over the course of the night, Fedar had adjusted their orbit and brought the *Friendship* into a stationary position above the landing area. The *Friendship's* speed was reduced to about 1,000 miles per hour to match the Earth's rotational velocity. There would be no burning reentry through the Earth's atmosphere at the orbital velocity of a typical Earth space vehicle. Instead, the gravitational field generator would first be activated to draw the ship closer to the Earth's gravitational field. Then, as it began to fall toward the Earth, the stabilizers would be activated and the gravitational field would be reversed to bring the *Friendship* gently to the landing point.

Fedar, Vilaria, Josh, Vinar and Banar were on the bridge. It was time to start to begin the final phase of their long journey. One hundred miles below, the world was waiting. Reporters and cameramen from media outlets the world over were gathering and setting up. Security around the base was very tight. A no-fly zone was established over the area and fighters were poised ready to shoot down any intruder.

The White House was deluged with requests to attend the landing and welcoming ceremony from Senators, Congressmen, foreign am-

bassadors, and various other people who considered themselves important enough to warrant an invitation. It was a political and logisti-
cal nightmare. President Trump decided that the VIP section would
be limited to the National Security Adviser, Secretary of Defense,
Joint Chiefs, key Congressional leaders, and the ambassadors from
the five permanent members of the Security Council. Due to quarantine restrictions, there would be no handshakes or close contact with
the Senians, so all the dignitaries were getting was a front row seat to
the landing.

Fedar touched the command sequence to set the landing procedure in motion. The coordinates were programmed into the ship's
computer and everything would proceed automatically. They watched
from the bridge as the Earth grew closer until they entered the strato-
sphere. The Air Force was on full alert in case there was any attempt
by a foreign power to intrude into U.S. airspace. All was quiet. General Florence was in open contact with General Ruskoff. He had
been assured that there would not be a Russian attempt to harm the
craft. The Russians knew that the Americans would not hesitate to
down any craft that entered U.S. airspace. One of the Russian generals had proposed an all out assault against the craft in order to prevent the alien technology falling into Americans hands. President
Putin rejected that proposal.

The Americans and the Russians watched in wonder as their intelligence satellites showed the *Friendship* slowly descending into the
atmosphere. How was it that the Senians could bring their craft out
of Earth orbit without any of the hazards they had come to believe
were an integral part of space travel?

The pace of their descent quickened after they entered the strato-
sphere. Soon they were in free fall and starting to wobble. Fedar activated the vertical stabilizers and the ship leveled out into a smooth
descent. Work and travel along the northeast U.S. had all but come to
a halt as people watched with their eyes, binoculars, and telescopes
for the first sign of the craft. The television cameras at Edwards Air
Force Base, with their telephoto lenses, were fixed upon the sky.

It was a clear day, not unlike the many clear days Josh had experienced on Senia. After twenty minutes, they were at about 20,000 feet altitude. The densely populated East Coast came into view. Three F-16s streaked by, rocking their wings back and forth as if to say "hello." The gravitational field generator had broken their fall and they were now descending at about 70 miles per hour and could be seen with the naked eye from Earth. Television cameras at Edwards and all along the coast were now following their descent as billions of people across the planet watched in amazement and near disbelief. The lull in the myriad battles across the planet continued from the previous day.

It would only be a few more minutes before they would land. Their descent had now slowed to about thirty miles per hour. Fedar activated the landing system and three legs descended from the underbelly of the ship in tripod formation. Fedar had been advised by General Ronkowski to bring the ship down as quickly as possible. They would be most vulnerable to an attack from the ground when they came within range of a hand held missile. There were no imminent threats, but General Ronkowski did not want to take any chances.

When they were about five hundred feet above the base, their descent slowed to around ten miles per hour. The *Friendship* now loomed large over the landing area as the cameras continued to roll against the steady buzz of the reporters' conversations. After a few more tense minutes that seemed like an eternity, the craft gently landed on the pavement. One would have expected cheers or applause from the small audience. Instead, there was stunned silence. The reporters stopped their incessant gabbing and let the event speak for itself.

Fedar had kept the outer rim rotating at near full velocity in case it was necessary to quickly escape from a missile. After they landed, the outer rim slowly decelerated and the high pitched hum faded away. Fedar opened the shuttle bay door. It was now time for them to depart.

Fedar would be the first to exit. He took the elevator, along with

Josh, Vilaria and Vinar, down to the first level. The gravitational field generator for the first level was fully operational, holding everything in place.

News media and guests were cordoned off several hundred feet from the ship. The events close to the ship would be recorded by one Pentagon camera crew, which would transmit its signal live to the news media outlets. The camera moved into place underneath the shuttle bay as the shuttle bay door slowly opened. The shuttle craft could be seen in the upside-down position, but it had been secured to the floor, so the reverse gravitational field was not evident. It became evident when, to the astonishment of billions of viewers, the door to the ship opened and Fedar, Vilaria, Josh and Vinar walked into the shuttle bay upside down.

Fedar strapped himself into the cradle of the cable and pulley system that would lower him to the ground. Vilaria, Josh and Vinar left the shuttle bay, as they would no longer be supported by the gravitational field when Fedar was lowered to the ground. Minar manually operated the control for the shuttle bay gravitational field generator, lowering the gravitational field so that Fedar would be slowly drawn in by the Earth's gravity. Fedar started his descent to the ground. Once outside the ship, his cradle pivoted around as he entered the Earth's gravity so that he was now with his feet toward the ground. After fully within the pull of the Earth's gravity, Minar continued to slowly lower him to the ground.

Everyone cheered and applauded as he touched the ground. From there, the cheers and applause spread through the billions of people watching around the globe. The news cameras zoomed in on Fedar, showing his wise and stately countenance and his exaggerated cranium. If there was need of any additional proof, it was clear that he was not of the Earth. He waved in a gesture of friendship to the crowd of onlookers. The cheers and applause continued.

Fedar stayed by the craft and no one approached due to quarantine restrictions. One by one, all aboard the craft except Minar and Elar were lowered to the ground. They were needed to operate the gravitational field generator and maintain the ship's systems until it could be placed in standby mode.

Josh, Fela, Rosilea, Vinar, Josar and Misha gathered together as a family. Vilaria and Valdar held hands as mother and son, Minar being unable to join them. The cameras rolled as they all waved their hands in the air toward the cheering onlookers.

It was time for President Trump to speak. The cheers died down as he approached the podium, midway between and facing the Senians and the gathered guests.

"This is an historic moment for our world. We have wondered for thousands of years whether there could be life elsewhere in our universe. Now, with your coming to Earth, we learn that, not only is there life elsewhere in the universe, it is very similar to our own.

This is a time of great promise for humankind. Our world has many troubles, and we are hopeful that with your help, we will be able to greatly advance the human condition here on Earth, and one day, throughout our universe, which you have shown us, is possible.

On behalf of all of the people of the United States, and all of the people of our great planet Earth, I extend to you our fervent welcome."

There was another round of cheers and applause as President Trump went back to his place in the crowd and Fedar approached the podium.

"My name is Fedar Sonderia. I am the commander of the Senian mission to Earth. Our mission to Earth is of great importance to the people of Senia, as well as Earth. We seek to have Earth join with us in friendship against dark and evil forces that threaten both Senia and Earth. I will be explaining this to your leaders.

I want to express my appreciation to one of your own people, Josh Rinaldi, who willingly went with us when we last visited Earth in your year 1977 and taught us one of your languages so that we could communicate with you on this visit. Josh and Fela, our linguist, have since married and now have a child, Rosilea, and two grandchildren, Josar and Misha.

Most of us will never be returning to Senia, which is over sixteen of your light years from Earth. Our lives from here on will be as one of you, helping you to live in harmony with your beautiful planet, eradicate disease, and explore our galaxy.

We come in peace and friendship."

Fedar walked back to the ship as the crowd applauded and cheered. The audience of guests and reporters lingered for about fifteen minutes and then disbursed. Fedar and the others waited beneath the *Explorer* until the crowd disbursed and then boarded the ship to begin the quarantine period.

The Americans and Senians agreed that it was best for the crew to stay aboard ship during the quarantine period. Human blood samples and specimens of all Earth diseases that the Senians might be in danger of contracting while in the United States would be provided to the Senians by the Center for Disease Control. Similarly, Senian blood samples would be provided to CDC for analysis as to any pathogens that could possible spread to the Earth population. The Senians would be immunized against any Earth diseases for which there was a vaccine and for which they were not already immunized. If it turned out that the Senians were carrying a pathogen for which there was no immunity on Earth, a vaccine would be developed before the Senians were allowed to come in contact with anyone. There was a reasonable degree of certainty that would not be necessary, as Josh had not developed any illnesses after his quarantine from the crew was removed.

Where to locate the *Explorer* was another important consideration. A secret hanger was being prepared at the Davis Monthan Air Base in Arizona. It was large enough to hold the ship, so there would be no construction that could be detected by Russian satellites. The ship would be flown there secretly at night. Everyone realized that the *Friendship* would be perceived as a threat by America's adversaries and that it was of the utmost importance to protect the *Friendship* from sabotage or outright attack.

After the crew was back aboard ship, Fedar gathered them in the central area. The *Friendship* was still operating on its own power and stood ready to make a quick exit if necessary. Everyone was cheerful, things having appeared to have gone so well.

Fedar addressed the crew:

"Our long journey has come to and end, but our mission is not over. There will be much for us to do in the coming days and we should never let down our guard. We have to stay prepared for any contingency. I thank all of you for your dedication and sacrifice in being a part of this mission. If we are successful, we will have built an alliance with Earth that will provide us with the uranium that we need to maintain our planetary defenses."

At the White House, everyone was ebullient over the apparent success of the events of the last two days. They all gathered in the East Room over wine and various canapés hastily prepared by the White House kitchen. President Trump and the First Lady were there, freely moving among the staff. At least for a little while, the pressured pace of the White House stopped for all to celebrate.

News media the world over continued to have a field day analyzing and pontificating about the developments. Everybody who was anybody had an opinion to offer about what this could mean for the future. The discussion was mostly very optimistic, even overly so. The Senians were going to help Earth conquer disease, eliminate pollution, live in peace, and travel to the stars. Still, there was no discounting the fact that the Senians were a ray of hope for a beleaguered planet.

EPILOGUE - AFTER THE LANDING

The Earth's many wars did not stop after the Senian landing. Slowly but surely, the guns began to fire, the shells flew, limbs were blown through the air, and blood continued to flow. The *Friendship* spent only two days at Edwards. In the dead of night, Fedar piloted the ship to its new secret location.

Josh desperately wanted to see his brother and what remained of the family that he knew, but quarantine would not permit it while at Edwards, and then they were gone. Instead, they spoke and saw each other over the ship's audio-visual system, linked into the system at the Davis Monthan Base.

They remained under quarantine for twenty days. During that time, they spent many hours tuned in to the almost infinite variety of viewing channels, absorbing news of events all over the planet and vastly expanding their knowledge of Earth's many ethnic groups and cultures.

The Center for Disease Control was unable to detect any pathogens in the Senian's blood that appeared to represent a threat to Earth. Initially, it was some brave scientists from the CDC that decided to mingle with the Senians. They were eager to see the *Friendship*'s medical lab and begin their work with the Senians on perfecting a vaccine for the H5N1 virus that would be less susceptible to being rendered ineffective by mutation. A team of three people entered the ship through the ramp that was now constructed to the second level.

Zofar took the lead in analyzing the DNA of the virus and developing a virus with an altered DNA structure that mimicked the most common elements of the virus. The work continued for several months. During that time, additional scientists from several private companies that were working on developing an H5N1 vaccine were brought into the fold, as they would be needed to produce the vaccine. Josh and Fedar insisted that the companies not be allowed to make large profits from the use of Senian technology. An agreement was reached whereby the Senians did not profit at all and the private companies recovered their costs of production with a small profit. It took several months to start producing the vaccine in large quantities. After that, the tide quickly turned in the battle against the H5N1 pandemic, and within about a year, the pandemic was brought under control.

The development of the H5N1 vaccine with Senian technology and guidance was closely followed by news media across the globe. It did much to allay fears about the Senians and demonstrate the promise that lay ahead.

After the quarantine was lifted, Josh, Fela and Fedar were approved for travel throughout the United States. Their first trip was to Washington D.C. aboard an Air Force transport for discussions with military leaders at the Pentagon regarding the licensing and protection of certain technologies that were deemed to be necessary for the national security of the United States and its allies. Fedar was fully cooperative, but wanted to secure licensing fees to initially fund their foundation and provide for the Senians after they left the *Friendship*. Josh retained patent attorneys to draw up the licensing agreements. The Senians received an up-front licensing fee of $100 million, with guarantees of a steady stream of revenue after the equipment went into production.

The Senians' gravitational field generation technology was by far the most significant new technology, but there were others as well. The Senians were well advanced in their development of laser weapons that could rapidly locate and destroy incoming missiles or jets in aerial combat. They could precisely locate and destroy vehicles on the ground, decreasing the risk of civilian casualties.

Congress quickly approved whatever was needed to bring the Senian military technology into production. Within several years, Seoul, Tel Aviv, and other cities suffering under the threat of missile attack were provided the new defensive systems.

After the threat of missile attack against Seoul was removed, the South Koreans initiated a renewed effort to reach an accommodation with the North Korean regime, insisting that there be complete disarmament of nuclear weapons and protection of basic human rights in exchange for stronger economic ties. The North Koreans responded with increased belligerency, threatening to vastly increase their arsenal of nuclear capable missiles to counter the new defensive systems. The talks failed to make progress for over a year, while the North Koreans continued to aggressively pursue their ballistic missile program. The accuracy of their long-range ballistic missile gradually improved until President Trump, in his second term, decided that the United States could not stand idly by and let the North Koreans conduct any further missile testing.

In the summer of 2021, the North Koreans began preparations for another test. A fleet of ten laser equipped starships was still in production at a secret location. With Vinar in command, the *Friendship* entered orbit over the test site. The North Koreans were warned that if they continued with the test, their missile would be shot down. Their response was that they would consider the downing of their missile an act of war and attack South Korea and Japan with "righteous fury," including nuclear weapons. President Trump responded that if they did, they would be annihilated. The Chinese government tried to broker a resolution of the matter, but the North Koreans insisted upon their right to conduct the missile test as a means of defense against "American imperialism."

It was a time of great international tension, as no one could be sure of the outcome. There was no guarantee that the *Friendship* would be able to destroy the missile, although it was considered likely. North Korea massed hundreds of thousands of troops along the demilitarized zone. The United States brought in two aircraft carrier groups, their jets armed with tactical nuclear weapons. South Korea mobilized all of its forces to repel a ground assault. Citizens fled Seoul en masse and the city ground to a virtual halt. The whole of Southeast Asia was a tinderbox, preparing for all out war.

There would be no advance notice from the North Koreans as to when the test would occur. The missile was on the launch pad and it stayed there for several days while the diplomatic efforts continued. Then, while the talks were still underway, shortly after mid-day, the missile was launched. The launch was immediately detected by the carrier battle groups and other systems in the vicinity. It could be readily seen by the *Friendship* hovering about seventy miles over the launch site. Vinar quickly maneuvered the *Friendship* into position to down the missile. It had not reached the peak of its trajectory when Vinar fired both lasers at it, causing it to explode in a stunning aerial display of the *Friendship*'s military capability. The events were recorded by the *Friendship*, while American, Chinese, and Russian warships watched in awe from below.

The next move was up to the North Koreans. The world anxiously waited as the North Korean military command debated whether to launch the attack. There were some who argued that attack meant sure annihilation and that it was time to stand down. Some argued for more time to decide. A few argued to make good on their threats and attack.

Cooler heads prevailed. The Supreme Leader, faced with the immediate consequences of a reckless attack against South Korea and Japan, gave the command for their forces to stand down. The Chinese were notified that the North Koreans would not launch an attack and wished to continue with the negotiations with the South Koreans and the United States. Over the next several weeks, North Korean forces were gradually withdrawn from across the demilitarized zone and the negotiations gained momentum. The South Koreans sweetened the pot with a variety of economic benefits. The generals that had advocated pursuing the attack against South Korea lost favor with the Supreme Leader as he came to realize that their effort to develop a nuclear attack force had been neutralized by the Senian technology. Over the course of several months, a treaty was eventually agreed upon that called for complete disarmament of the Korean Peninsula. The Chinese, realizing how close they had come to a nuclear war in Asia, were very instrumental in bringing it about.

This, the first aerial display of Senian military capability against ballistic missiles caused a renewed sense of great alarm with some of the Russian generals. Would the United States built a fleet of starships capable of effectively neutralizing their land and sea based missile forces? Some of the Chinese generals were similarly concerned. General Ruskoff was among those who advocated initiating negotiations with the Americans to limit the development of such forces. The Russian's bargaining card was that they would be forced to greatly expand their missile force in the absence of an agreement, and that the creation of such a force would be in violation of the Start II Treaty.

The American position was that they wanted to eliminate all land based ballistic missile forces. They invited nuclear attack of the American and Russian land mass and were not needed as a deterrent considering their submarine and bomber forces. In exchange, the Americans would limit their development of a starship fleet to the ten ships that were currently under construction. This force, they argued, was necessary to defend against the erroneous release of a missile and would be beneficial to both sides. It would also prevent other nuclear powers, such as India and Pakistan, from engaging in an accidental or intentional nuclear exchange. The Americans would not give up their technology, but would allow Russian commanders to be aboard these ships as observers. It would be a long and complicated process, but in the year 2023 a treaty was finally agreed upon and ratified by the Senate.

The Senians prospered in their new life on Earth, along with many others in the United States and across the globe who reaped the benefits of Senian technology. Within five years, the Senia – Earth Foundation found itself to be the stewards of hundreds of billions of dollars derived from the licensing of Senian medical and other technologies and the creation of public companies to exploit these technologies. Josh, Fela and the Senians settled along the Oregon coast in a heavily secured compound of 35 acres. The foundation's headquarters was located a few miles from the compound. Fedar initially headed up the foundation, but after a few years, turned the reins over to Josh, content to live out the remainder of his years exploring Earth's vast literature from his perch above the Pacific.

Vilaria, Banar, Elar, Minar, and Zenar were given command positions in the U.S. Air Force, focusing on development of the new fleet of starships. Vinar went to work with NASA. Bandar, who was still fascinated with horticultural systems, developed a hydroponics farm in Oregon where he grew a variety of Senian fruits and vegetables that quickly became very much in demand due to their unique flavors.

In addition to the new fleet of Air Force starships, the Senia-Earth Foundation constructed a starship, about the size of the *Friendship*, to transport highly refined uranium back to Senia. The U.S. military cooperated fully, providing the uranium. The starship departed Earth in the year 2025. Vilaria and Minar left the Air Force to pilot the mission, along with Valdar, who was now a young man of twenty Earth years. Valdar and Misha had fallen in love and she went with him. It was a very sad day for Vinar and Rosilea, but they knew from their own experience that they could not stand in the way. The rest of the crew was made up of several Americans and one Russian, eager to brave the rigors of space travel in order to see a new world.

After the starship fleet was in service, the *Friendship* was outfitted for a manned mission to Mars with American, Russian and Chinese cosmonauts. Vinar was in command of the mission. It was grand day in the year 2028 when the *Friendship* departed.

Relations between the United States, Russia and China had improved greatly over the years. When the Senians first landed, Russia and China were moving closer to an attempt to destroy the United States economically by flooding the market with U.S. Treasury bonds, devaluing the dollar and creating inflation. This plan was abandoned after the licensing of Senian technology led to the development of a myriad of new industries and a resurgence of the American economy. It became apparent that this effort would fail and end up costing them hundreds of billions of foreign exchange. Instead, Russia and China stepped up their participation with the United States and its allies in the battle against Islamic extremism.

About a year after the landing, Josh, Fela, Rosilea, Vinar, Josar, Misha, and two security guards finally took a trip to New York to visit Nathans in Coney Island. They were chauffeured there in a long black limo and were quite the sight when the bulbous-headed Senians exited the limo to stand in line at the hot dog counter. It caused a stir as a crowd gathered around them. Some people took pictures with their cell phones, which quickly went viral on the net. Josh was surprised to find that it stood there just as he remembered it from the late 1960s. At that time a hot dog was twenty-five cents. Now it was four dollars. Still, it was the same hot dog and the French fries were still the best on the planet.

This story ends with Josh and Fela walking along the beach at sunset in the year 2028. After the launch of the mission to Mars from Cape Kennedy, they rented a house at Crescent Beach, not far from where Josh had parked his van on the beach back in 1977. He was now 77 years old. They walked to the spot where Fedar had landed the shuttle craft. Josh thought about those intense moments when he decided whether to board the craft. Had he made the right decision? He thought so. He had fulfilled his desire to do something meaningful with his life. There was still much for others to do, but there was now the promise that humankind could live in harmony with spaceship Earth and reach for the stars.

REFERENCES

Historyorb.com, *Historical Events, 1990-1994*: search for "Soviet Union USSR Gorbachev Yeltsin"

Historyorb.com, *Historical Events, 1512, 1978-1995, 2000*

U.S. News and World Report, *Carter's B-1 Shocker* (July 11, 1977)

U.S. News and World Report, *Worldgram* (July 11, 1977)

U.S. News and World Report, *As the Carter Team Sizes Up the World* (July 18, 1977)

U.S. News and World Report, *A Fresh Warning to Americans About U.S.-Soviet Arms Talks* (July 18, 1977)

U.S. News and World Report, *Is Energy Use Overheating World?* (July 25, 1977)

U.S. News and World Report, *Worldgram* (August 1, 1977)

U.S. News and World Report, *A New Cabinet Agency Takes On Energy Crisis* (August 15, 1977)

U.S. News and World Report, *Coming Soon: Gasoline at a Dollar a Gallon* (August 15, 1977)

U.S. News and World Report, *The Chinese Puzzle That Vance Will Try to Solve* (August 22, 1977)

U.S. News and World Report, *Historic Treaty With Panama: Toughest Test Yet to Come* (August 22, 1977)

U.S. News and World Report, *Surprise Attack By Russia, Still "Unthinkable?"* (September 5, 1977)

U.S. News and World Report, *Behind Carter's Gamble in the Middle East* (October 17, 1977)

U.S. News and World Report, *Why the Energy Program is Such a Mess* (October 24, 1977)

U.S. News and World Report, *Washington Whispers* (November 14,

1994)

U.S. News and World Report, *Taking a Byte Out of the Bottom Line* (November 14, 1994)

Wikipedia, *1972 Nixon Visit to China* (March 21, 2015)

Wikipedia, *1982 Lebanon War* (March 22, 2015)

Wikipedia, *1983 Beirut Barracks Bombing* (March 23, 2015)

Wikipedia, *1993 World Trade Center Bombing* (March 31, 2015)

Wikipedia, *Boris Yeltsin* (March 26, 2015)

Wikipedia, *Cold War* (1985-91) (March 19, 2015)

Wikipedia, *David Stockman* (March 18, 2015)

Wikipedia, *Deng Xiaoping* (March 21, 2015)

Wikipedia, *Gulf War* (March 26, 2015)

Wikipedia, *History of Computing Hardware* (March 22, 2015)

Wikipedia, *History of the Internet* (March 22, 2015)

Wikipedia, *Influenza A Virus Subtype H5N1* (March 30, 2015)

Wikipedia, *Iran Hostage Crisis* (March 13, 2015)

Wikipedia, *Iraq War* (March 31, 2015)

Wikipedia, *Mikhail Gorbachev* (March 26, 2015)

Wikipedia, *Nelson Mandela* (March 30, 2015)

Wikipedia, *Nuclear Program of Iran* (March 31, 2015)

Wikipedia, *Presidency of Ronald Reagan* (March 18, 2015)

Wikipedia, *Reagan Doctrine* (March 18, 2015)

Wikipedia, *Rockwell B-1 Lancer* (March 18, 2015)

Wikipedia, *Ronald Reagan* (March 19, 2015)

Wikipedia, *Ruhollah Khomeini* (March 16, 2015)

Wikipedia, *September 11 Attacks* (March 31, 2015)

Wikipedia, *Shapour Bakhtiar* (March 16, 2015)

Wikipedia, *Soviet War in Afghanistan* (March 19, 2015)

Wikipedia, *Timeline of the Arab Spring* (April 1, 2015)

Wikipedia, *Timeline of the Nuclear Program of Iran* (March 31, 2015)

Wikipedia, *Vladimir Putin* (March 29, 2015)

Wikipedia, *War in Afghanistan* (March 31, 2015)